The Last of the Chiefs: A Story of the Great Sioux War

Joseph A. Altsheler

CONTENTS

Chapter I
The Train

The boy in the third wagon was suffering from exhaustion. The days and days of walking over the rolling prairie, under a brassy sun, the hard food of the train, and the short hours of rest, had put too severe a trial upon his delicate frame. Now, as he lay against the sacks and boxes that had been drawn up to form a sort of couch for him, his breath came in short gasps, and his face was very pale. His brother, older, and stronger by far, who walked at the wheel, regarded him with a look in which affection and intense anxiety were mingled. It was not a time and place in which one could afford to be ill.

Richard and Albert Howard were bound together by the strongest of brotherly ties. Richard had inherited his father's bigness and powerful constitution, Albert his mother's slenderness and fragility. But it was the mother who lived the longer, although even she did not attain middle age, and her last words to her older son were: "Richard, take care of Albert. " He had promised, and now was thinking how he could keep the promise.

It was a terrible problem that confronted Richard Howard. He felt no fear on his own account. A boy in years, he was a man in the ability to care for himself, wherever he might be. In a boyhood spent on an Illinois farm, where the prairies slope up to the forest, he had learned the ways of wood and field, and was full of courage, strength, and resource.

But Albert was different. He had not thrived in the moist air of the great valley. Tall enough he was, but the width of chest and thickness of bone were lacking. Noticing this, the idea of going to California had come to the older brother. The great gold days had passed years since, but it was still a land of enchantment to the youth of the older states, and the long journey in the high, dry air of the plains would be good for Albert. There was nothing to keep them back. They had no property save a little money—enough for their equipment, and a few dollars over to live on in California until they could get work.

To decide was to start, and here they were in the middle of the vast country that rolled away west of the Missouri, known but little, and full of dangers. The journey had been much harder than the older boy had expected. The days stretched out, the weeks trailed away, and still the plains rolled before them.

The summer had been of the hottest, and the heated earth gave back the glare until the air quivered in torrid waves. Richard had drawn back the cover of the wagon that his brother might breathe the air, but he replaced it now to protect him from the overpowering beams. Once more he anxiously studied the country, but it gave him little hope. The green of the grass was gone, and most of the grass with it. The brown undulations swept away from horizon to horizon, treeless, waterless, and bare. In all that vast desolation there was nothing save the tired and dusty train at the very center of it.

"Anything in sight, Dick? " asked Albert, who had followed his brother's questioning look.

Dick shook his head.

"Nothing, Al, " he replied.

"I wish we'd come to a grove, " said the sick boy.

He longed, as do all those who are born in the hills, for the sight of trees and clear, running water.

"I was thinking, Dick, " he resumed in short, gasping tones, "that it would be well for us, just as the evening was coming on, to go over a swell and ride right into a forest of big oaks and maples, with the finest little creek that you ever saw running through the middle of it. It would be pleasant and shady there. Leaves would be lying about, the water would be cold, and maybe we'd see elk coming down to drink. "

"Perhaps we'll have such luck, Al, " said Dick, although his tone showed no such hope. But he added, assuming a cheerful manner: "This can't go on forever; we'll be reaching the mountains soon, and then you'll get well. "

"How's that brother of yours? No better, I see, and he's got to ride all the time now, making more load for the animals. "

It was Sam Conway, the leader of the train, who spoke, a rough man of middle age, for whom both Dick and Albert had acquired a deep dislike. Dick flushed through his tan at the hard words.

"If he's sick he had the right to ride, " he replied sharply. "We've paid our share for this trip and maybe a little more. You know that. "

Conway gave him an ugly look, but Dick stood up straight and strong, and met him eye for eye. He was aware of their rights and he meant to defend them. Conway, confronted by a dauntless spirit, turned away, muttering in a surly fashion:

"We didn't bargain to take corpses across the plains. "

Fortunately, the boy in the wagon did not hear him, and, though his eyes flashed ominously, Dick said nothing. It was not a time for quarreling, but it was often hard to restrain one's temper. He had realized, soon after the start, when it was too late to withdraw, that the train was not a good one. It was made up mostly of men. There were no children, and the few women, like the men, were coarse and rough. Turbulent scenes had occurred, but Dick and Albert kept aloof, steadily minding their own business.

"What did Conway say? " asked Albert, after the man had gone.

"Nothing of any importance. He was merely growling as usual. He likes to make himself disagreeable. I never saw another man who got as much enjoyment out of that sort of thing. "

Albert said nothing more, but closed his eyes. The canvas cover protected him from the glare of the sun, but seemed to hold the heat within it. Drops of perspiration stood on his face, and Dick longed for the mountains, for his brother's sake.

All the train fell into a sullen silence, and no sound was heard but the unsteady rumble of the wheels, the creak of an ungreased axle, and the occasional crack of a whip. Clouds of dust arose and were whipped by the stray winds into the faces of the travelers, the fine particles burning like hot ashes. The train moved slowly and heavily, as if it dragged a wounded length over the hard ground.

Dick Howard kept his position by the side of the wagon in which his brother lay. He did not intend that Albert should hear bitter words leveled at his weakness, and he knew that his own presence was a deterrent. The strong figures and dauntless port of the older youth inspired respect. Moreover, he carried over his shoulder a repeating rifle of the latest pattern, and his belt was full of cartridges. He and Albert had been particular about their arms. It was a necessity. The plains and the mountains were subject to all the dangers of Indian warfare, and they had taken a natural youthful pride in buying the finest of weapons.

The hot dust burned Dick Howard's face and crept into his eyes and throat. His tongue lay dry in his mouth. He might have ridden in one of the wagons, too, had he chosen. As he truly said, he and Albert had paid their full share, and in the labor of the trail, he was more efficient than anybody else in the train. But his pride had been touched by Conway's words. He would not ride, nor would he show any signs of weakness. He strode on by the side of the wagon, head erect, his step firm and springy.

The sun crept slowly down the brassy arch of the heavens, and the glare grew less blinding. The heat abated, but Albert Howard, who had fallen asleep, slept on. His brother drew a blanket over him, knowing that he could not afford to catch cold, and breathed the cooler air himself, with thankfulness. Conway came back again, and was scarcely less gruff than before, although he said nothing about Albert.

"Bright Sun says than in another day or two we'll be seeing the mountains, " he vouchsafed; "and I'll be glad of it, because then we'll be coming to water and game. "

"I'd like to be seeing them now, " responded Dick; "but do you believe everything that Bright Sun says? "

"Of course I do. Hasn't he brought us along all right? What are you driving at? "

His voice rose to a challenging tone, in full accordance with the nature of the man, whenever anyone disagreed with him, but Dick Howard took not the least fear.

"I don't altogether like Bright Sun, " he replied. "Just why, I can't say, but the fact remains that I don't like him. It doesn't seem natural for an Indian to be so fond of white people, and to prefer another race to his own. "

Conway laughed harshly.

"That shows how much you know, " he said. "Bright Sun is smart, smarter than a steel trap. He knows that the day of the red is passing, and he's going to train with the white. What's the use of being on the losing side? It's what I say, and it's what Bright Sun thinks. "

The man's manner was gross and materialistic, so repellent that Dick would have turned away, but at that moment Bright Sun himself approached. Dick regarded him, as always, with the keenest interest and curiosity mixed with some suspicion. Yet almost anyone would have been reassured by the appearance of Bright Sun. He was a splendid specimen of the Indian, although in white garb, even to the soft felt hat shading his face. But he could never have been taken for a white man. His hair was thick, black, and coarse, his skin of the red man's typical coppery tint, and his cheek bones high and sharp. His lean but sinewy and powerful figure rose two inches above six feet. There was an air about him, too, that told of strength other than that of the body. Guide he was, but leader he looked.

"Say, Bright Sun, " exclaimed Conway coarsely, "Dick Howard here thinks you're too friendly with the whites. It don't seem natural to him that one of your color should consort so freely with us. "

Dick's face flushed through the brown, and he shot an angry glance at Conway, but Bright Sun did not seem to be offended.

"Why not? " he asked in perfect English. "I was educated in a mission school. I have been with white people most of my life, I have read your books, I know your civilization, and I like it. "

"There now! " exclaimed Conway triumphantly. "Ain't that an answer for you? I tell you what, Bright Sun, I'm for you, I believe in you, and if anybody can take us through all right to California, you're the man. "

"It is my task and I will accomplish it, " said Bright Sun in the precise English he had learned at the mission school.

5

His eyes met Dick's for a moment, and the boy saw there a flash that might mean many things—defiance, primeval force, and the quality that plans and does. But the flash was gone in an instant, like a dying spark, and Bright Sun turned away. Conway also left, but Dick's gaze followed the Indian.

He did not know Bright Sun's tribe. He had heard that he was a Sioux, also that he was a Crow, and a third report credited him with being a Cheyenne. As he never painted his face, dressed like a white man, and did not talk of himself and his people, the curious were free to surmise as they chose. But Dick was sure of one thing: Bright Sun was a man of power. It was not a matter of surmise, he felt it instinctively.

The tall figure of the Indian was lost among the wagons, and Dick turned his attention to the trail. The cooling waves continued to roll up, as the west reddened into a brilliant sunset. Great bars of crimson, then of gold, and the shades in between, piled above one another on the horizon. The plains lost their brown, and gleamed in wonderful shimmering tints. The great desolate world became beautiful.

The train stopped with a rumble, a creak, and a lurch, and the men began to unharness the animals. Albert awoke with a start and sat up in the wagon.

"Night and the camp, Al, " said Dick cheerfully; "feel better, don't you?

"Yes, I do, " replied Albert, as a faint color came into his face.

"Thought the rest and the coolness would brace you up, " continued Dick in the same cheerful tone.

Albert, a tall, emaciated boy with a face of great refinement and delicacy, climbed out of the wagon and looked about. Dick busied himself with the work of making camp, letting Albert give what help he could.

But Dick always undertook to do enough for two—his brother and himself—and he really did enough for three. No other was so swift and skillful at taking the gear off horse or mule, nor was there a stronger or readier arm at the wheel when it was necessary to complete the circle of wagons that they nightly made. When this was done, he went out on the prairie in search of buffalo chips for the fire, which he was fortunate enough to find without any trouble.

Before returning with his burden, Dick stood a few moments looking back at the camp. The dusk had fully come, but the fires were not yet lighted, and he saw only the shadowy forms of the wagons and flitting figures about them. But much talked reached his ears, most of it coarse and rough, with a liberal sprinkling of oaths. Dick sighed. His regret was keener than ever that Albert and he were in such company. Then he looked the other way out upon the fathomless plains, where the night had gathered, and the wind was moaning among the swells. The air was now chill enough to make him shiver, and he gazed with certain awe into the black depths. The camp, even with all its coarseness and roughness, was better, and he walked swiftly back with his load of fuel.

They built a dozen fires within the circle of the wagons, and again Dick was the most active and industrious of them all, doing his share, Albert's, and something besides. When the fires were lighted they burned rapidly and merrily, sending up great tongues of red or yellow flame, which shed a flickering light over wagons, animals, and men. A pleasant heat was suffused and Dick began to cook supper for Albert and himself, bringing it from the wagon in which his brother and he had a share. He fried bacon and strips of dried beef, boiled coffee, and warmed slices of bread over the coals.

He saw with intense pleasure that Albert ate with a better appetite than he had shown for days. As for himself, he was as hungry as a horse—he always was on this great journey—and since there was plenty, he ate long, and was happy.

Dick went to the wagon, and returned with a heavy cloak, which he threw over Albert's shoulders.

"The night's getting colder, " he said, "and you mustn't take any risks, Al. There's one trouble about a camp fire in the open—your face can burn while your back freezes. "

Content fell over the camp. Even rough men of savage instincts are willing to lie quiet when they are warm and well fed. Jokes, coarse but invariably in good humor, were exchanged. The fires still burned brightly, and the camp formed a core of light and warmth in the dark, cold wilderness.

Albert, wrapped in the cloak, lay upon his side and elbow gazing dreamily into the flames. Dick sat near him, frying a piece of bacon on the end of a stick. Neither heard the step behind them because it was noiseless, but both saw the tall figure of Bright Sun, as he came up to their fire.

"Have a piece of bacon, Bright Sun, " said Dick hospitably, holding out the slice to him, and at the same time wondering whether the Indian would take it.

Bright Sun shook his head.

"I thank you, " he replied, "but I have eaten enough. How is Mr. Albert Howard now? "

Dick appreciated the inquiry, whether or not it was prompted by sympathy.

"Good, " he replied. "Al's picking up. Haven't seen him eat as he did to-night for months. If he keeps on this way, he'll devour a whole buffalo as soon as he's able to kill one. "

Bright Sun smiled, and sat down on the ground near them. It seemed to the boy, a keen observer of his kind, that he wished to talk. Dick was willing.

"Do you know, " asked Bright Sun, "that reports of gold in the region to the north, called by you the Black Hills, have come to us? "

"I heard some one speak of it two or three days ago, " replied Dick, "but I paid no attention to it. "

Bright Sun looked thoughtfully into the fire, the glow of which fell full upon his face, revealing every feature like carving. His nose was hooked slightly, and to Dick it now looked like the beak of an eagle. The somber eyes, too, expressed brooding and mastery alike.

Despite himself, Dick felt again that he was in the presence of power, and he was oppressed by a sense of foreboding.

"It was worth attention, " said Bright Sun in the slow, precise tones of one who speaks a language not his own, but who speaks it perfectly. "The white man's gold is calling to him loudly. It calls all through the day and night. Do these men with whom you travel go to anything certain far over on the coast of the Western ocean? No, they are leaves blown by the wind. The wind now blows in the direction of the Black Hills, where the gold is said to be, and to-morrow the wagon train turns its head that way. "

Dick sat up straight, and Albert, wrapped in his blanket, leaned forward to listen.

"But the engagement with us all, " said Dick, "was to go to the Pacific. Albert and I paid our share for that purpose. Conway knows it. "

The Indian looked at Dick. The boy thought he saw a flickering smile of amusement in his eyes, but it was faint, and gone in a moment.

"Conway does not care for that, " said the Indian. "Your contracts are nothing to him. This is the wilderness, and it stretches away for many hundreds of miles in every direction. The white man's law does not come here. Moreover, nearly all wish him to turn to the North and the gold. "

Albert suddenly spoke, and his tone, though thin from physical weakness, was quick, intense, and eager.

"Why couldn't we go on with them, Dick? " he said. "We have nothing definite on the Pacific coast. We are merely taking chances, and if the Black Hills are full of gold, we might get our share! "

Dick's eyes glistened. If one had to go, one might make the best of it. The spirit of romance was alive within him. He was only a boy.

"Of course we'll go, Al, " he said lightly, "and you and I will have a tone of gold inside a year. "

Bright Sun looked at the two boys, first one and then the other, stalwart Dick and weak Albert. It seemed to Dick that he saw a new expression in the Indian's eyes, one that indicated the shadow of regret. He resented it. Did Bright Sun think that Albert and he were not equal to the task?

"I am strong, " he said; "I can lift and dig enough for two; but Albert will also be strong, after we have been a little while in the mountains. "

"You might have strength enough. I do not doubt it, " said Bright Sun softly, "but the Black Hills are claimed by the Sioux. They do not wish the white men to come there, and the Sioux are a great and powerful tribe, or rather a nation of several allied and kindred tribes, the most powerful Indian nation west of the Mississippi. "

Bright Sun's voice rose a little toward the last, and the slight upward tendency gave emphasis and significance to his words. The brooding eyes suddenly shot forth a challenging light.

"Are you a Sioux? " asked Dick involuntarily.

Bright Sun bent upon him a look of gentle reproof.

"Since I have taken the ways of your race I have no tribe, " he replied. "But, as I have said, the Sioux claim the Black Hills, and they have many thousands of warriors, brave, warlike, and resolved to keep the country. "

"The government will see that there is no war, " said Dick.

"Governments can do little in a wilderness, " replied Bright Sun.

Dick might have made a rejoinder, but at that moment a burly figure came into the light of the fire. It was Sam Conway, and he glanced suspiciously at the Indian and the two boys.

"Are you telling 'em, Bright Sun, when we'll reach California? " he asked.

Bright Sun gave him an oblique glance. The Indian seldom looks the white man in the face, but it was obvious that Bright Sun was not afraid of the leader. Conway, as well as the others, knew it.

"No, " he replied briefly.

"It's just as well that you haven't, " said Conway briskly, "'cause we're not going to California at all—at least not this year. It's the wish and general consensus of this here train that we turn to the North, go into the Black Hills, and fill our wagons with gold. "

"So it's decided, then, is it? " asked Dick.

"Yes, it's decided, " replied Conway, his tone now becoming positively brutal, "and if you and your brother don't like it, you know what you can do. "

"Keep on alone for the coast, I suppose, " said Dick, looking him steadily in the face.

"If you put it that way. "

"But we don't choose, " said Dick, "Al and I have an interest in one wagon and team, and we're going to hold on to it. Besides, we're quite willing to try our luck in the Black Hills, too. We're going with you. "

Conway frowned, but Dick also was not afraid of him, and knew that he could not turn the two boys out on the prairie. They had a full right to go with the train.

"That settles it, " he said, turning away. "You can do as you please, but what happens after we get into the Black Hills is another thing. Likely, we'll scatter. "

The sound of his retreating footsteps quickly died away in the darkness, and Bright Sun, too, slid among the shadows. He was gone so quickly and quietly that it gave Dick an uncanny feeling.

"What do you make of it, Al? " he asked his brother. "What does Bright Sun mean by what he said to us? "

The glow of the flame fell across Albert's pale face, and, by the light of it, Dick saw that he was very thoughtful. He seemed to be looking over and beyond the fire and the dark prairie, into time rather than space.

"I think it was a warning, Dick, " replied Albert at last. "Maybe Bright Sun intended it for only you and me. But I want to go up there in the Black Hills, Dick. "

"And so do I. It'll be easier for you, Al, than the trip across the continent. When you are a mile and a half or two miles above the sea, you'll begin to take on flesh like a bear in summer. Besides, the gold, Al! think of the gold! "

Albert smiled. He, too, was having happy thoughts. The warm glow of the fire clothed him and he was breathing easily and peacefully. By and by he sank down in his blanket and fell into a sound sleep. Dick himself did not yet have any thought of slumber. Wide-awake visions were pursuing one another through his brain. He saw the mountains, dark and shaggy with pine forests, the thin, healing air over them, and the beds of gold in their bosom, with Albert and himself discovering and triumphant.

The fire died down, and glowed a mass of red embers. The talk sank. Most of the men were asleep, either in their blankets or in the wagons. The darkness thickened and deepened and came close up to the fires, a circling rim of blackness. But Dick was still wakeful, dreaming with wide-open eyes his golden dreams.

As the visions followed one after another, a shadow which was not a part of any of them seemed to Dick to melt into the uttermost darkness beyond the fires. A trace of something familiar in the figure impressed him, and, rising, he followed swiftly.

The figure, still nebulous and noiseless, went on in the darkness, and another like it seemed to rise from the plain and join it. Then they were lost to the sight of the pursuer, seeming to melt into and become a part of the surrounding darkness. Dick, perplexed and uneasy, returned to the fire. The second shadow must certainly have been that of a stranger. What did it mean?

He resumed his seat before the red glow, clasping his arms around his knees, a splendid, resourceful youth whom nature and a hardy life had combined to make what he was. His brother still slept soundly and peacefully, but the procession of golden visions did not pass again through Dick's brain; instead, it was a long trail of clouds, dark and threatening. He sought again and again to conjure the clouds away and bring back the golden dreams, but he could not.

The fire fell to nothing, the triumphant darkness swept up and blotted out the last core of light, the wind, edged with ice, blew in from the plains. Dick shivered, drew a heavy blanket around his own shoulders, and moved a little, as he saw the dim figure of Bright Sun passing at the far edge of the wagons, but quickly relapsed into stillness.

Sleep at last pulled down his troubled lids. His figure sank, and, head on arms, he slumbered soundly.

Chapter II
King Bison

"Up! Up, everybody! " was the shout that reached Dick's sleeping ears. He sprang to his feet and found that the gorgeous sun was flooding the prairie with light. Already the high, brilliant skies of the Great West were arching over him. Men were cooking breakfast. Teamsters were cracking their whips and the whole camp was alive with a gay and cheerful spirit. Everybody seemed to know now that they were going for the gold, and, like Dick, they had found it in fancy already.

Breakfast over, the train took up its march, turning at a right angle from its old course and now advancing almost due north. But this start was made with uncommon alacrity and zeal. There were no sluggards now. They, too, had golden visions, and, as if to encourage them, the aspect of the country soon began to change, and rapidly to grow better. The clouds of dust that they raised were thinner. The bunch grass grew thicker. Off on the crest of a swell a moving figure was seen now and then. "Antelope, " said the hunters. Once they passed a slow creek. The water was muddy, but it contained no alkali, and animals and men drank eagerly. Cottonwoods, the first trees they had seen in days, grew on either side of the stream, and they rested there awhile in the shade, because the sun was now out in full splendor, and the vast plains shimmered in the heat.

Albert resumed his place in the wagon. Dick had a horse which, on becoming foot-sore, had been allowed to rest for a few days, and was now well. He mounted it and galloped on ahead. The clouds were all gone away and the golden visions had come back. He felt so strong, so young, and the wonderful air of the plains was such a tonic that he urged his horse to a gallop, and it was hard for him to keep from shouting aloud in joy. He looked eagerly into the north, striving already for a sight of the dark mountains that men called the Black Hills. The blue gave back nothing but its own blue.

His horse seemed to share his spirits, and swung along with swift and easy stride. Dick looked back presently, and saw that the train which had been winding like a serpent over the plains was lost to sight behind the swells. The surface of the earth had become more rolling as they advanced northward, and he knew that the train, though out of sight, was nor far away.

He enjoyed for the moment the complete absence of all human beings save himself. To be alone then meant anything but loneliness. He galloped to the crest of a higher swell than usual, and then stopped short. Far off on the plain he saw tiny moving figures, a dozen or so, and he was sure that they were antelope. They had seen antelope before at a great distance, but had not bothered about them. Now the instincts of the hunter rose in Dick, and he resolved to make a trial of his skill.

He found in one of the depressions between the swells a stunted cottonwood, to which he hitched his horse, knowing it would be well hidden there from the observation of the herd. He then advanced on foot. He had heard that the antelope was a slave to its own curiosity, and through that weakness he intended to secure his game.

When he had gone about half the distance he sank down on his hands and knees and began to crawl, a laborious and sometimes painful operation, burdened as he was with his rifle, and unused to such methods of locomotion. Presently he noticed a flutter among the antelope, a raising of timid heads, an alarmed looking in his direction. But Dick was prepared. He lay flat upon his face, and dug the point of the long hunting knife that he carried into the ground, while the wind blew out the folds of the red handkerchief which he had tied to the handle.

Mr. Big Buck Antelope, the chief of the herd and a wary veteran, saw the waving red spot on the horizon and his interest was aroused, despite his caution. What a singular thing! It must be investigated! It might be some new kind of food very good for Mr. Big Buck's palate and stomach, and no provident antelope could afford to let such an opportunity pass.

He was trembling all over with curiosity, and perhaps his excitement kept him from seeing the dark shape that blurred with the earth just beyond the red something, or he may have taken it for a shadow. At any event, his curiosity kept him from paying heed to it, and he began to approach. His steps were hesitating, and now and then he drew away a little, but that singular red object lured him on, and yard by yard he drew nearer.

He suddenly saw the black shadow beyond the fluttering red object detach itself from the ground, and resolve into a terrible shape. His heart sprang up in his bosom, and he was about to rush madly away, but it was too late. A stream of fire shot forth from the dark object and the buck fell, a bullet through him.

Dick prepared the animal for dressing, thinking of the tender, juicy steaks that Albert would enjoy, and then throwing the body across the horse, behind him, rode back to the train, proud of his success.

Conway frowned and said grudging words. He did not like, he said, for anybody to leave the train without his permission, and it was foolish, anyhow, for a boy to be galloping about as he pleased over the prairie; he might get lost, and there would be nobody to take care of the other boy, the sick one. Dick made an easy diplomatic reply. He knew that Conway merely wished to be unpleasant, but Dick was of a very good nature, and he was particularly averse just then to quarreling with anybody. He was too full of the glory of living. Instead, he offered some of the antelope steaks to Conway, who churlishly accepted them, and that night he broiled others for Albert and himself, dividing the rest among the men.

Albert found antelope steak tender and juicy, and he ate with an increasing appetite. Dick noted the increase with pleasure.

"I wish I could go out and kill antelope, " said Albert.

Dick laughed cheerfully.

"Kill antelope, " he said. "Why, Al, in six months you'll be taking a grizzly bear by the neck and choking him to death with your two hands. "

"Wish I could believe it, " said Albert.

But Dick went to sleep early that night, and slept peacefully without dreams or visions, and the next morning the train resumed its sanguine march. They were still ascending, and the character of the country continued to improve. Bunch grass steadily grew thicker and buffalo chips were numerous. The heat in the middle of the day was still great, but the air was so dry and pure that it was not oppressive. Albert dismounted from the wagon, and walked for several miles by the side of his brother.

"Shouldn't be surprised if we saw buffalo, " said Dick. "Heard 'em talking about it in the train. Bright Sun says these are favorite grazing grounds, and there's still a lot of buffalo scattered about the plains. "

Albert showed excitement.

"A buffalo herd! " he exclaimed. "Do you think it can really happen, Dick? I never thought I'd see such a thing! I hope it'll come true! "

It came true much sooner than Albert hoped.

Scarcely a half hour after he spoke, Bright Sun, who was at the head of the column, stopped his pony and pointed to indistinct tiny shadows just under the horizon.

"Buffalo! " he said tersely, and after a moment's pause he added: "A great herd comes! "

Dick and Albert were on foot then, but they heard his words and followed his pointing finger with the deepest interest. The tiny black shadows seemed to come out of the horizon as if they stepped from a wall. They grew in size and number, and all the west was filled with their forms.

The train resumed its march, bending off under the guidance of Bright Sun a little toward the west, and it was obvious that the herd would pass near. Dick and Albert rejoiced, because they wished to see the buffaloes at close quarters, and Dick was hoping also for a shot. Others, too, in the train, although their minds were set on gold, began to turn their attention now to the herd. The sport and the fresh meat alike would be welcome. It was Dick's impulse to mount his horse and gallop away again, gun in hand, but he made a supreme conquest over self and remained. He remembered Albert's longing words about the antelope, his wish that he, too, tireless, might be able to pursue the game. Dick remained quietly by his brother's side.

The whole train stopped presently at Conway's order on the crest of a swell, and drew itself up in a circle. Many of the men were now mounted and armed for an attack upon the herd, but at the suggestion of Bright Sun they waited a little, until the opportunity should become more convenient.

"It is a big herd, " said Bright Sun; "perhaps the biggest that one can ever see now. "

It certainly seemed immense to Dick and Albert. The great animals came on in an endless stream from the blue wall of the horizon. The vast procession steadily broadened and lengthened and it moved with unceasing step toward the south. The body of it was solid black, with figures which at the distance blended into one mass, but on the flanks hung stragglers, lawless old bulls or weaklings, and outside there was a fringe of hungry wolves, snapping and snarling, and waiting a chance to drag down some failing straggler.

Far over the plain spread the herd, thousands and tens of thousands, and the earth shook with their tread. Confused, bellowings and snortings arose, and the dust hung thick.

Dick and Albert stared with intent eyes at the wonderful scene. The herd was drawing nearer and nearer. It would pass only a few hundred yards from the crest on which the train stood. Already the hunters were shouting to one another and galloping away, but Dick did not stir from Albert's side. Albert's eyes were expanded, and the new color in his face deepened. His breath cam in the short, quick fashion of one who is excited. He suddenly turned to his brother.

"The men are off! Why aren't you with them Dick? " he exclaimed.

"I thought I wouldn't go, " replied Dick evasively. "There'll be enough without me. "

Albert stared. Not hunt buffalo when one could. It was unbelievable. Then he comprehended. But he would not have it that way! It was noble of Dick, but it should not be so for a moment. He cried out, a note of anxiety in this voice:

"No, Dick, you shall not say here with me! My time will come later on! Jump on your horse, Dick, and join 'em! I won't forgive you if you don't! "

Dick saw that Albert was in earnest, and he knew that it would be better for them both now if he should go.

"All right, Al! " he cried, "I'll pick out a good fat one. " He jumped on his horse and in a moment was galloping at full speed over the plain toward the great herd which now rushed on, black and thundering.

Dick heard shots already from those who had preceded him, and the exultant shouts of the men mingled with the roar of mighty tramplings. But it was not all triumph for the men, few of whom were experienced. Two or three had been thrown by shying horses, and with difficulty escaped being trodden to death under the feet of the herd. The herd itself was so immense that it did not notice these few wasps on a distant flank, and thundered steadily on southward.

Dick's own horse, frightened by such a tremendous sight, shied and jumped, but the boy had a sure seat and brought him around again. Dick himself was somewhat daunted by the aspect of the herd. If he and his hose got in the way, they would go down forever, as surely as if engulfed by an avalanche.

The horse shied again and made a mighty jump, as a huge bull, red-eyed and puffing, charged by. Dick, who was holding his rifle in one hand, slipped far over, and with great difficulty regained his balance on the horse's back. When he was secure again, he turned his mount and galloped along for some distance on the flank of the herd, seeking a suitable target for his bullet. The effect was dizzying. So many thousands were rushing beside him that the shifting panorama made him wink his eyes rapidly. Vast clouds of dust floated about, now and then enveloping him, and that made him wink his eyes, too. But he continued, nevertheless, to seek for his target a fat cow. Somehow he didn't seem to see anything just then but old bulls. They were thick on the flanks of the herd either as stragglers or protectors, and Dick was afraid to press in among them in his search for the cow.

His opportunity came at last. A young cow, as fat as one could wish, was thrown on the outside by some movement of the herd, caught, as it were, like a piece of driftwood in an eddy, and Dick instantly fired at her. She staggered and went down, but at the same instant a huge, shaggy bull careened against Dick and his horse. It was not so much a charge as an accident, the chance of Dick's getting in the bull's way, and the boy's escape was exceedingly narrow.

His horse staggered and fell to his knees. The violence of the shock wrested Dick's rifle from his hand, and he was barely quick enough to grasp it as it was sliding across the saddle. But he did save it, and the horse, trembling and frightened, recovered his feet. By that time the old bull and his comrades were gone.

Dick glanced around and was relieved to see that nobody had noticed his plight. They were all too much absorbed in their own efforts to pay any heed to him. The body took a deep, long breath. He had killed a buffalo, despite his inexperience. There was the cow to show for it.

The herd thundered off to the southward, the clouds of dust and the fringe of wolves following it. About a dozen of their number had fallen before the rifles, but Dick had secured the fattest and the tenderest. Albert, as proud as Dick himself of his triumph, came down on the plain and helped as much as he could in skinning and cutting up the cow. Dick wished to preserve the robe, and they spread it out on the wagon to dry.

The train made no further attempt to advance that day, but devoted the afternoon to a great feast. Bright Sun showed them how to cook the tenderest part of the hump in the coals, and far into the night the fires blazed.

"We will see no more buffaloes for a while, " said Bright Sun. "To-morrow we reach another little river coming down from the hills, and the ground becomes rough. "

Bright Sun told the truth. They reached the river about noon of the next day, and, as it flowed between steep banks, the crossing was difficult. It took many hours to get on the other side, and two or three axles were broken by the heavy jolts. Conway raged and swore, calling them a clumsy lot, and some of the men refused to take his abuse, replying to his hard words with others equally as hard. Pistols were drawn and there was promise of trouble, but it was finally stopped, partly by the persuasion of others, and partly of its own accord. The men were still feeling the desire for gold too strongly to fight while on the way to it. Dick and Albert kept aloof from these contentions, steadily minding their own business, and they found, as others do, that it paid.

They came presently into a better country, and the way led for a day or two through a typical part of the Great Plains, not a flat region, but one of low, monotonous swells. Now and then they crossed a shallow little creek, and occasionally they came to pools, some of which were tinged with alkali. There were numerous small depressions, two or three feet deep, and Dick knew that they were "buffalo wallows. " He and Albert examined them with interest.

"This is buffalo country again, " said Dick. "Everything proves it. The grass here is the best that we have seen in a long time, and I imagine that it's just the sort of place they would love. "

The grass was, indeed, good, as Dick had said, not merely clumps of it, but often wide, carpeted spaces. It was somewhat dry, and turning brown, but so big and strong an animal as the buffalo would not mind it. In fact, they saw several small groups of buffaloes grazing at a distance, usually on the crest of one of the low swells. As they already had plenty of buffalo meat, the men of the train did not trouble them, and the great animals would continue to crop the grass undisturbed.

About a week after the buffalo hunt they camped in a great plain somewhat flatter than any that they had encountered hitherto, and drew up the wagons in a loose circle.

The day had been very hot, but, as usual on the plains, the night brought coolness. The fire which Dick made of buffalo chips was not only useful, but it felt pleasant, too, as they sat beside it, ate their supper, and watched the great inclosing circle of darkness creep up closer and closer to the camp. There was not much noise about them. The men were tired, and as soon as they ate their food they fell asleep in the wagons or on the ground. The tethered horses and mules stirred a little for a while, but they, too, soon rested in peace.

"You take the wagon, Al, " said Dick, "but I think I'll sleep on the ground. "

Albert said good night and disappeared in the wagon. Dick stood up and looked over the camp. Only two or three fires were yet burning, and not a dozen men were awake. He saw dark figures here and there on the ground, and knew that they were those of sleepers. Three sentinels had been posted, but Dick was quite sure from the general character of the train that later on they would sleep like the others. All his instincts of order and fitness rebelled against the management of this camp.

Dick rolled himself in his blanket and lay down by the little fire that he had built. The dry, clean earth made a good bed, and with his left elbow under his head he gazed into the fire, which, like all fires of buffalo chips, was now rapidly dying, leaving little behind but light ashes that the first breeze would scatter through space.

He watched the last blaze sink and go out, he saw the last coal die, then, when a few sparks flew upward, there was blank darkness where the fire had been. All the other fires were out, too, and only the dim figures of the wagons showed. He felt, for a little while, as if he were alone in the wilderness, but he was not afraid. All was darkness below, and the wind was moaning, but overhead was a blue sky filled with friendly stars.

Dick could not go to sleep for a long time. From the point where he lay he could now see two of the sentinels walking back and forth, rifle on shoulder. He did not believe that they would continue to do so many hours, and he had a vague sort of desire to prove that he was right. Having nothing else to do he watched them.

The nearer sentinel grew lazier in his walk, and his beat became shorter. At last he dropped his rifle to the ground, leaned his folded arms on its muzzle, and gazed toward the camp, where, so far as he could see, there was nothing but darkness and sleep. The other presently did the same. Then they began short walks back and forth, but soon both sat down on the ground, with their rifles between their knees, and after that they did not stir. Watching as closely as he could Dick could not observe the slightest movement on the part of either, and he knew that they were asleep. He laughed to himself, pleased, in a way, to know that he had been right, although it was only another evidence of the carelessness and indifference general throughout the train.

He fell asleep himself in another half hour, but he awoke about midnight, and he was conscious at once that he had been awakened not by a troubled mind, but by something external and unusual. He was lying with his right ear to the ground, and it seemed to him that a slight trembling motion ran through the solid earth. He did not so much hear it as feel it, and tried to persuade himself that it was mere fancy, but failed. He sat up, and he no longer observed the trembling, but when he put his ear to the ground again it was stronger.

It could not be fancy. It was something real and extraordinary. He glanced at the sentinels, but they were sound asleep. He felt a desire to rouse somebody, but if it proved to be nothing they would laugh at him, or more likely call him hard names. He tried ear to earth once more. The trembling was still growing in strength, and mixed with it was a low, groaning sound, like the swell of the sea on the shore. The sound came with the wind from the north.

Dick sprang to his feet. There, in the north was a faint light which grew with amazing rapidity. In a minutes almost it seemed to redden the whole northern heavens, and the groaning sound became a roll, like that of approaching thunder.

A shadow flitted by Dick.

"What is it, Bright Sun?? What is it? " exclaimed the boy.

"The dry grass burns, and a mighty buffalo herd flees before it. "

Then Bright Sun was gone, and the full sense of their danger burst upon Dick in overwhelming tide. The flames came on, as fast as a horse's gallop, and the buffaloes, in thousands and tens of thousands, were their vanguard. The camp lay directly in the path of fire and buffalo. The awakened sentinels were on their feet now, and half-clad men were springing from the wagons.

Dick stood perfectly still for perhaps a minute, while the fire grew brighter and the thunder of a myriad hoofs grew louder. Then he remembered what he had so often read and heard, and the crisis stirred him to swift action. While the whole camp was a scene of confusion, of shouts, of oaths, and of running men, he sped to its south side, to a point twenty or thirty yards from the nearest wagon. There he knelt in the dry grass and drew his box of matches from his pocket. It happened that Conway saw.

"What are you doing, you boy? " he cried, threateningly.

But Dick did not care for Conway just then.

"Back fire! Back fire! " he shouted, and struck a match. It went out, but he quickly struck another, shielded it with one hand and touched the tiny flame to the grass. A flame equally tiny answered, but in an instant it leaped into the size and strength of a giant. The blaze rose

23

higher than Dick's head, ran swiftly to right and left, and then roared away to the south, eating up everything in its path.

"Well done, " said a voice at Dick's elbow. "It is the only thing that could save the train. "

It was Bright Sun who spoke, and he had come so silently that Dick did not see him until then.

Conway understood now, but without a word of approval he turned away and began to give orders, mixed with much swearing. He had a rough sort of efficiency, and spurred by his tongue and their own dreadful necessity, the men worked fast. The horses and mules, except three or four which had broken loose and were lost, were hitched to the wagons in half the usual time. There were no sluggards now.

Dick helped, and Albert, too, but to both it seemed that the work would never be done. The back fire was already a half mile away, gathering volume and speed as it went, but the other was coming on at an equal pace. Deer and antelope were darting past them, and the horses and mules were rearing in terror.

"Into the burned ground, " shouted Conway, "an' keep the wagons close together! "

No need to urge the animals. They galloped southward over earth which was still hot and smoking, but they knew that something was behind them, far more terrible than sparks and smoke.

Dick made Albert jump into their own wagon, while he ran beside it. As he ran, he looked back, and saw a sight that might well fill the bravest soul with dread. A great black line, crested with tossing horns, was bearing down on them. The thunder of hoofs was like the roar of a hurricane, but behind the herd was a vast wall of light, which seemed to reach from the earth to the heavens and which gave forth sparks in myriads. Dick knew that they had been just in time.

They did not stop until they had gone a full quarter of a mile, and then the wagons were hastily drawn up in a rude circle, with the animals facing the center, that is, the inside, and still rearing and neighing in terror. Then the men, rifle in hand, and sitting in the rear of the wagons, faced the buffalo herd.

Dick was with the riflemen, and, like the others, he began to fire as soon as the vanguard of the buffaloes was near enough. The wagons were a solid obstacle which not even King Bison could easily run over, but Dick and Albert thought the herd would never split, although the bullets were poured into it at a central point like a driven wedge.

But the falling buffaloes were an obstacle to those behind them, and despite their mad panic, the living became conscious of the danger in front. The herd split at last, the cleft widened to right and left, and then the tide, in two great streams, flowed past the wagon train.

Dick ceased firing and sat with Albert on the tail of the wagon. The wall of fire, coming to the burned ground, went out in the center, but the right and left ends of it, swinging around, still roared to the southward, passing at a distance of a quarter of a mile on either side.

Dick and Albert watched until all the herd was gone, and when only smoke and sparks were left, helped to get the camp into trim again. Conway knew that the boy had saved them, but he gave him no thanks.

It took the ground a long time to cool, and they advanced all the next day over a burned area. They traveled northward ten days, always ascending, and they were coming now to a wooded country. They crossed several creeks, flowing down from the higher mountains, and along the beds of these they found cottonwood, ash, box elder, elm, and birch. On the steeper slops were numerous cedar brakes and also groves of yellow pine. There was very little undergrowth, but the grass grew in abundance. Although it was now somewhat dry, the horses and mules ate it eagerly. The buffaloes did not appear here, but they saw many signs of bear, mule deer, panther or mountain lion, and other game.

They camped one night in a pine grove by the side of a brook that came rushing and foaming down from the mountains, and the next morning Albert, who walked some distance from the water, saw a silver-tip bear lapping the water of the stream. The bear raised his head and looked at Albert, and Albert stopped and looked at the bear. The boy was unarmed, but he was not afraid. The bear showed no hostility, only curiosity. He gazed a few moments, stretched his nose as if he would sniff the air, then turned and lumbered away

25

among the pines. Albert returned to camp, but he said nothing of the bear to anybody except Dick.

"He was such a jolly, friendly looking fellow, Dick, " he said, "that I didn't want any of these men to go hunting him. "

Dick laughed.

"Don't you worry about that, Al, " he said. "They are hunting gold, not bears. "

On the twelfth day they came out on a comparatively level plateau, where antelope were grazing and prairie chickens whirring. It looked like a fertile country, and they were glad of easy traveling for the wagons. Just at the edge of the pine woods that they were leaving was a beautiful little lake of clear, blue water, by which they stayed half a day, refreshing themselves, and catching some excellent fish, the names of which they did not know.

"How much long, Bright Sun, will it take us to reach the gold country? " asked Conway of the Indian, in Dick's hearing.

"About a week, " replied Bright Sun. "The way presently will be very rough and steep, up! up! up! and we can go only a few miles a day, but the mountains are already before us. See! "

He pointed northward and upward, and there before them was the misty blue loom that Dick knew was the high mountains. In those dark ridges lay the gold that they were going to seek, and his heart throbbed. Albert and he could do such wonderful things with it.

They were so high already that the nights were crisp with cold; but at the edge of the forest, running down to the little lake, fallen wood was abundant, and they built that night a great fire of fallen boughs that crackled and roared merrily. Yet they hovered closely, because the wind, sharp with ice, was whistling down from the mountains, and the night air, even in the little valley, was heavy with frost. Dick's buffalo robe was dry now, and he threw it around Albert, as he sat before the fire. It enveloped the boy like a great blanket, but far warmer, the soft, smooth fur caressing his cheeks, and as Albert drew it closer, he felt very snug indeed.

"We cross this valley to-morrow, " said Dick, "and then we begin a steeper climb. "

"Then it will be mountains, only mountains, " said Bright Sun. "We go into regions which no white men except the fur hunters, have ever trod. "

Dick started. He had not known that the Indian was near. Certainly he was not there a moment ago. There was something uncanny in the way in which Bright Sun would appear on noiseless footstep, like a wraith rising from the earth.

"I shall be glad of it, Bright Sun, " said Albert. "I'm tired of the plains, and they say that the mountains are good for many ills. "

Bright Sun's enigmatic glance rested upon Albert a moment.

"Yes, " he said, "the mountains will cure many ills. "

Dick glanced at him, and once more he received the impression of thought and power. The Indian's nose curved like an eagle's beak, and the firelight perhaps exaggerated both the curve and its effect. The whole impression of thought and force was heightened by the wide brow and the strong chin.

Dick looked back into the fire, and when he glanced around a few moments again, Bright Sun was not there. He had gone as silently as he had come.

"That Indian gives me the shivers sometimes, " he said to Albert. "What do you make of him? "

"I don't know, " replied the boy. "Sometimes I like him and sometimes I don't. "

Albert was soon asleep, wrapped in the buffalo robe, and Dick by and by followed him to the same pleasant land. The wind, whistling as it blew down from the mountains, grew stronger and colder, and its tone was hostile, as if it resented the first presence of white men in the little valley by the lake.

Chapter III
The Pass

They resumed the journey early the next day, Bright Sun telling Conway that they could reach the range before sunset, and that they would find there an easy pass leading a mile or two farther on to a protected and warm glen.

"That's the place for our camp, " said Conway, and he urged the train forward.

The traveling was smooth and easy, and they soon left the little blue lake well behind, passing through a pleasant country well wooded with elm, ash, birch, cottonwood, and box elder, and the grass growing high everywhere. They crossed more than one clear little stream, a pleasant contrast to the sluggish, muddy creeks of the prairies.

The range, toward which the head of the train was pointing, now came nearer. The boys saw its slopes, shaggy with dark pine, and they knew that beyond it lay other and higher slopes, also dark with pine. The air was of a wonderful clearness, showing in the east and beyond the zenith a clear silver tint, while the west was pure red gold with the setting sun.

Nearer and nearer came the range. The great pines blurred at first into an unbroken mass, now stood out singly, showing their giant stems. Afar a flash of foamy white appeared, where a brook fell in a foamy cascade. Presently they were within a quarter of a mile of the range, and its shadow fell over the train. In the west the sun was low.

"The pass is there, straight ahead, " said Bright Sun, pointing to the steep range.

"I don't see any opening, " said Conway.

"It is so narrow and the pines hide it, " rejoined Bright Sun, "but it is smooth and easy. "

Albert was at the rear of the train. He had chosen to walk in the later hours of the afternoon. He had become very tired, but, unwilling to confess it even to himself, he did not resume his place in the wagon. His weariness made him lag behind.

Albert was deeply sensitive to the impressions of time and place. The twilight seemed to him to fall suddenly like a great black robe. The pines once more blurred into a dark, unbroken mass. The low sun in the west dipped behind the hills, and the rays of red and gold that it left were chill and cold.

"Your brother wishes to see you. He is at the foot of the creek that we crossed fifteen minutes ago. "

It was Bright Sun who spoke.

"Dick wants to see me at the crossing of the creek! Why, I thought he was ahead of me with the train! " exclaimed Albert.

"No, he is waiting for you. He said that it was important, " repeated Bright Sun.

Albert turned in the darkening twilight and went back on the trail of the train toward the crossing of the creek. Bright Sun went to the head of the train, and saw Dick walking there alone and looking at the hills.

"Your brother is behind at the creek, " said Bright Sun. "He is ill and wishes you. Hurry! I think it is important! "

"Albert at the creek, ill? " exclaimed Dick in surprise and alarm. "Why, I thought he was here with the train! "

But Bright Sun had gone on ahead. Dick turned back hastily, and ran along the trail through the twilight that was now fast merging into the night.

"Al, ill and left behind! " he exclaimed again and again. "He must have overexerted himself! "

His alarm deepened when he saw how fast the darkness was increasing. The chill bars of red and gold were gone from the west. When he looked back he could see the train no more, and heard only the faint sound of the cracking of whips. The train was fast disappearing in the pass.

But Dick had become a good woodsman and plainsman. His sense of direction was rarely wrong, and he went straight upon the trail for the creek. Night had now come but it was not very dark, and presently he saw the flash of water. It was the creek, and a few more steps took him there. A figure rose out of the shadows.

"Al! " he cried. "Have you broken down? Why didn't you get into the wagon? "

"Dick, " replied Albert in a puzzled tone, "there's nothing the matter with me, except that I'm tired. Bright Sun told me that you were here waiting for me, and that you had something important to tell me. I couldn't find you, and now you come running. "

Dick stopped in amazement.

"Bright Sun said I was waiting here for you, and had something important to tell you? " exclaimed Dick. "Why, he told me that you were ill, and had been left unnoticed at the crossing! "

The two boys stared at each other.

"What does it mean? " they exclaimed together.

From the dark pass before them came a sound which in the distance resembled the report of a firecracker, followed quickly by two or three other sounds, and then by many, as if the whole pack had been ignited at once. But both boys knew it was not firecrackers. It was something far more deadly and terrible—a hail of rifle bullets. They looked toward the pass and saw there pink and red flashes appearing and reappearing. Shouts, and mingled with them a continuous long, whining cry, a dreadful overnote, came to their ears.

"The train has been attacked! " cried Dick. "It has marched straight into an ambush! "

"Indians? " exclaimed Albert, who was trembling violently from sheer physical and mental excitement.

"It couldn't be anything else! " replied Dick. "This is their country! And they must be in great force, too! Listen how the fight grows! "

The volume of the firing increased rapidly, but above it always rose that terrible whining note. The red and pink flashes in the pass danced and multiplied, and the wind brought the faint odor of smoke.

"We must help! " exclaimed Dick. "One can't stand here and see them all cut down! "

He forgot in his generous heart, at that moment, that he disliked Conway and all his men, and that he and Albert had scarcely a friend in the train. He thought only of doing what he could to beat back the Indian attack, and Albert felt the same impulse. Both had their rifles—fine, breech-loading, repeating weapons, and with these the two might do much. No one ever parted with his arms after entering the Indian country.

"Come on, Albert! " exclaimed Dick, and the two ran toward the pass. But before they had gone a hundred yards they stopped as if by the same impulse. That terrible whining note was now rising higher and higher. It was not merely a war whoop, it had become also a song of triumph. There was a certain silvery quality in the night air, a quality that made for illumination, and Dick thought he saw dusky forms flitting here and there in the mouth of the pass behind the train. It was only fancy, because he was too far away for such perception, but in this case fancy and truth were the same.

"Hurry, Dick! Let's hurry! " exclaimed the impulsive and generous Albert. "If we don't, we'll be too late to do anything! "

They started again, running as fast as they could toward that space in the dark well where the flashes of red and blue came and went. Dick was so intent that he did not hear the short, quick gasps of Albert, but he did hear a sudden fall beside him and stopped short. Albert was lying on his back unconscious. A faint tinge of abnormal red showed on his lips.

"Oh, I forgot! I forgot! " groaned Dick.

Such sudden and violent exertion, allied with the excitement of the terrible moment, had overpowered the weak boy. Dick bent down in grief. At first he thought his brother was dead, but the breath still came.

Dick did not know what to do. In the pass, under the shadow of night, the pines, and the mountain wall, the battle still flared and crackled, but its volume was dying. Louder rose the fierce, whining yell, and its note was full of ferocity and triumph, while the hoarser cries of the white men became fewer and lower. Now Dick really saw dusky figures leaping about between him and the train. Something uttering a shrill, unearthly cry of pain crashed heavily through the bushes near him and quickly passed on. It was a wounded horse, running away.

Dick shuddered. Then he lifted Albert in his arms, and he had the forethought, even in that moment of excitement and danger, to pick up Albert's rifle also. Strong as he naturally was, he had then the strength of four, and, turning off at a sharp angle, he ran with Albert toward a dense thicket which clustered at the foot of the mountain wall.

He went a full three hundred yards before he was conscious of weariness, and he was then at the edge of the thicket, which spread over a wide space. He laid Albert down on some of last year's old leaves, and then his quick eyes caught the sight of a little pool among some rocks. He dipped up the water in his felt hat, and after carefully wiping the red stain from his brother's lips, poured the cold fluid upon his face.

Albert revived, sat up, and tried to speak, but Dick pressed his hand upon his mouth.

"Nothing above a whisper, Al, " he said softly. "The fight is not yet wholly over, and the Sioux are all about. "

"I fainted, " said Albert in a whisper. "O Dick, what a miserable, useless fellow I am! But it was the excitement and the run! "

"It was doubtless a lucky thing that you fainted, " Dick whispered back. "If you hadn't, both of us would probably be dead now. "

"It's not all over yet, " said Albert.

"No, but it soon will be. Thank God, we've got our rifles. Do you feel strong enough to walk now, Al? The deeper we get into the thicket the better it will be for us. "

Albert rose slowly to his feet, rocked a little, and then stood straight.

Only a few flashes were appearing now in the pass. Dick knew too well who had been victorious. The battle over, the Sioux would presently be ranging for stragglers and for plunder. He put one arm under Albert, while he carried both of the rifles himself. They walked on through the thicket and the night gradually darkened. The silvery quality was gone from the air, and the two boys were glad. It would not be easy to find them now. In the pass both the firing and the long, whining whoop ceased entirely. The flashes of red or blue appeared no more. Silence reigned there and in the valley. Dick shivered despite himself. For the moment the silence was more terrible than the noise of battle had been. Black, ominous shadows seemed to float down from the mountains, clothing all the valley. A chill wind came up, moaning among the pines. The valley, so warm and beautiful in the day, now inspired Dick with a sudden and violent repulsion. It was a hateful place, the abode of horror and dread. He wished to escape from it.

They crossed the thicket and came up against the mountain wall. But it was not quite so steep as it had looked in the distance, and in the faint light Dick saw the trace of a trail leading up the slope among the pines. It was not the trail of human beings, merely a faint path indicating that wild animals, perhaps cougars, had passed that way.

"How are you feeling, Al? " he asked, repeating his anxious query.

"Better. My strength has come back, " replied his brother.

"Then we'll go up the mountain. We must get as far away as we can from those fiends, the Sioux. Thank God, Al, we're spared together! "

Each boy felt a moment of devout thankfulness. They had not fallen, and they were there together! Each also thought of the singular message that Bright Sun had given to them, but neither spoke of it.

They climbed for more than half an hour in silence, save for an occasional whisper. The bushes helped Albert greatly. He pulled himself along by means of them, and now and then the two boys stopped that he might rest. He was still excited under the influence of the night, the distant battle, and their peril, and he breathed in short gasps, but did not faint again. Dick thrust his arm at intervals under his brother's and helped him in the ascent.

After climbing a quarter of an hour, they stopped longer than usual and looked down at the pass, which Dick reckoned should be almost beneath them. They heard the faint sound of a shot, saw a tiny beam of red appear, then disappear, and after that there was only silence and blank darkness.

"It's all over now, " whispered Albert, and it was a whisper not of caution, but of awe.

"Yes, it's all over, " Dick said in the same tone. "It's likely, Al, that you and I alone out of all that train are alive. Conway and all the others are gone. "

"Except Bright Sun, " said Albert.

The two boys looked at each other again, but said nothing. They then resumed their climbing, finding it easier this time. They reached a height at which the undergrowth ceased, but the pines, growing almost in ordered rows, stretched onward and upward.

Dick sent occasional glances toward the pass, but the darkness there remained unbroken. Every time he turned his eyes that way he seemed to be looking into a black well of terror.

Both Dick and Albert, after the first hour of ascent, had a feeling of complete safety. The Sioux, occupied with their great ambush and victory, would not know there had been two stragglers behind the train, and even had they known, to search for them among the dense forests of distant mountain slopes would be a futile task. Dick's mind turned instead to the needs of their situation, and he began to appreciate the full danger and hardship of it.

Albert and he were right in feeling thankful that they were spared together, although they were alone in the wilderness in every sense of the word. It was hundreds of miles north, east, south, and west to the habitations of white men. Before them, fold on fold, lay unknown mountains, over which only hostile savages roamed. Both he and Albert had good rifles and belts full of cartridges, but that was all. It was a situation to daunt the most fearless heart, and the shiver that suddenly ran over Dick did not come from the cold of the night.

They took a long rest in a little clump of high pines and saw a cold, clear moon come out in the pale sky. They felt the awful sense of desolation and loneliness, for it seemed to them that the moon was looking down on an uninhabited world in which only they were left. They heard presently little rustlings in the grass, and thought at first it was another ambush, though they knew upon second thought that it was wild creatures moving on the mountain side.

"Come, Al, " said Dick. "Another half hour will put us on top of the ridge, and then I think it will be safe for us to stop. "

"I hope they'll be keeping a good room for us at the hotel up there, " said Albert wanly.

Dick tried to laugh, but it was a poor imitation and he gave it up.

"We may find some sort of a sheltered nook, " he said hopefully.

Dick had become conscious that it was cold, since the fever in his blood was dying down. Whenever they stopped and their bodies relaxed, they suffered from chill. He was deeply worried about Albert, who was in no condition to endure exposure on a bleak mountain, and wished now for the buffalo robe they had regarded as such a fine trophy.

They reached the crest of the ridge in a half hour, as Dick had expected, and looking northward in the moonlight saw the dim outlines of other ridges and peaks in a vast, intricate maze. A narrow, wooded valley seemed to occupy the space between the ridge on which they stood and the next one parallel to it to the northward.

"It ought to be a good place down there to hide and rest, " said Albert.

"I think you're right, " said Dick, "and we'll go down the slope part of the way before we camp for the night. "

They found the descent easy. It was still open forest, mostly pine with a sprinkling of ash and oak, and it was warmer on the northern side, the winds having but little sweep there.

The moon became brighter, but it remained cold and pitiless, recking nothing of the tragedy in the pass. It gave Dick a chill to look at it. But he spent most of the time watching among the trees for some sheltered spot that Nature had made. It was over an hour before he found it, a hollow among rocks, with dwarf pines clustering thickly at the sides and in front. It was so well hidden that he would have missed it had he not been looking for just such a happy alcove, and at first he was quite sure that some wild animal must be using it as a den.

He poked in the barrel of his rifle, but nothing flew out, and then, pulling back the pine boughs, he saw no signs of a previous occupation.

"It's just waiting for us, Al, old fellow, " he said gayly, "but nothing of this kind is so good that it can't be made better. Look at all those dead leaves over there under the oaks. Been drying ever since last year and full of warmth. "

They raked the dead leaves into the nook, covering the floor of it thickly, and piling them up on the sides as high as they would stay, and then they lay down inside, letting the pine boughs in front fall back into place. It was really warm and cozy in there for two boys who had been living out of doors for weeks, and Dick drew a deep, long breath of content.

"Suppose a panther should come snooping along, " said Albert, "and think this the proper place for his bed and board? "

"He'd never come in, don't you fear. He'd smell us long before he got here, and then strike out in the other direction. "

Albert was silent quite a while, and as he made no noise, Dick thought he was asleep. But Albert spoke at last, though he spoke low and his tone was very solemn.

"Dick, " he said, "we've really got a lot to be thankful for. You know that. "

"I certainly do, " said Dick with emphasis. "Now you go to sleep, Al."

Albert was silent again, and presently his breathing became very steady and regular. Dick touched him and saw that he was fast asleep. Then the older boy took off his coat and carefully spread it on the younger, after which he raked a great lot of the dry leaves over himself, and soon he, too, was sound asleep.

Dick awoke far in the night and stirred in his bed of leaves. But the movement caused him a little pain, and he wondered dimly, because he had not yet fully come through the gates of sleep, and he did not remember where he was or what had happened. A tiny shaft of pale light fell on his forehead, and he looked up through pine branches. It was the moon that sent the beam down upon him, but he could see nothing else. He stirred again and the little pain returned. Then all of it came back to him.

Dick reached out his hand and touched Albert. His brother was sleeping soundly, and he was still warm, the coat having protected him. But Dick was cold, despite the pines, the rocks, and the leaves. It was the cold that had caused the slight pain in his joints when he moved, but he rose softly lest he wake Albert, and slipped outside, standing in a clear space between the pines.

The late moon was of uncommon brilliancy. It seemed a molten mass of burnished silver, and its light fell over forest and valley, range and peak. The trees on the slopes stood out like lacework, but far down in the valley the light seemed to shimmer like waves on a sea of silver mist. It was all inexpressibly cold, and of a loneliness that was uncanny. Nothing stirred, not a twig, not a blade of grass. It seemed to Dick that if even a leaf fell on the far side of the mountain he could hear it. It was a great, primeval world, voiceless and unpeopled, brooding in a dread and mystic silence.

Dick shivered. He had shivered often that night, but now the chill went to the marrow. It was the chill the first man must have felt when he was driven from the garden and faced the globe-girdling forest. He came back to the rock covert and leaned over until he could hear his brother breathing beneath the pine boughs. Then he felt the surge of relief, of companionship—after all, he was not alone in the wilderness! —and returned to the clear space between the pines. There he walked up and down briskly, swinging his arms, exercising all his limbs, until the circulation was fully restored and he was warm again.

Dick felt the immensity of the problem that lay before him—one that he alone must solve if it were to be solved at all. He and Albert had escaped the massacre, but how were they to live in that wilderness of mountains? It was not alone the question of food. How were they to save themselves from death by exposure? Those twinges in his knees had been warning signs. Oddly enough, his mind now fastened upon one thing. He was longing for the lost buffalo robe, his first great prize. It had been so large and so warm, and the fur was so soft. It would cover both Albert and himself, and keep them warm on the coldest night. If they only had it now! He thought more of that robe just then than he did of the food that they would need in the morning. Cast forth upon a primeval world, this first want occupied his mind to the exclusion of all others.

He returned to the rocky alcove presently, and lay down again. He was too young and too healthy to remain awake long, despite the full measure of their situation, and soon he slept soundly once more. He was first to awake in the morning, and the beam that struck upon his forehead was golden instead of silver. It was warm, too, and cheerful, and as Dick parted the branches and looked out, he saw that the sun was riding high. It had been daylight a full three hours at least, but it did not matter. Time was perhaps the only commodity of which he and Albert now had enough and to spare.

He took his coat off Albert and put it on himself, lest Albert might suspect, and then began to sing purposely, with loudness and levity, an old farm rhyme that had been familiar to the boys of his vicinity:

"Wake up, Jake, the day is breaking. The old cow died, her tail shaking. "

Albert sat up, rubbed his eyes, and stared at Dick and the wilderness.

"Now look at him! " cried Dick. "He thinks he's been called too early. He thinks he'd like to sleep eight or ten hours longer! Get up, little boy! Yes, it's Christmas morning! Come and see what good old Santa has put in your stocking! "

Albert yawned again and laughed. Really, Dick was such a cheerful, funny fellow that he always kept one in good spirits. Good old Dick!

"Old Santa filled our stockings, all right, " continued Dick, "but he was so busy cramming 'em full of great forests and magnificent scenery that he forgot to leave any breakfast for us, and I'm afraid we'll have to hustle for it. "

They started down the mountain slope, and presently they came to a swift little brook, in which they bathed their faces, removing, at the same time, fragments of twigs and dried leaves from their hair.

"That was fine and refreshing, " said Dick, "but it doesn't fill my stomach. Al, I could bite a tenpenny nail in half and digest both pieces, too. "

"I don't care for nails, " said Albert, "but I think I could gnaw down a good-sized sapling. Hold me, Dick, or I'll be devouring a pine tree."

Both laughed, and put as good a face on it as they could, but they were frightfully hungry, nevertheless. But they had grown up on farms, and they knew that the woods must contain food of some kind or other. They began a search, and after a while they found wild plums, now ripe, which they ate freely. They then felt stronger and better, but, after all, it was a light diet and they must obtain food of more sustenance.

"There are deer, of course, in this valley, " said Dick, fingering his rifle, "and sooner or later we'll get a shot at one of them, but it may be days, and—Al—I've got another plan. "

"What is it? "

"You know, Al, that I can travel pretty fast anywhere. Now those Sioux, after cutting down the train and wiping out all the people, would naturally go away. They'd load themselves up with spoil and scoot. But a lot, scattered here and there, would be left behind. Some of the teams would run away in all the shooting and shouting. And, Al, you and I need those things! We must have them if we are going to live, and we both want to live! "

"Do you mean, Dick, that you're going back down there in that awful pass? "

"That's just about what I had on my mind, " replied Dick cheerfully; "and now I've got it off, I feel better. "

"But you can never get back alive, Dick! " exclaimed Albert, his eyes widening in horror at the memory of what they had seen and heard the night before.

"Get back alive? Why, of course I will, " responded Dick. "And I'll do more than that, too. You'll see me come galloping up the mountain, bearing hogsheads and barrels of provisions. But, seriously, Al, it must be done. If I don't go, we'll starve to death. "

"Then I'm going, too. "

"No, Al, old boy, you're not strong enough just yet, though you will be soon. There are certainly no Sioux in this little valley, and it would be well if you were to go back up the slope and stay in the pine shelter. It's likely that I'll be gone nearly all day, but don't be worried. You'll have one of the rifles with you, and you know how to use it. "

Albert had a clear and penetrating mind, and he saw the truth of Dick's words. They went back up the slope, where he crept within the pine shelter and lay down on the leaves, while Dick went alone on his mission.

Chapter IV
Treasure-Trove

When Dick passed the crest of the ridge and began the descent toward the fatal pass, his heart beat heavily. The terror and shock of the night before, those distant shots and shouts, returned to him, and it was many minutes before he could shake off a dread that was almost superstitious in its nature. But youth, health, and the sunlight conquered. The day was uncommonly brilliant. The mountains rolled back, green on the slopes, blue at the crests, and below him, like a brown robe, lay the wavering plain across which they had come.

Dick could see no sign of human life down there. No rejoicing Sioux warrior galloped over the swells, no echo of a triumphant war whoop came to his ear. Over mountain and plain alike the silence of the desert brooded. But high above the pass great black birds wheeled on lazy pinions.

Dick believed more strongly than ever that the Sioux had gone away. Savage tribes do not linger over a battlefield that is finished; yet as he reached the bottom of the slope his heart began to beat heavily again, and he was loath to leave the protecting shadow of the pines. He fingered his rifle, passing his hand gently over the barrel and the trigger. It was a fine weapon, a beautiful weapon, and just at this moment it was a wonderful weapon. He felt in its full force, for the first time in his life, what the rifle meant to the pioneer.

The boy, after much hesitation and a great searching of eye and ear, entered the pass. At once the sunlight dimmed. Walls as straight as the side of a house rose above him three of four hundred feet, while the distance between was not more than thirty feet. Dwarf pines grew here and there in the crannies of the cliffs, but mostly the black rock showed. Dwarf pines also grew at the bottom of the pass close to either cliff, and Dick kept among them, bending far down and advancing very slowly.

Fifty yards were passed, and still there was no sound save a slight moaning through the pass, which Dick knew was the sigh of the wind drawn into the narrow cleft. It made him shudder, and had he not been of uncommon courage he would have turned back.

He looked up. The great black birds, wheeling on lazy pinions, seemed to have sunk lower. That made him shudder, too, but it was another confirmation of his belief that all the Sioux had gone. He went eight or ten yards farther and then stopped short. Before him lay two dead horses and an overturned wagon. Both horses had been shot, and were still in their gear attached to the wagon.

Dick examined the wagon carefully, and as he yet heard and saw no signs of a human being save himself, his courage grew. It was a big wagon of the kind used for crossing the plains, with boxes around the inside like lockers. Almost everything of value had been taken by the Sioux, but in one of the lockers Dick was lucky enough to find a large, heavy, gray blanket. He rolled it up at once, and with a strap cut from the horse's gear tied it on his back, after the fashion of a soldier on the march.

"The first great treasure! " he murmured exultantly. "Now for the next! "

He found in the same wagon, jammed under the driver's seat and hidden from hasty view, about the half of a side of bacon—ten pounds, perhaps. Dick fairly laughed when he got his hands upon it, and he clasped it lovingly, as if it were a ten-pound nugget of pure gold. But it was far better than gold just then. He wrapped it in a piece of canvas which he cut from the cover of the wagon, and tied it on his back above the blanket.

Finding nothing more of value in the wagon, he resumed his progress up the pass. It was well for Dick that he was stout-hearted, and well for him, too, that he was driven by great need, else he would surely have gone back.

He was now come into the thick of it. Around him everywhere lay the fallen, and the deeds done in Indian warfare were not lacking. Sam Conway lay upon his side, and brutal as the man had been, Dick felt grief when he saw him. Here were others, too, that he knew, and he counted the bodies of the few women who had been with the train. They had died probably in the battle like the rest. They, like the men, had been hardened, rough, and coarse of speech and act, but Dick felt grief, too, when he saw them. Nearly all the animals had been slain also in the fury of the attack, and they were scattered far up the pass.

Dick resolutely turned his face away from the dead and began to glean among the wagons for what the Sioux might have left. All these wagons were built like the first that he had searched, and he was confident that he would find much of value. Nor was he disappointed. He found three more blankets, and in their own wagon the buffalo robe that he had lamented. Doubtless, its presence there was accounted for by the fact that the Sioux did not consider a buffalo robe a trophy of their victory over white men.

Other treasures were several boxes of crackers, about twenty boxes of sardines, three flasks of brandy, suitable for illness, a heavy riding cloak, a Virginia ham, two boxes of matches, a small iron skillet, and an empty tin canteen. He might have searched further, but he realized that time was passing, and that Albert must be on the verge of starvation. He had forgotten his own hunger in the excitement of seek and find, but it came back now and gnawed at him fiercely. Yet he would not touch any of the food. No matter how great the temptation he would not take a single bite until Albert had the same chance.

He now made all his treasures into one great package, except the buffalo robe. That was too heavy to add to the others, and he tied it among the boughs of a pine, where the wolves could not reach it. Then, with the big pack on his back, he began the return. It was more weight than he would have liked to carry at an ordinary time, but now in his elation he scarcely felt it. He went rapidly up the slope and by the middle of the afternoon was going down the other side.

As he approached the pine alcove he whistled a familiar tune, popular at the time—"Silver Threads Among the Gold. " He knew that Albert, if he were there—and he surely must be there—would recognize his whistle and come forth. He stopped, and his heart hammered for a moment, but Albert's whistle took up the second line of the air and Albert himself came forth jauntily.

"We win, Al, old boy! " called Dick. "Just look at this pack! "

"I can't look at anything else, " replied Albert in the same joyful tones. "It's so big that I don't see you under it. Dick, have you robbed a treasure ship? "

"No, Al, " replied Dick, very soberly. "I haven't robbed a treasure ship, but I've been prowling with success over a lost battlefield—a ghoul I believe they call such a person, but it had to be done. I've enough food here to last a week at least, and we may find more. "

He put down his pack and took out the bacon. As Albert looked at it he began unconsciously to clinch and unclinch his teeth. Dick saw his face, and, knowing that the same eager look was in his own, he laughed a little.

"Al, " he said, "you and I know now how wolves often feel, but we're not going to behave like wolves. We're going to light a fire and cook this bacon. We'll take the risk of the flame or smoke being seen by Sioux. In so vast a country the chances are all in our favor. "

They gathered up pine cones and other fallen wood, and with the help of the matches soon had a fire. Then they cut strips of bacon and fried them on the ends of sharpened sticks, the sputter making the finest music in their ears.

Never before had either tasted food so delicious, and they ate strip after strip. Dick noticed with pleasure how the color came into Albert's cheeks, and how his eyes began to sparkle. Sleeping under the pines seemed to have benefited instead of injuring him, and certainly there was a wonderful healing balm in the air of that pine-clad mountain slope. Dick could feel it himself. How strong he was after eating! He shook his big shoulders.

"What are you bristling up about? " asked Albert.

"Merely getting ready to start again, " replied Dick. "You know the old saying, Al, 'you've got to hit while the iron's hot. ' More treasure is down there in the pass, but if we wait it won't stay there. Everything that we get now is worth more to us than diamonds. "

"It's so, " said Albert, and then he sighed sadly as he added, "How I wish I were strong enough to go with you and help! "

"Just you wait, " said Dick. "You'll be as strong as a horse in a month, and then you'll have to do all the work and bring me my breakfast in the morning as I lie in bed. Besides, you'd have to stay here and guard the treasure that we already have. Better get into the pine den. Bears and wolves may be drawn by the scent of the food, and they might think of attacking you. "

They put out the fire, and while Albert withdrew into the pine shelter, Dick started again over the mountain. The sun was setting blood red in the west, and in the east the shadows of twilight were advancing. It required a new kind of courage to enter the pass in the night, and Dick's shudders returned. At certain times there is something in the dark that frightens the bravest and those most used to it.

Dick hurried. He knew the way down the mountain now, and after the food and rest he was completely refreshed. But as fast as he went the shadows of twilight came faster, and when he reached the bottom of the mountain it was quite dark. The plain before him was invisible, and the forest on the slope behind him was a solid robe of black.

Dick set foot in the pass and then stopped. It was not dread but awe that thrilled him in every vein. He saw nothing before him but the well of darkness that was the great slash in the mountains. The wind, caught between the walls, moaned as in the day, and he knew perfectly well what if was, but it had all the nature of a dirge, nevertheless. Overhead a few dim stars wavered in a dusky sky.

Dick forced himself to go on. It required now moral, as well as physical, courage to approach that lost battlefield lying under its pall of night. Never was the boy a greater hero than at that moment. He advanced slowly. A bush caught him by the coat and held him an instant. He felt as if he had been seized in a man's grasp. He reached the first wagon, and it seemed to him, broken and rifled, an emblem of desolation. As he passed it a strange, low, whining cry made his backbone turn to ice. But he recovered and forced an uneasy little laugh at himself. It was only a wolf, the mean coyote of the prairies!

He came now into the space where the mass of the wagons and the fallen lay. Dark figures, low and skulking, darted away. More wolves! But one, a huge timber wolf, with a powerful body and long fangs, stood up boldly and stared at him with red eyes. Dick's own eyes were used to the darkness now, and he stared back at the wolf, which seemed to be giving him a challenge. He half raised his rifle, but the monster did not move. It was a stranger to guns, and this wilderness was its own.

It was Dick's first impulse to fire at the space between the red eyes, but he restrained it. He had not come there to fight with wolves, nor to send the report of a shot through the mountains. He picked up a stone and threw it at the wolf, striking him on the flank. The monster turned and stalked sullenly away, showing but little sign of fear. Dick pursued his task, and as he advanced something rose and, flapping heavily, sailed away. The shiver came again, but his will stopped it.

He was now in the center of the wreckage, which in the darkness looked as if it had all happened long ago. Nearly every wagon had been turned over, and now and then dark forms lay between the wheels. The wind moaned incessantly down the pass and over the ruin.

Overcoming his repulsion, Dick went to work. The moon was now coming out and he could see well enough for his task. There was still much gleaning left by the quick raiders, and everything would be of use to Albert and himself, even to the very gear on the fallen animals. He cut off a great quantity of this at once and put it in a heap at the foot of the cliff. Then he invaded the wagons and again brought forth treasures better than gold.

He found in one side box some bottles of medicine, the simple remedies of the border, which he packed very carefully, and in another he discovered half a sack of flour—fifty pounds, perhaps. A third rewarded him with a canister of tea and a twenty-pound bag of ground coffee. He clutched these treasures eagerly. They would be invaluable to Albert.

Continuing his search, he was rewarded with two pairs of heavy shoes, an ax, a hatchet, some packages of pins, needles, and thread, and a number of cooking utensils—pots, kettles, pans, and skillets. Just as he was about to quit for the purpose of making up his pack, he noticed in one of the wagons a long, narrow locker made into the side and fastened with a stout padlock. The wagon had been plundered, but evidently the Sioux had balked at the time this stout box would take for opening, and had passed on. Dick, feeling sure that it must contain something of value, broke the padlock with the head of the ax. When he looked in he uttered a cry of delight at his reward.

He brought forth from the box a beautiful double-barreled breech-loading shotgun, and the bounty of chance did not stop with the gun, for in the locker were over a thousand cartridges to fit it. Dick foresaw at once that it would be invaluable to Albert and himself in the pursuit of wild ducks, wild geese, and other feathered game. He removed some of the articles from his pack, which was already heavy enough, and put the shotgun and cartridges in their place. Then he set forth on the return journey.

As he left the wagons and went toward the mouth of the pass, he heard soft, padding sounds behind him, and knew that the wolves were returning, almost on his heels. He looked back once, and saw a pair of fiery red eyes which he felt must belong to the monster, the timber wolf, but Dick was no longer under the uncanny spell of the night and the place; he was rejoicing too much in his new treasures, like a miser who has just added a great sum to his hoard, to feel further awe of the wolves, the darkness, and a new battlefield.

Dick's second pack was heavier than his first, but as before, he trod lightly. He took a different path when he left the pass, and here in the moonlight, which was now much brighter, he saw the trace of wheels on the earth. The trace ran off irregularly through the short bushes and veered violently to and fro like the path of a drunken man. Dick inferred at once that it had been made, not by a wagon entering the pass, but by one leaving it, and in great haste. No doubt the horses or mules had been running away in fright at the firing.

Dick's curiosity was excited. He wished to see what had become of that wagon. The trail continued to lead through the short bushes that covered the plain just before entering the pass, and then turned off sharply to the right, where it led to an abrupt little canyon or gully about ten feet deep. The gully also was lined with bushes, and at first Dick could see nothing else, but presently he made out a wagon lying on its side. No horses or mules were there; undoubtedly, they had torn themselves loose from the gear in time to escape the fall.

Dick laid down his pack and descended to the wagon. He believed that in such a place it had escaped the plundering hands of the hasty Sioux, and his belief was correct. The wagon, a large one, was loaded with all the articles necessary for the passage of the plains. Although much tossed about by the fall, nothing was hurt.

Here was a treasure-trove, indeed! Dick's sudden sense of wealth was so overpowering that he felt a great embarrassment. How was he to take care of such riches? He longed at that moment for the strength of twenty men, that he might take it all at once and go over the mountain to Albert.

It was quite a quarter of an hour before he was able to compose himself thoroughly. Then he made a hasty examination of the wagon, so far as its position allowed. He found in it a rifle of the same pattern as that used by Albert and himself, a sixteen-shot repeater, the most advanced weapon of the time, and a great quantity of cartridges to fit. There was also two of the new revolvers, with sufficient cartridges, another ax, hatchets, saws, hammers, chisels, and a lot of mining tools. The remaining space in the wagon was occupied by clothing, bedding, provisions, and medicines.

Dick judged that the wolves could not get at the wagon as it lay, and leaving it he began his third ascent of the slope. He found Albert sound asleep in the pine alcove with his rifle beside him. He looked so peaceful that Dick was careful not to awaken him. He stored the second load of treasure in the alcove, and, wrapping one of the heavy blankets around himself, slept heavily.

He told Albert the next day of the wagon in the gully, and nothing could keep him from returning in the morning for salvage. He worked there two or three days, carrying heavy loads up the mountain, and finally, when it was all in their den, he and Albert felt equipped for anything. Nor had the buffalo robe been neglected. It was spread over much of the treasure. Albert, meanwhile, had assumed the functions of cook, and he discharged them with considerable ability. His strength was quite sufficient to permit of his collecting firewood, and he could fry bacon and make coffee and tea beautifully. But they were very sparing of the coffee and tea, as they also were of the flour, although their supplies of all three of these were greatly increased by the wagon in the gully. In fact, the very last thing that Dick had brought over the mountain was a hundred-pound sack of flour, and after accomplishing this feat he had rested a long time.

Both boys felt that they had been remarkably fortunate while this work was going on. One circumstance, apparently simple in itself, had been a piece of great luck, and that was the absence of rain. It was not a particularly rainy country, but a shower could have made them thoroughly miserable, and, moreover, would have been extremely dangerous for Albert. But nights and days alike remained dry and cool, and as Albert breathed the marvelous balsamic air he could almost feel himself transfused with its healing property. Meanwhile, the color in his cheeks was steadily deepening.

"We've certainly had good fortune, " said Dick.

"Aided by your courage and strength, " said Albert. "It took a lot of nerve to go down there in that pass and hunt for what the Sioux might have left behind. "

Dick disclaimed any superior merit, but he said nothing of the many tremors that he felt while performing the great task.

An hour or two later, Albert, who was hunting through their belongings, uttered a cry of joy on finding a little package of fishhooks. String they had among their stores, and it was easy enough to cut a slim rod for a pole.

"Now I can be useful for something besides cooking, " he said. "It doesn't require any great strength to be a fisherman, and I'm much mistaken if I don't soon have our table supplied with trout. "

There was a swift creek farther down the slope, and, angling with much patience, Albert succeeded in catching several mountain trout and a larger number of fish of an unknown species, but which, like the trout, were very good to eat.

Albert's exploit caused him intense satisfaction, and Dick rejoiced with him, not alone because of the fish, but also because of his brother's triumph.

Chapter V
The Lost Valley

They spent a week on the slope, sleeping securely and warmly under their blankets in the pine alcove, and fortune favored them throughout that time. It did not rain once, and there was not a sign of the Sioux. Dick did not revisit the pass after the first three days, and he knew that the wolves and buzzards had been busy there. But he stripped quite clean the wagon which had fallen in the gully, even carrying away the canvas cover, which was rainproof. Albert wondered that the Sioux had not returned, but Dick had a very plausible theory to account for it.

"The Sioux are making war upon our people, " he said, "and why should they stay around here? They have cut off what is doubtless the first party entering this region in a long time, and now they have gone eastward to meet our troops. Beside, the Sioux are mostly plains Indians, and they won't bother much about these mountains. Other Indians, through fear of the Sioux, will not come and live here, which accounts for this region being uninhabited. "

"Still a wandering band of Sioux might come through at any time and see us, " said Albert.

"That's so, and for other reasons, too, we must move. It's mighty fine, Al, sleeping out in the open when the weather's dry and not too cold, but I've read that the winter in the northwestern mountains is something terrible, and we've got to prepare for it. "

It was Dick's idea to go deeper into the mountains. He knew very well that the chance of their getting out before spring were too slender to be considered, and he believed that they could find better shelter and a more secure hiding place farther in. So he resolved upon a journey of exploration, and though Albert was now stronger, he must go alone. It was his brother's duty to remain and guard their precious stores. Already bears and mountain lions, drawn by the odors of the food, had come snuffing about the alcove, but they always retreated from the presence of either of the brothers. One huge silver tip had come rather alarmingly close, but when Dick shouted at him he, too, turned and lumbered off among the pines.

"What you want to guard against, Al, " said Dick, "is thieves rather than robbers. Look out for the sneaks. We'll fill the canteen and all our iron vessels with water so that you won't have to go even to the brook. Then you stay right here by the fire in the daytime, and in the den at night. You can keep a bed of coals before the den when you're asleep, and no wild animal will ever come past it. "

"All right, Dick, " said Albert courageously; "but don't you get lost over there among those ranges and peaks. "

"I couldn't do it if I tried, " replied Dick in the same cheerful tone. "You don't know what a woodsman and mountaineer I've become, Al, old boy! "

Albert smiled. Yet each boy felt the full gravity of the occasion when the time for Dick's departure came, at dawn of a cool morning, gleams of silver frost showing here and there on the slopes. Both knew the necessity of the journey, however, and hid their feelings.

"Be back to-morrow night, Al, " said Dick.

"Be ready for you, Dick, " said Albert.

Then they waved their hands to each other, and Dick strode away toward the higher mountains. He was well armed, carrying his repeating rifle and the large hunting knife which was useful for so many purposes. He had also thrust one of the revolvers into his belt.

Flushed with youth and strength, and equipped with such good weapons, he felt able to take care of himself in any company into which he might be thrown.

He reached the bottom of the slope, and looking back, saw Albert standing on a fallen log. His brother was watching him and waved his hand. Dick waved his in reply, and then, crossing the creek, began the ascent of the farther slope. There the pines and the distance rendered the brothers invisible to each other, and Dick pressed on with vigor. His recent trips over the lower slopes for supplies had greatly increased his skill in mountain climbing, and he did not suffer from weariness. Up, up, he went, and the pines grew shorter and scrubbier. But the thin, crisp air was a sheer delight, and he felt an extraordinary pleasure in mere living.

Dick looked back once more from the heights toward the spot where their camp lay and saw lying against the blue a thin gray thread that only the keenest eye would notice. He knew it to be the smoke from Albert's fire and felt sure that all was well.

While the slope which he was ascending was fairly steep, it was easy enough to find a good trail among the pines. There was little undergrowth and the ascent was not rocky. When Dick stood at last on the crest of the ridge he uttered a cry of delight and amazement.

The slope on which he stood was merely a sort of gate to the higher mountains, or rather it was a curtain hiding the view.

Before him, range on range and peak on peak, lay mighty mountains, some of them shooting up almost three miles above the sea, their crests and heads hid in eternal snow. Far away to northward and westward stretched the tremendous maze, and it seemed to Dick to have no end. A cold, dazzling sunlight poured in floods over the snowy summits, and he felt a great sense of awe. It was all so grand, so silent, and so near to the Infinite. He saw the full majesty of the world and of the Power that had created it. For a little while his mission and all human passions and emotions floated away from him; he was content merely to stand there, without thinking, but to feel the immensity and majesty of it all.

Dick presently recovered himself and with a little laugh came back to earth. But he was glad to have had those moments. He began the descent, which was rougher and rockier than the ascent had been, but the prospect was encouraging. The valley between the ridge on the slope of which he stood and the higher one beyond it seemed narrow, but he believed that he would find in it the shelter and hiding that he and Albert wished.

As he went down the slope became steeper, but once more the pines, sheltered from the snows and cruel winds, grew to a great size. There was also so much outcropping of rock that Dick was hopeful of finding another alcove deep enough to be converted into a house.

When nearly down, he caught a gleam among the trees that he knew was water, and again he was encouraged. Here was a certainty of one thing that was an absolute necessity. Soon he was in the valley, which he found exceedingly narrow and almost choked with a growth of pine, ash, and aspen, a tiny brook flowing down its center.

He was tired and warm from the long descent and knelt down and drank from the brook. Its waters were as cold as ice, flowing down from the crest of one of the great peaks clad, winter and summer, in snow.

Dick followed the brook for fully a mile, seeking everywhere a suitable place in which he and his brother might make a home, but he found none. The valley resembled in most of its aspects a great canyon, and all the fertile earth on either side of the brook was set closely with pine, ash, and aspen. These would form a shelter from winds, but they would not protect from rain and the great colds and snows of the high Rockies.

Dick noticed many footprints of animals at the margin of the stream, some of great size, which he had no doubt were made by grizzlies or silver tips. He also believed that the beaver might be found farther down along this cold and secluded water, but he was not interested greatly just then in animals; he was seeking for that most necessary of all things—something that must be had—a home.

It seemed to him at the end of his estimated mile that the brook was going to flow directly into the mountain which rose before him many hundreds of feet; but when he came to the rocky wall he found that the valley turned off at a sharp angle to the left, and the stream, of course, followed it, although it now descended more rapidly, breaking three times into little foamy falls five or six feet in height. Then another brook came from a deep cleft between the mountains on the eastern side and swelled with its volume the main stream, which now became a creek.

The new valley widened out to a width of perhaps a quarter of a mile, although the rocky walls on either side rose to a great height and were almost precipitous. Springs flowed from these walls and joined the creek. Some of them came down the face of the cliffs in little cascades of foam and vapor, but others spouted from the base of the rock. Dick knelt down to drink from one of the latter, but as his face approached the water he jumped away. He dipped up a little of it in his soft hat and tasted it. It was brackish and almost boiling hot.

Dick was rather pleased at the discovery. A bitter and hot spring might be very useful. He had imbibed—like many others—from the teaching of his childhood that any bitter liquid was good for you. As he advanced farther the valley continued to spread out. It was now perhaps a half mile in width, and well wooded. The creek became less turbulent, flowing with a depth of several feet in a narrow channel.

The whole aspect of the valley so far had been that of a wilderness uninhabited and unvisited. A mule deer looked curiously at Dick, then walked away a few paces and stood there. When Dick glanced back his deership was still curious and gazing. A bear crashed through a thicket, stared at the boy with red eyes, then rolled languidly away. Dick was quick to interpret these signs. They were unfamiliar with human presence, and he was cheered by the evidence. Yet at the end of another hundred yards of progress he sank down suddenly among some bushes and remained perfectly silent, but intently watchful.

He had seen a column of smoke rising above the pines and aspens. Smoke meant fire, fire meant human beings, and human beings, in that region, meant enemies. He had no doubt that Sioux were at the foot of that column of smoke. It was a tragic discovery. He was looking for a home for Albert and himself somewhere in this valley, but there could be no home anywhere near the Sioux. He and his brother must turn in another direction, and with painful effort lug their stores over the ridges.

But Dick was resolved to see. There were great springs of courage and tenacity in his nature, and he wished, moreover, to prove his new craft as a woodsman and mountaineer. He remained awhile in the bushes, watching the spire, and presently, to his amazement, it thinned quickly and was gone. It had disappeared swiftly, while the smoke from a fire usually dies down. It was Dick's surmise that the Sioux had put out their fire by artificial means and then had moved on. Such an act would indicate a fear of observation, and his curiosity increased greatly.

But Dick did not forget his caution. He crouched in the bushes for quite a while yet, watching the place where the smoke had been, but the sky remained clear and undefiled. He heard nothing and saw nothing but the lonely valley. At last he crept forward slowly, and with the greatest care, keeping among bushes and treading very softly. He advanced in this manner three or four hundred yards, to the very point which must have been the base of the spire of smoke—he had marked it so well that he could not be mistaken—

and from his leafy covert saw a large open space entirely destitute of vegetation. He expected to see there also the remains of a camp fire, but none was visible, not a single charred stick, nor a coal.

Dick was astonished. A new and smoking camp fire must leave some trace. One could not wipe it away absolutely. He remained a comparatively long time, watching in the edge of the bushes beside the wide and open space.

He still saw and heard nothing. Never before had a camp fire vanished so mysteriously and completely, and with it those who had built it. At last, his curiosity overcoming his caution, he advanced into the open space, and now saw that it fell away toward the center. Advancing more boldly, he found himself near the edge of a deep pit.

The pit was almost perfectly round and had a diameter of about ten feet. So far as Dick could judge, it was about forty feet deep and entirely empty. It looked like a huge well dug by the hand of man.

While Dick was gazing at the pit, an extraordinary and terrifying thing happened. The earth under his feet began to shake. At first he could not believe it, but when he steadied himself and watched closely, the oscillating motion was undoubtedly there. It was accompanied, too, by a rumble, dull and low, but which steadily grew louder. It seemed to Dick that the round pit was the center of this sound.

Despite the quaking of the earth, he ventured again into the open space and saw that the pit had filled with water. Moreover, this water was boiling, as he could see it seething and bubbling. As he looked, clouds of steam shot up to a height of two or three hundred feet, and Dick, in alarm, ran back to the bushes. He knew that this was the column of vapor he had first seen from a distance, but he was not prepared for what followed.

There was an explosion so loud that it made Dick jump. Then a great column of water shot up from the boiling pit to a height of perhaps fifty feet, and remained there rising and falling. From the apex of this column several great jets rose, perhaps, three times as high.

The column of hot water glittered and shimmered in the sun, and Dick gazed in wonder and delight. He had read enough to recognize the phenomenon that he now saw. It was a geyser, a column of hot water shooting up, at regular intervals and with great force, from the unknown deeps of the earth.

As he gazed, the column gradually sank, the boiling water in the pit sank, too, and there was no longer any rumble or quaking of the earth. Dick cautiously approached the pit again. It was as empty as a dry well, but he knew that in due time the phenomenon would be repeated. He was vastly interested, but he did not wait to see the recurrence of the marvel, continuing his way down the valley over heaps of crinkly black slag and stone, which were age-old lava, although he did not know it, and through groves of pine and ash, aspen, and cedar. He saw other round pits and watched a second geyser in eruption. He saw, too, numerous hot springs, and much steamy vapor floating about. There were also mineral springs and springs of the clearest and purest cold water. It seemed to Dick that every minute of his wanderings revealed to him some new and interesting sight, while on all sides of the little valley rose the mighty mountains, their summits in eternal snow.

A great relief was mingled with the intense interest that Dick felt. He had been sure at first that he saw the camp fires of the Sioux, but after the revulsion it seemed as if it were a place never visited by man, either savage or civilized. As he continued down the valley, he noticed narrow clefts in the mountains opening into them from either side, but he felt sure from the nature of the country that they could not go back far. The clefts were four in number, and down two of them came considerable streams of clear, cold water emptying into the main creek.

The valley now narrowed again and Dick heard ahead a slight humming sound which presently grew into a roar. He was puzzled at first, but soon divined the cause. The creek, or rather little river, much increased in volume by the tributary brooks, made a great increase of speed in its current. Dick saw before him a rising column of vapor and foam, and in another minute or two stood beside a fine fall, where the little river took a sheer drop of forty feet, then rushed foaming and boiling through a narrow chasm, to empty about a mile farther on into a beautiful blue lake.

Dick, standing on a high rock beside the fall, could see the lake easily. Its blue was of a deep, splendid tint, and on every side pines and cedars thickly clothed the narrow belt of ground between it and the mountains. The far end seemed to back up abruptly against a mighty range crowned with snow, but Dick felt sure that an outlet must be there through some cleft in the range. The lake itself was of an almost perfect crescent shape, and Dick reckoned its length at seven miles, with a greatest breadth, that is, at the center, of about two miles. He judged, too, from its color and its position in a fissure that its depth must be very great.

The surface of the lake lay two or three hundred feet lower than the rock on which Dick was standing, and he could see its entire expanse, rippling gently under the wind and telling only of peace and rest. Flocks of wild fowl flew here and there, showing white or black against the blue of its waters, and at the nearer shore Dick thought he saw an animal like a deer drinking, but the distance was too great to tell certainly.

He left the rock and pursued his way through dwarf pines and cedars along the edge of the chasm in which the torrent boiled and foamed, intending to go down to the lake. Halfway he stopped, startled by a long, shrill, whistling sound that bore some resemblance to the shriek of a distant locomotive. The wilderness had been so silent before that the sound seemed to fill all the valley, the ridges taking it up and giving it back in one echo after another until it died away among the peaks. In a minute or so the whistling shriek was repeated and then two or three times more.

Dick was not apprehensive. It was merely a new wonder in that valley of wonders, and none of these wonders seemed to have anything to do with man. The sound apparently came from a point two or three hundred yards to his left at the base of the mountain, and turning, Dick went toward it, walking very slowly and carefully through the undergrowth. He had gone almost the whole distance seeing nothing but the mountain and the forest, when the whistling shriek was suddenly repeated so close to him that he jumped. He sank down behind a dwarf pine, and then he saw not thirty feet away the cause of the sound.

A gigantic deer, a great grayish animal, stood in a little open space, and at intervals emitted that tremendous whistle. It stood as high as a horse, and Dick estimated its weight at more than a thousand pounds. He was looking at a magnificent specimen of the Rocky Mountain elk, by far the largest member of the deer tribe that he had ever seen. The animal, the wind blowing from him toward Dick, was entirely unsuspicious of danger, and the boy could easily have put a bullet into his heart, but he had no desire to do so. Whether the elk was whistling to his mate or sending a challenge to a rival bull he did not know, and after watching and admiring him for a little while he crept away.

But Dick was not wholly swayed by sentiment. He said to himself as he went away among the pines: "Don't you feel too safe, Mr. Elk, we'll have to take you or some of your brethren later on. I've heard that elk meat is good. "

He resumed his journey and was soon at the edge of the lake, which at this point had a narrow sandy margin. Its waters were fresh and cold, and wold duck, fearless of Dick, swam within a few yards of him. The view here was not less majestic and beautiful than it had been from the rock, and Dick, sensitive to nature, was steeped in all its wonder and charm. He was glad to be there, he was glad that chance or Providence had led him to this lovely valley. He felt no loneliness, no fear for the future, he was content merely to breathe and feel the glory of it permeate his being.

He picked up a pebble presently and threw it into the lake. It sank with the sullen plunk that told unmistakably to the boy's ears of great depths below. Once or twice he saw a fish leap up, and it occurred to him that here was another food supply.

He suddenly pulled himself together with a jerk. He could not sit there all day dreaming. He had come to find a winter home for Albert and himself, and he had not yet found it. But he had a plan from which he had been turned aside for a while by the sight of the lake, and now he went back to carry it out.

There were two clefts opening into the mountains from his side of the river, and he went into the first on the return path. It was choked with pine and cedars and quickly ended against a mountain wall, proving to be nothing but a very short canyon. There was much outcropping of rock here, but nothing that would help toward a shelter, and Dick went on to the second cleft.

This cleft, wider than the other, was the one down which the considerable brook flowed, and the few yards or so of fertile ground on either side of the stream produced a rank growth of trees. They were so thick that the boy could see only a little distance ahead, but he believed that this slip of a tributary valley ran far back in the mountains, perhaps a dozen miles.

He picked his way about a mile and then came suddenly upon a house. It stood in an alcove protected by rocks and trees, but safe from snow slide. It was only a log hut of one room, with the roof broken in and the door fallen from its hinges, but Dick knew well enough the handiwork of the white man. As he approached, some wild animal darted out of the open door and crashed away among the undergrowth, but Dick knew that white men had once lived there. It was equally evident that they had long been gone.

It was a cabin of stout build, its thick logs fitted nicely together, and the boards of the roof had been strong and well laid. Many years must have passed to have caused so much decay. Dick entered and was saluted by a strong, catlike odor. Doubtless a mountain lion had been sleeping there, and this was the tenant that he had heard crashing away among the undergrowth. On one side was a window closed by a sagging oaken shutter, which Dick threw open. The open door and window established a draught, and as the clean sweet air blew through the cabin the odor of the cat began to disappear.

Dick examined everything with the greatest interest and curiosity. There was a floor of puncheons fairly smooth, a stone fireplace, a chimney of mud and sticks, dusty wooden hooks, and rests nailed into the wall, a rude table overturned in a corner, and something that looked like a trap. It was the last that told the tale to Dick. When he examined it more critically, he had no doubt that it was a beaver trap.

Nor did he have any doubt but that this hut had been built by beaver trappers long ago, either by independent hunters, or by those belonging to one of the great fur companies. The beaver, he believed, had been found on this very brook, and when they were all taken the trappers had gone away, leaving the cabin forever, as they had left many another one. It might be at least forty years old.

Dick laughed aloud in his pleasure at this good luck. The cabin was dusty, dirty, disreputable, and odorous, but that draught would take away all the odors and his stout arm could soon repair the holes in the roof, put the door back on its hinges, and straighten the sagging window shutter. Here was their home, a house built by white men as a home, and now about to be used as such again. Dick did not feel like a tenant moving in, but like an owner. It would be a long, hard task to bring their supplies over the range but Albert and he had all the time in the world. It was one of the effects of their isolation to make Dick feel that there was no such thing as time.

He took another survey of the cabin. It was really a splendid place, a palace in its contrast with the surrounding wilderness, and he laughed with pure delight. When it was swept and cleaned, and a fire blazing on the flat stone that served for a hearth, while the cold winds roared without, it would be the snuggest home west of the Missouri. He was so pleased that he undertook at once some primary steps in the process of purification. He cut a number of small, straight boughs, tied them together with a piece of bark, the leaves at the head thus forming a kind of broom, and went to work.

He raised a great dust, which the draught blew into his eyes, ears, and nose, and he retreated from the place, willing to let the wind take it away. He would finish the task some other day. Then the clear waters of the brook tempted him. Just above the cabin was a deep pool which may have been the home of the beaver in an older time. Now it was undisturbed, and the waters were so pure that he could see the sand and rock on the bottom.

Still tingling from the dust, he took off his clothes and dived head foremost into the pool. He came up shivering and sputtering. It was certainly the coldest water into which he had ever leaped! After such a dash one might lie on a slab of ice to warm. Dick forgot that every drop in the brook had come from melting snows far up on the peaks, but, once in, he resolved to fight the element. He dived again, jumped up and down, and kicked and thrashed those waters as no beaver had ever done. Gradually he grew warm, and a wonderful exhilaration shot through every vein. Then he swam around and around and across and across the pool, disporting like a young white water god.

Dick was thoroughly enjoying himself, but when he began to feel cold again in seven or eight minutes he sprang out, ran up and down the bank, and rubbed himself with bunches of leaves until he was dry. After he had dressed, he felt that he had actually grown in size and strength in the last half hour.

He was now ravenously hungry. His absorption in his explorations and discoveries had kept him from thinking of such a thing as food until this moment, but when Nature finally got in her claim she made it strong and urgent. He had brought cold supplies with him, upon which he feasted, sitting in the doorway of the cabin. Then he noticed the lateness of the hour. Shadows were falling across the snow on the western peaks and ridges. The golden light of the sun was turning red, and in the valley the air was growing misty with the coming twilight.

He resolved to pass the night in the cabin. He secured the window shutter again, tied up the fallen door on rude bark hinges, and fastened it on the inside with a stick—hasps for the bar were there yet—but before retiring he took a long look in the direction in which Albert and their camp lay.

A great range of mountains lay between, but Dick felt that he could almost see his brother, his camp fire, and the pine alcove. He was Albert's protector, and this would be the first entire night in the mountains in which the weaker boy had been left alone, but Dick was not apprehensive about him. He believed that their good fortune would still endure, and secure in that belief he rolled himself up in the blanket which he had brought in a little pack on his back, and laid himself down in the corner of the cabin.

The place was not yet free from dust and odor, but Dick's hardy life was teaching him to take as trifles things that civilization usually regarded as onerous, and he felt quite comfortable where he lay. He knew that it was growing cold in the gorge, and the shelter of the cabin was acceptable. He saw a little strip of wan twilight through a crack in the window, but it soon faded and pitchy darkness filled the narrow valley.

Dick fell into a sound sleep, from which he awoke only once in the night, and then it was a noise of something as of claws scratching at the door which stirred him. The scratch was repeated only once or twice, and with it came the sound of heavy, gasping puffs, like a big animal breathing. Then the creature went away, and Dick, half asleep, murmured: "I've put you out of your house, my fine friend, bear or panther, whichever you may be. " In another minute he was wholly asleep again and did not waken until an edge of glittering sunlight, like a sword blade, came through the crack in the window and struck him across the eyes.

He bathed a second time in the pool, ate what was left of the food, and started on the return journey, moving at a brisk pace. He made many calculations on the way. It would take a week to move all their goods over the range to the cabin, but, once there, he believed that they would be safe for a long time; indeed, they might spend years in the valley, if they wished, and never see a stranger.

It was afternoon when he approached the pine alcove, but the familiar spire of smoke against the blue had assured him already that Albert was there and safe. In fact, Albert saw him first. He had just returned from the creek, and, standing on a rock, a fish in his hand, hailed his brother, who was coming up the slope.

"Halloo, Dick! " he shouted. "Decided to come home, have you? Hope you've had a pleasant visit. "

"Fine trip, Al, old man, " Dick replied. "Great place over there. Think we'd better move to it. "

"That so? Tell us about it. "

Dick, ever sensitive to Albert's manner and appearance, noticed that the boy's voice was fuller, and he believed that the dry, piny air of the mountains was still at its healing work. He joined Albert, who was waiting for him, and who, after giving his hand a hearty grasp, told him what he had found.

Chapter VI
Castle Howard

Albert agreed with Dick that they should begin to more at once, and his imagination was greatly stirred by Dick's narrative. "Why, it's an enchanted valley! " he exclaimed. "And a house is there waiting for us, too! Dick, I want to see it right away! "

Dick smiled.

"Sorry, but you'll have to wait a little, Al, old man, " he said. "You're not strong enough yet to carry stores over the big range, though you will be very soon, and we can't leave our precious things here unguarded. So you'll have to stay and act as quartermaster while I make myself pack mule. When we have all the things over there, we can fasten them up in our house, where bears, panthers, and wolves can't get at them. "

Albert made a wry face, but he knew that he must yield to necessity. Dick began the task the next morning, and it was long, tedious, and most wearing. More than once he felt like abandoning some of their goods, but he hardened his resolution with the reflection that all were precious, and not a single thing was abandoned.

It was more than a week before it was all done, and it was not until the last trip that Albert went with him, carrying besides his gun a small pack. The weather was still propitious. Once there had been a light shower in the night, but Albert was protected from it by the tarpaulin which they had made of the wagon cover, and nothing occurred to check his progress. He ate with an appetite that he had never known before, and he breathed by night as well as by day the crisp air of the mountains tingling with the balsam of the pines. It occurred to Dick that to be marooned in these mountains was perhaps the best of all things that could have happened to Albert.

They went slowly over the range toward the enchanted valley, stopping now and then because Albert, despite his improvement, was not yet equal to the task of strenuous climbing, but all things continued auspicious. There was a touch of autumn on the foliage, and the shades of red and yellow were appearing on the leaves of all the trees except the evergreens, but everything told of vigorous life. As they passed the crest of the range and began the descent of the slope toward the enchanted valley, a mule deer crashed from the covert and fled away with great bounds. Flocks of birds rose with whirrings from the bushes. From some point far away came the long, whistling sound that made Albert cry out in wonder. But Dick laughed.

"It's the elk, " he said. "I saw one when I first came into the valley. I think they are thick hereabout, and I suspect that they will furnish us with some good winter food. "

Albert found the valley all that Dick had represented it to be, and more. He watched the regular eruptions of the geysers with amazement and delight; he insisted on sampling the mineral springs, and intended to learn in time their various properties. The lake, in all its shimmering aspects, appealed to his love of the grand and beautiful, and he promptly named it "The Howard Sea, after its discoverer, you know, " he said to Dick. Finally, the cabin itself filled him with delight, because he foresaw even more thoroughly than Dick how suitable it would be for a home in the long winter months. He installed himself as housekeeper and set to work at once.

The little cabin was almost choked with their supplies, which Dick had been afraid to leave outside for fear that the provisions would be eaten and the other things injured by the wild animals, and now they began the task of assorting and putting them into place.

The full equipment of the wagon that Dick had found in the gully, particularly the tools, proved to be a godsend. They made more racks on the walls—boring holes with the augers and then driving in pegs—on which they laid their axes and extra rifles. In the same manner they made high shelves, on which their food would be safe from prowling wild beasts, even should they succeed in breaking in the door. But Dick soon made the latter impossible by putting the door on strong hinges of leather which he made from the gear that he had cut from the horses. He also split a new bar from one of the young ash trees and strengthened the hasps on the inside. He felt now that when the bar was in place not even the heaviest grizzly could force the door.

The task of mending the roof was more difficult. He knew how to split rude boards with his ax, but he had only a few nails with which to hold them in place. He solved the problem by boring auger holes, into which he drove pegs made from strong twigs. The roof looked water-tight, and he intended to reenforce it later on with the skins of wild animals that he expected to kill—there had been no time yet for hunting.

Throughout these operations, which took about a week, they slept in the open in a rude tent which they made of the wagon cover and set beside the cabin, for two reasons: because Dick believed the open air at all times to be good for Albert, and because he was averse to using the cabin as a dormitory until it was thoroughly cleansed and aired.

Albert made himself extremely useful in the task of refurbishing the cabin. He brushed out all the dust, brought water from the brook and scrubbed the floor, and to dry the latter built their first fire on the hearth with pine cones and other fallen wood. As he touched the match to it, he did not conceal his anxiety.

"The big thing to us, " he said, "is whether or not this chimney will draw. That's vital, I tell you, Dick, to a housekeeper. If it puffs out smoke and fills the cabin with it, we're to have a hard time and be miserable. If it draws like a porous plaster and takes all the smoke up it, then we're to have an easy time of it and be happy. "

Both watched anxiously as Albert touched the match to some pine shavings which were to form the kindling wood. The shavings caught, a light blaze leaped up, there came a warning crackle, and smoke, too, arose. Which way would it go? The little column wavered a moment and then shot straight up the chimney. It grew larger, but still shot straight up the chimney. The flames roared and were drawn in the same direction.

Albert laughed and clapped his hands.

"It's to be an easy time and a happy life! " he exclaimed. "Those old beaver hunters knew what they were about when they built this chimney! "

"You can cook in here, Al, " said Dick; "but I suggest that we sleep in the tent until the weather grows bad. "

Dick had more than one thing in mind in making this suggestion about the tent and sleeping. The air of the cabin could be close at night even with the window open, but in the tent with the flap thrown back—they never closed it—they breathed only a fresh balsamic odor, crisp with the coolness of autumn. He had watched Albert all the time. Now and then when he had exerted himself more than usual, the younger boy would cough, and at times he was very tired, but Dick, however sharply he watched, did not see again the crimson stain on the lips that he had noticed the night of the flight from the massacre.

But the older brother, two years older only, in fact, but ten years older, at least, in feeling, did notice a great change in Albert, mental as well as physical. The younger boy ceased to have periods of despondency. While he could not do the things that Dick did, he was improving, and he never lamented his lack of strength. It seemed to him a matter of course, so far as Dick could judge, that in due time he should be the equal of the older and bigger boy in muscle and skill.

Albert, moreover, had no regrets for the world without. Their life with the wagon train had been far from pleasant, and he had only Dick, and Dick had only him. Now the life in the enchanted valley, which was a real valley of enchantments, was sufficient for him. Each day brought forth some new wonder, some fresh and interesting detail. He was a capable fisherman, and he caught trout in both the brook and the river, while the lake yielded to his line other and larger fish, the names of which neither boy knew, but which proved to be of delicate flavor when broiled over the coals. Just above them was a boiling hot spring, and Albert used the water from this for cooking purposes. "Hot and cold water whenever you please, " he said to Dick. "Nothing to do but to turn the tap. "

Dick smiled; he, too, was happy. He enjoyed life in the enchanted valley, where everything seemed to have conspired in their favor. When they had been there about a week, and their home was ready for any emergency, Dick took his gun and went forth, the hunting spirit strong within him. They had heard the elk whistling on the mountain side nearly every day, and he believed that elk meat would prove tender and good. Anyway he would see.

Dick did not feel much concern about their food supply. He believed that vast quantities of big game would come into this valley in the winter to seek protection from the mighty snows of the northern Rockies, but it was just as well to begin the task of filling the larder.

He came out into the main valley and turned toward the lake. Autumn was now well advanced, but in the cool sunshine the lake seemed more beautiful than ever. Its waters were golden to-day, but with a silver tint at the edges where the pine-clad banks overhung it. Dick did not linger, however. He turned away toward the slopes, whence the whistling call had come the oftenest, and was soon among the pines and cedars. He searched here an hour or more, and at last he found two feeding, a male and a female.

Dick had the instinct of the hunter, and already he had acquired great skill. Creeping through the undergrowth, he came within easy shot of the animals, and he looked at them a little before shooting. The bull was magnificent, and he, if any, seemed a fit subject for the bullet, but Dick chose the cow, knowing that she would be the tenderer. Only a single shot was needed, and then he had a great task to carry the hide and the body in sections to the cabin. They ate elk steaks and then hung the rest in the trees for drying and jerking. Dick, according to his previous plan, used the skin to cover the newly mended places in the roof, fastening it down tightly with small wooden pegs. His forethought was vindicated two days later when a great storm came. Both he and Albert had noticed throughout the afternoon an unusual warmth in the air. It affected Albert particularly, as it made his respiration difficult. Over the mountains in the west they saw small dark clouds which soon began to grow and unite. Dick thought he knew what it portended, and he and his brother quickly taking down the tent, carried it and all its equipment inside the cabin. Then making fast the door and leaving the window open, they waited.

The heat endured, but all the clouds became one that overspread the entire heavens. Despite the lateness of the season, the thunder, inexpressibly solemn and majestic, rumbled among the gorges, and there was a quiver of lightening. It was as dark as twilight.

The rain came, roaring down the clefts and driving against the cabin with such force that they were compelled to close the window. How thankful Dick was now for Albert's sake that they had such a secure shelter! Nor did he despise it for his own.

The rain, driven by a west wind, poured heavily, and the air rapidly grew colder. Albert piled dry firewood on the hearth and lighted it. The flames leaped up, and warmth, dryness, and cheer filled all the little cabin. Dick had been anxiously regarding the roof, but the new boards and the elk skin were water-tight. Not a drop came through. Higher leaped the flames and the rosy shadows fell upon the floor.

"It's well we took the tent down and came in here, " said Albert. "Listen to that! "

The steady, driving sweep changed to a rattle and a crackle. The rain had turned to hail, and it was like the patter of rifle fire on the stout little cabin.

"It may rain or hail or snow, or do whatever it pleases, but it can't get at us, " said Albert exultingly.

"No, it can't, " said Dick. "I wonder, Al, what Bright Sun is doing now? "

"A peculiar Indian, " said Albert thoughtfully, "but it's safe to say that wherever he is he's planning and acting. "

"At any rate, " said Dick, "we're not likely to know it, whatever it is, for a long time, and we won't bother trying to guess about it. "

It hailed for an hour and then changed to rain again, pouring down in great steadiness and volume. Dick opened the window a little way once, but the night was far advanced, and it was pitchy black outside. They let the coals die down to a glowing bed, and then, wrapping themselves in their blankets, they slept soundly all through the night and the driving rain, their little cabin as precious to them as any palace was ever to a king.

Albert, contrary to custom, was the first to awake the next morning. A few coals from the fire were yet alive on the hearth, and the atmosphere of the room, breathed over and over again throughout the night, was close and heavy. He threw back the window shutter, and the great rush of pure cold air into the opening made his body thrill with delight. This was a physical pleasure, but the sight outside gave him a mental rapture even greater. Nothing was falling now, but the rain had turned back to hail before it ceased, and all the earth was in glittering white. The trees in the valley, clothed in ice, were like lace work, and above them towered the shining white mountains.

Albert looked back at Dick. His brother, wrapped in his blanket, still slept, with his arm under his head and his face toward the hearth. He looked so strong, so enduring, as he lay there sleeping soundly, and Albert knew that he was both. But a curious feeling was in the younger boy's mind that morning. He was glad that he had awakened first. Hitherto he had always opened his eyes to find Dick up and doing. It was Dick who had done everything. It was Dick who had saved him from the Sioux; it was Dick who had practically carried him over the first range; Dick had found their shelter in the pine alcove; Dick had labored day and night, day after day, and night after night, bringing the stores over the mountain from the lost train, then he had found their new home in the enchanted valley, which Albert persisted in calling it, and he had done nearly all the hard work of repairing and furnishing the cabin.

It should not always be so. Albert's heart was full of gratitude to this brother of his who was so brave and resourceful, but he wanted to do his share. The feeling was based partly on pride and partly on a new increase of physical strength. He took a deep inhalation of the cold mountain air and held it long in his lungs. Then he emitted it slowly. There was no pain, no feeling of soreness, and it was the first time he could remember that it had been so. A new thrill of pleasure, keener and more powerful than any other, shook him for a moment. It was a belief, nay, a certainty, or at least a conviction, that he was going to be whole and sound. The mountains were doing their kindly healing. He could have shouted aloud with pleasure, but instead he restrained himself and went outside, softly shutting the door behind him.

Autumn had gone and winter had come in a night. The trees were stripped of every leaf and in their place was the sheathing of ice. The brook roared past, swollen for the time to a little river. The air, though very cold, was dry despite the heavy rain of the night before. Albert shivered more than once, but it was not the shiver of weakness. It did not bite to the very marrow of him. Instead, when he exercised legs and arms vigorously, warmth came back. He was not a crushed and shriveled thing. Now he laughed aloud in sheer delight. He had subjected himself to another test, and he had passed it in triumph.

He built up the fire, and when Dick awoke, the pleasant aroma of cooking filled the room.

"Why, what's this, Al? " exclaimed the big youth, rubbing his eyes.

"Oh, I've been up pretty near an hour, " replied Albert airily. "Saw that you were having a fine sleep, so I thought I wouldn't disturb you. "

Dick looked inquiringly at him. He thought he detected a new note in his brother's voice, a note, too, that he liked.

"I see, " he said; "and you've been at work sometime, Do you feel fully equal to the task? "

Albert turned and faced his brother squarely.

"I've been thinking a lot, and feeling a lot more this morning, " he replied. "I've been trying myself out, as they say, and if I'm not well I'm traveling fast in that direction. Hereafter I share the work as well as the rewards. "

Albert spoke almost defiantly, but Dick liked his tone and manner better than ever. He would not, on any account, have said anything in opposition at this moment.

"All right, Al, old fellow. That's agreed, " he said.

Chapter VII
An Animal Progression

The thin sheath of ice did not last long. On the second day the sun came out and melted it in an hour. Then a warm wind blew and in a few more hours the earth was dry. On the third day Albert took his repeating rifle from the hooks on the wall and calmly announced that he was going hunting.

"All right, " said Dick; "and as I feel lazy I'll keep house until you come back. Don't get chewed up by a grizzly bear. "

Dick sat down in the doorway of the cabin and watched his brother striding off down the valley, gun on shoulder, figure very erect. Dick smiled; but it was a smile of pride, not derision.

"Good old Al! He'll do! " he murmured.

Albert followed the brook into the larger valley and then went down by the side of the lake. Though a skillful shot, he was not yet a good hunter, but he knew that one must make a beginning and he wanted to learn through his own mistakes.

He had an idea that game could be found most easily in the forest that ran down the mountain side to the lake, and he was thinking most particularly just then of elk. He had become familiar with the loud, whistling sound, and he listened for it now but did not hear it.

He passed the spot at which Dick had killed the big cow elk and continued northward among the trees that covered the slopes and flat land between the mountain and the lake. This area broadened as he proceeded, and, although the forest was leafless now, it was so dense and there was such a large proportion of evergreens, cedars, and pines that Albert could not see very far ahead. He crossed several brooks pouring down from the peaks. All were in flood, and once or twice it was all that he could do with a flying leap to clear them, but he went on, undiscouraged, keeping a sharp watch for that which he was hunting.

Albert did not know much about big game, but he remembered hearing Dick say that elk and mule deer would be likely to come into the valley for shelter at the approach of winter, and he was hopeful that he might have the luck to encounter a whole herd of the big elk. Then, indeed, he would prove that he was an equal partner with Dick in the work as well as the reward. He wished to give the proof at once.

He had not been so far up the north end of the valley before, and he noticed that here was quite an expanse of flat country on either side of the lake. But the mountains all around the valley were so high that it seemed to Albert that deer and other wild animals might find food as well as shelter throughout the winter. Hence he was quite confident, despite his poor luck so far, that he should find big game soon, and his hunting fever increased. He had never shot anything bigger than a rabbit, but Albert was an impressionable boy, and his imagination at once leaped over the gulf from a rabbit to a grizzly bear.

He had the lake, an immense and beautiful blue mirror, on his right and the mountains on his left, but the space between was now nearly two miles in width, sown thickly in spots with pine and cedar, ash and aspen, and in other places quite open. In the latter the grass was green despite the lateness of the season, and Albert surmised that good grazing could be found there all through the winter, even under the snow. Game must be plentiful there, too.

The way dropped down a little into a sheltered depression, and Albert heard a grunt and a great puffing breath. A huge dark animal that had been lying among some dwarf pines shuffled to its feet and Albert's heart slipped right up into his throat. Here was his grizzly, and he certainly was a monster! Every nerve in Albert was tingling, and instinct bade him run. Will had a hard time of it for a few moments, struggling with instinct, but will conquered, and, standing his ground, Albert fired a bullet from his repeater at the great dark mass.

The animal emitted his puffing roar again and rushed, head down, but blindly. Then Albert saw that he had roused not a grizzly bear but an enormous bull buffalo, a shaggy, fierce old fellow who would not eat him, but who might gore or trample him to death. His aspect was so terrible that will again came near going down before instinct, but Albert did not run. Instead, he leaped aside, and, as the buffalo rushed past, he fired another bullet from his repeater into his body just back of the fore legs.

The animal staggered, and Albert staggered, too, from excitement and nervousness, but he remembered to take aim and fire again and again with his heavy repeater. In his heat and haste he did not hear a shout behind him, but he did see the great bull stagger, then reel and fall on his side, after which he lay quite still.

Albert stood, rifle in hand, trembling and incredulous. Could it be he who had slain the mightiest buffalo that ever trod the earth? The bull seemed to his distended eyes and flushed brain to weigh ten tons at least, and to dwarf the biggest elephant. He raised his hand to his forehead and then sat down beside his trophy, overcome with weakness.

"Well, now, you have done it, young one! I thought I'd get a finger in this pie, but I came up too late! Say, young fellow, what's your name? Is it Daniel Boone or Davy Crockett? "

It was Dick who had followed in an apparently casual manner. He had rushed to his brother's rescue when he saw the bull charging, but he had arrived too late—and he was glad of it; the triumph was wholly Albert's.

Albert, recovering from his weakness, looked at Dick, looked at the buffalo, and then looked back at Dick. All three looks were as full of triumph, glory, and pride as any boy's look could be.

"He's as big as a mountain, isn't he, Dick? " he said.

"Well, not quite that, " replied Dick gravely. "A good-sized hill would be a better comparison. "

The buffalo certainly was a monster, and the two boys examined him critically. Dick was of the opinion that he belonged to the species known as the wood bison, which is not numerous among the mountains, but which is larger than the ordinary buffalo of the plains. The divergence of type, however, is very slight.

"He must have been an outlaw, " said Dick; "a vicious old bull compelled to wander alone because of his bad manners. Still, it's likely that he's not the only buffalo in our valley. "

"Can we eat him? " asked Albert.

"That's a question. He's sure to be tough, but I remember how we used to make steak tender at home by beating it before it was cooked. We might serve a thousand pounds or two of this bull in that manner. Besides, we want that robe. "

The robe was magnificent, and both boys felt that it would prove useful. Dick had gained some experience from his own buffalo hunt on the plains, and they began work at once with their sharp hunting knives. It was no light task to take the skin, and the beast was so heavy that they could not get it entirely free until they partly chopped up the body with an ax that Dick brought from the cabin. Then it made a roll of great weight, but Dick spread it on the roof of their home to cure. They also cut out great sections of the buffalo, which they put in the same place for drying and jerking.

While they were engaged at this task, Albert saw a pair of fiery eyes regarding them from the undergrowth.

"See, Dick, " he said, "what is that? "

Dick saw the eyes, the lean ugly body behind it, and he shuddered. He knew. It was the timber wolf, largest and fiercest of the species, brother to him whom he had seen prowling about the ruined wagon train. The brute called up painful memories, and, seizing his rifle, he fired at a spot midway between the red eyes. The wolf uttered a howl, leaped high in the air, and fell dead, lying without motion, stretched on his side.

"I didn't like the way he looked at us, " explained Dick.

A horrible growling and snapping came from the bushes presently.

"What's that? " asked Albert.

"It's only Mr. Timber Wolf's brethren eating up Mr. Timber Wolf, now that he is no longer of any use to himself. "

Albert shuddered, too.

It was nightfall when they took away the last of the buffalo for which they cared, and as they departed they heard in the twilight the patter of light feet.

"It's the timber wolves rushing for what we've left, " said Dick. "Those are big and fierce brutes, and you and I, Al, must never go out without a rifle or a revolver. You can't tell what they'll try, especially in the winter. "

The entire roof of the cabin was covered the next day with the buffalo robe and the drying meat, and birds of prey began to hover above it. Albert constituted himself watchman, and, armed with a long stick, took his place on the roof, where he spent the day.

Dick shouldered one of the shotguns and went down to the lake. There he shot several fine teal, and in one of the grassy glades near it he roused up prairie hen. Being a fine shot, he secured four of these, and returned to the cabin with his acceptable spoil.

They had now such a great supply of stores and equipment that their place was crowded and they scarcely had room for sleeping on the floor.

"What we need, " said Dick, "is an annex, a place that can be used for a storehouse only, and this valley, which has been so kind to us, ought to continue being kind and furnish it. "

The valley did furnish the annex, and it was Albert who found it. He discovered a little further up the cleft an enormous oak, old and decayed. The tree was at lease seven feet through, and the hollow itself was fully five feet in diameter, with a height of perhaps fourteen feet. It was very rough inside with sharp projections in every direction which had kept any large animal from making his den there, but Albert knew at once that the needed place had been found. Full of enthusiasm he ran for Dick, who came instantly to see.

"Fine, " said Dick approvingly. "We'll call it the 'Annex, ' sure enough, and we'll get to work right away with our axes. "

They cut out all the splinters and other projections, smoothing off the round walls and the floor, and they also extended the hollow overhead somewhat.

"This is to be a two-story annex, " said Dick. "We need lots of room."

High up they ran small poles across, fixing them firmly in the tree on either side, and lower down they planted many wooden pegs and hooks on which they might hang various articles.

"Everything will keep dry in here, " said Albert. "I would not mind sleeping in the Annex, but when the door is closed there won't be a particle of air. "

It was the "door" that gave them the greatest trouble. The opening by which they entered the hollow was about four feet high and a foot and a half across, and both boys looked at it a long time before they could see a way to solve the puzzle.

"That door has to be strong enough to keep everything out, " said Dick. "We mean to keep most of our meat supply in there, and that, of course, will draw wild animals, little and big; it's the big ones we've got to guard against. "

After strenuous thinking, they smoothed off all the sides of the opening in order that a flat surface might fit perfectly against them. Then Dick cut down a small oak, and split out several boards—not a difficult task for him, as he had often helped to make boards in Illinois. The boards were laid together the width of the opening and were held in place by cross pieces fastened with wooden pegs. Among their stores were two augers and two gimlets, and they were veritable godsends; they enabled the boys to make use of pegs and to save the few nails that they had for other and greater emergencies.

The door was made, and now came the task to "hang" it. "Hang" was merely a metaphorical word, as they fitted it into place instead. The wood all around the opening was about a foot thick, and they cut it out somewhat after the fashion of the lintels of a doorway. Then they fitted in the door, which rested securely in its grooves, but they knew that the claws of a grizzly bear or mountain lion might scratch it out, and they intended to make it secure against any such mischance.

With the aid of hatchet and auger they put three wooden hooks on either side of the doorway, exactly like those that defend the door of a frontier cabin, and into these they dropped three stout bars. It was true that the bars were on the outside, but no wild animal would have the intelligence enough to pry up those three bars and scratch the door out of place. Moreover, it could not happen by accident. It took them three laborious days to make and fit this door, but when the task was done they contemplated it with just pride.

"I call that about the finest piece of carpenter's work ever done in these mountains, " said Albert in tones suffused with satisfaction.

"Of course, " said Dick. "Why shouldn't it be, when the best carpenters in the world did the job? "

The two laughed, but their pride was real and no jest. It was late in the afternoon when they finished this task, and on the way to the cabin Albert suddenly turned white and reeled. Dick caught him, but he remained faint for sometime. He had overtasked himself, and when they reached the cabin Dick made him lie down on the great buffalo robe while he cooked supper. But, contrary to his former habit, Albert revived rapidly. The color returned to his face and he sprang up presently, saying that he was hungry enough to eat a whole elk. Dick felt a might sense of relief. Albert in his zeal had merely overexerted himself. It was not any relapse. "Here's the elk steak and you can eat ten pounds of it if you want it, " he said.

They began early the next morning to move supplies to the Annex. High up in the hollow they hung great quantities of dried meat of buffalo, elk, and mule deer. They also stored there several elk and mule deer skins, two wolf skins, and other supplies that they thought they would not need for a while. But in the main it was what they called a smokehouse, as it was universally known in the Mississippi Valley, their former home—that is, a place for keeping meat cured or to be cured.

This task filled the entire day, and when the door was securely fastened in place they returned to the cabin. After supper Dick opened the window, from which they could see the Annex, as they had cut away a quantity of the intervening bushes. Albert meanwhile put out the last coals of the fire. Then he joined Dick at the window. Both had an idea that they were going to see something interesting.

The valley filled with darkness, but the moon came out, and, growing used to the darkness, they could see the Annex fairly well.

Dick wet his finger and held it up.

"The wind is blowing from the Annex toward us, " he said.

"That's good, " said Albert, nodding.

They watched for a long time, hearing only the dry rustling of the light wind among the bare boughs, but at last Dick softly pushed his shoulder against Albert's. Albert nodded again, with comprehension. A small dark animal came into the open space around the Annex. The boys had difficulty in tracing his outlines at first, but once they had them fixed, they followed his movements with ease. He advanced furtively, stopping at intervals evidently both to listen and look. Some other of his kind, or not of his kind, might be on the same quest and it was his business to know.

"Is it a fox? " whispered Albert.

"I think not, " replied Dick in the same tone. "It must be a wolverine. He scents the good things in the Annex and he wants, oh, how he wants, the taste of them! "

The little dark animal, after delicate maneuvering, came close up to the tree, and they saw him push his nose against the cold bark.

"I know just how he feels, " whispered Albert with some sympathy. "It's all there, but he must know the quest is hopeless. "

The little animal went all around the tree nosing the cold bark, and then stopped again at the side of the door.

"No use, sir, " whispered Albert. "That door won't open just because you're hungry. "

The little animal suddenly cocked up his head and darted swiftly away into the shadows. But another and somewhat larger beast came creeping into the open, advancing with caution toward the Annex.

"Aha! " whispered Dick. "Little fellow displaced by a bigger one. That must be a wild cat. "

The wild cat went through the same performance. He nosed eagerly at the door, circled the tree two or three times, but always came back to the place where that tempting, well-nigh irresistible odor assailed him. The boys heard a low growl and the scratching of sharp claws on the door.

"Now he's swearing and fighting, " whispered Albert, "but it will do him no good. Save your throat and your claws, old fellow. "

"Look, he's gone! " whispered Dick.

The wild cat suddenly tucked his tail between his legs and fled from the opening so swiftly that they could scarcely see him go.

"And here comes his successor, " whispered Albert. "I suppose, Dick, we might call this an arithmetical or geometrical progression. "

An enormous timber wolf stalked into the clear space. He bore no resemblance to the mean, sneaking little coyote of the prairie. As he stood upright his white teeth could be seen, and there was the slaver of hunger on his lips. He, too, was restive, watchful, and suspicious, but it did not seem to either Dick or Albert that his movements betokened fear. There was strength in his long, lean body, and ferocity in his little red eyes.

"What a hideous brute! " whispered Albert, shuddering.

"And as wicked as he is ugly, " replied Dick. "I hate the sight of these timber wolves. I don't wonder that the wild cat made himself scarce so quickly. "

"And he's surely hungry! " said Albert. "See how he stretches out his head toward our Annex, as if he would devour everything inside it!"

Albert was right. The big wolf was hungry, hungry through and through, and the odor that came from the tree was exquisite and permeating; it was a mingled odor of many things and everything was good. He had never before known a tree to give forth such a delightful aroma and he thrilled in every wolfish fiber as it tickled his nostrils.

He approached the tree with all the caution of his cautious and crafty race, and, as he laid his nose upon the bark, that mingled aroma of many things good grew so keen and powerful that he came as near as a big wolf can to fainting with delight. He pushed at the places where the door fitted into the tree, but nothing yielded. Those keen and powerful odors that penetrated delightfully to every marrow of him were still there, but he could not reach their source. A certain disappointment, a vague fear of failure mingled with his anticipation, and as the wolverine and the wild cat had done, he moved uneasily around the tree, scratching at the bark, and now and then biting it with teeth that were very long and cruel.

His troubled circuit brought him back to the door, where the aroma was finest and strongest. There he tore at the lowest bar with tooth and claw, but it did not move. He had the aroma and nothing more, and no big, strong wolf can live on odors only. The vague disappointment grew into a positive rage. He felt instinctively that he could not reach the good things that the wonderful tree held within itself, but he persisted. He bent his back, uttered a growl of wrath just as a man swears, and fell to again with tooth and claw.

"If I didn't know that door was so very strong, I'd be afraid he'd get it, " whispered Albert.

"Never fear, " Dick whispered back with confidence.

The big wolf suddenly paused in his effort. Tooth and claw were still, and he crouched hard against the tree, as if he would have his body to blend with its shadow. A new odor had come to his nostrils. It did not come from the tree. Nor was it pleasant. Instead, it told him of something hostile and powerful. He was big and strong himself, but this that came was bigger and stronger. The growl that had risen in his throat stopped at his teeth. A chill ran down his backbone and the hair upon it stood up. The great wolf was afraid, and he knew he was afraid.

"Look! " whispered Albert in rising excitement. "The wolf, too, is stealing away! He is scared by something! "

"And good cause he has to be scared, " said Dick. "See what's coming! "

A great tawny beast stood for a moment at the edge of the clearing. He was crouched low against the ground, but his body was long and powerful, with massive shoulders and fore arms. His eyes were yellow in the moonlight, and they stared straight at the Annex. The big wolf took one hasty frightened look and then fled silently in the other direction. He knew now that the treasures of the Annex were not for him.

"It's a cougar, " whispered Dick, "and it must be the king of them all. Did you ever see such a whopper? "

The cougar came farther into the clearing. He was of great size, but he was a cat—a huge cat, but a cat, nevertheless—and like a cat he acted. He dragged his body along the earth, and his eyes, now yellow, now green, in the moonlight, were swung suspiciously from side to side. He felt all that the wolf had felt, but he was even more cunning and his approach was slower. It was his habit to spring when close enough, but he saw nothing to spring at except a tree trunk, and so he still crept forward on noiseless pads.

"Now, what will Mr. Cougar do? " asked Albert.

"Just what the others have done, " replied Dick. "He will scratch and bite harder because he is bigger and stronger, but we've fixed our Annex for just such attacks. It will keep him out. "

Dick was right. The cougar or mountain lion behaved exactly as the others had done. He tore at the door, then he circled the tree two or three times, hunting in vain for an opening. Every vein in him was swollen with rage, and the yellowish-green eyes flared with anger.

"He'd be an ugly creature to meet just now, " whispered Dick. "He's so mad that I believe he'd attack an elephant. "

"He's certainly in no good humor, " replied Dick. "But look, Al! See his tail drop between his legs! Now what under the moon is about to happen? "

Albert, surcharged with interest and excitement, stared as Dick was staring. The mighty cat seemed suddenly to crumple up. His frame shrank, his head was drawn in, he sank lower to the earth, as if he would burrow into it, but he uttered no sound whatever. He was to both the boys a symbol of fear.

"What a change! What does it mean? " whispered Albert.

"It must mean, " replied Dick, "that he, too, has a master and that master is coming. "

The cougar suddenly bunched himself up and there was a flash of tawny fur as he shot through the air. A second leap and the trees closed over his frightened figure. Albert believed that he would not stop running for an hour.

Into the opening, mighty and fearless, shambled a monstrous beast. He had a square head, a long, immense body, and the claws of his great feet were hooked, many inches in length, and as sharp and hard as if made of steel. The figure of the beast stood for power and unbounded strength, and his movements indicated overwhelming confidence. There was nothing for him to fear. He had never seen any living creature that could do him harm. It was a gigantic grizzly bear.

Albert, despite himself, as he looked at the terrible brute, felt fear. It was there, unconfined, and a single blow of its paw could sweep the strongest man out of existence.

"I'm glad I'm in this cabin and that this cabin is strong, " he whispered tremulously.

"So am I, " said Dick, and his own whisper was a little shaky. "It's one thing to see a grizzly in a cage, and another to see him out here in the dark in these wild mountains. And that fellow must weigh at least a thousand pounds. "

King Bruin shambled boldly across the opening to the Annex. Why should he be careful? There might be other animals among the bushes and trees watching him, but they were weak, timid things, and they would run from his shadow. In the wan moonlight, which distorted and exaggerated, his huge bulk seemed to the two boys to grow to twice its size. When he reached the tree he reared up against it, growled in a manner that made the blood of the boys run cold, and began to tear with teeth and claws of hooked steel. The bark and splinters flew, and, for a moment, Dick was fearful lest he should force the door to their treasure. But it was only for a moment; not even a grizzly could break or tear his way through such a thickness of oak.

"Nothing can displace him, " whispered Albert. "He's the real king."

"He's not the king, " replied Dick, "and something can displace him."

"What do you mean? " asked Albert with incredulity.

"No beast is king. It's man, and man is here. I'm going to have a shot at that monster who is trying to rob us. We can reach him from here with a bullet. You take aim, too, Al. "

They opened the window a little wider, being careful to make no noise, and aimed their rifles at the bear, who was still tearing at the tree in his rage.

"Try to hit him in the heart, Al, " whispered Dick, "and I'll try to do the same. I'll count three in a whisper, and at the 'three' we'll fire together. "

The hands of both boys as they leveled their weapons were trembling, not with fear, but from sheer nervousness. The bear, meanwhile, had taken no notice and was still striving to reach the hidden treasures. Like the others, he had made the circuit of the Annex more than once, but now he was reared up again at the door, pulling at it with mighty tooth and claw. It seemed to both as they looked down the barrels of their rifles and chose the vulnerable spot that, monstrous and misshapen, he was constantly growing in size, so powerful was the effect of the moonlight and their imagination. But it was terrible fact to them.

They could see him with great distinctness, and so silent was the valley otherwise that they could hear the sound of his claws ripping across the bark. He was like some gigantic survival of another age. Dick waited until both his brother and himself grew steadier.

"Now don't miss, Albert, " he said.

He counted "One, two, three, " slowly, and at the "three! " the report of the two rifles came as one. They saw the great bear drop down from the tree, they heard an indescribable roar of pain and rage, and then they saw his huge bulk rushing down upon them. Dick fired three times and Albert twice, but the bear still came, and then Dick slammed the window shut and fastened it just as the full weight of the bear was hurled against the cabin.

Neither boy ever concealed from himself the fact that he was in a panic for a few moments. Their bullets seemed to have had no effect upon the huge grizzly, who was growling ferociously and tearing at the logs of the cabin. Glad they were that those logs were so stout and thick, and they stood there a little while in the darkness, their blood chilling at the sounds outside. Presently the roaring and tearing ceased and there was the sound of a fall. It was so dark in the cabin that the brothers could not see the faces of each other, but Dick whispered:

"Albert, I believe we've killed him, after all. "

Albert said nothing and they waited a full ten minutes. No sound whatever came to their ears. Then Dick opened the window an inch or two and peeped out. The great bear lay upon his side quite still, and Dick uttered a cry of joy.

"We've killed him, Al! we've killed him! " he cried.

"Are you sure? " asked Albert.

"Quite sure. He does not stir in the slightest. "

They opened the door and went out. The great grizzly was really dead. Their bullets had gone true, but his vitality was so enormous that he had been able to rush upon the cabin and tear at it in his rage until he fell dead. Both boys looked at him with admiration and awe; even dead, he was terrifying in every respect.

"I don't wonder that the cougar, big and strong as he was, slunk away in terror when he saw old Ephraim coming, " said Dick.

"We must have his skin to put with our two buffalo robes, " said Albert.

"And we must take it to-night, " said Dick, "or the wolves will be here while we sleep. "

They had acquired some skill in the art of removing furs and pelts, but it took them hours to strip the coat from the big grizzly. Then, as in the case of the buffalo, they cut away some portions of the meat that they thought might prove tender. They put the hide upon the roof to dry, and, their work over, they went to sleep behind a door securely fastened.

Dick was awakened once by what he thought was a sound of growling and fighting outside, but he was so sleepy that it made no impression upon him. They did not awake fully until nearly noon, and when they went forth they found that nothing was left of the great bear but his skeleton.

"The timber wolves have been busy, " said Dick.

Chapter VIII The Trap Makers

The hide of the bear, which they cured in good style, was a magnificent trophy; the fur was soft and long, and when spread out came near covering the floor of their cabin. It was a fit match for the robe of the buffalo. They did not know much about grizzlies, but they believed that no larger bear would ever be killed in the Rocky Mountains.

A few days later Dick shot another buffalo in one of the defiles, but this was a young cow and her flesh was tender. They lived on a portion of it from day to day and the rest they cured and put in the Annex. They added the robe to their store of furs.

"I'm thinking, " said Dick, "that you and I, Al, might turn fur hunters. " This seems to be an isolated corner of the mountains. It may have been tapped out long ago, but when man goes away the game comes back. We've got a comfortable house, and, with this as a basis, we might do better hunting furs here than if we were hunting gold in California, where the chances are always against you.

The idea appealed to Albert, but for the present they contented themselves with improving their house and surroundings. Other bears, cougars, and wolves came at night and prowled around the Annex, but it was secure against them all, and Dick and Albert never troubled themselves again to keep awake and watch for such intruders.

Winter now advanced and it was very cold, but, to Dick's great relief, no snow came. It was on Albert's account that he wished air and earth to remain dry, and it seemed as if Nature were doing her best to help the boy's recovery. The cough did not come again, he had no more spells of great exhaustion, the physical uplift became mental also, and his spirits, because of the rebound, fairly bubbled. He was full of ideas, continually making experiments, and had great plans in regard to the valley and Castle Howard, as he sometimes playfully called their cabin.

One of the things that pleased Albert most was his diversion of water from a hot spring about fifty yards from the cabin and higher up the ravine. He dug a trench all the way from the pool to the house, and the hot water came bubbling down to their very door. It cooled, of course, a little on the way, but it was still warm enough for cooking purposes, and Albert was hugely delighted.

"Hot water! Cold water! Whatever you wish, Dick, " he said; "just turn on the tap. If my inventive faculty keeps on growing, I'll soon have a shower bath, hot and cold, rigged up here. "

"It won't grow enough for that, " said Dick; "but I want to tell you, Al, that the big game in the valley is increasing at a remarkable rate. Although cold, it's been a very open winter so far, but I suppose the instinct of these animals warns them to seek a sheltered place in time. "

"Instinct or the habit of endless generations, " said Albert.

"Which may be the same thing, " rejoined Dick.

"There's a whole herd of elk beyond the far end of the lake, I've noticed on the cliffs what I take to be mountain sheep, and thirty or forty buffalos at least must be ranging about in here. "

"Then, " said Albert, "let's have a try at the buffaloes. Their robes will be worth a lot when we go back to civilization, and there is more room left in the Annex. "

They took their repeaters and soon proved Dick's words to be true. In a sheltered meadow three or more miles up the valley they found about twenty buffaloes grazing. Each shot down a fat cow, and they could have secured more had not the minds of both boys rebelled at the idea of slaughter.

"It's true we'd like to have the robes, " said Dick, "but we'd have to leave most of the carcasses rotting here. Even with the wonderful appetites that we've developed, we couldn't eat a whole buffalo herd in one winter. "

But after they had eaten the tongue, brisket, and tenderloin of the two cows, while fresh, these being the tenderest and best parts of the buffalo, they added the rest of the meat to their stores in the Annex. As they had done already in several cases, they jerked it, a most useful operation that observant Dick had learned when they were with the wagon train.

It took a lot of labor and time to jerk the buffaloes, but neither boy had a lazy bone in him, and time seemed to stretch away into eternity before them. They cut the flesh into long, thin strips, taking it all from the bones. Then all these pieces were thoroughly mixed with salt—fortunately, they could obtain an unlimited supply of salt by boiling out the water from the numerous salt springs in the valley—chiefly by pounding and rubbing. They let these strips remain inside the hides about three hours, then all was ready for the main process of jerking.

Albert had been doing the salting and Dick meanwhile had been getting ready the frame for the jerking. He drove four forked poles into the ground, in the form of a square and about seven feet apart. The forks were between four and five feet above the ground. On opposite sides of the square, from fork to fork, he laid two stout young poles of fresh, green wood. Then from pole to pole he laid many other and smaller poles, generally about an inch apart. They laid the strips of buffalo meat, taken from their salt bath, upon the network of small poles, and beneath they built a good fire of birch, ash, and oak.

"Why, it makes me think of a smokehouse at home, " said Albert.

"Same principle, " said Dick, "but if you let that fire under there go out, Al, I'll take one of those birch rods and give you the biggest whaling you ever had in your life. You're strong enough now to stand a good licking. "

Albert laughed. He thought his big brother Dick about the greatest fellow on earth. But he paid assiduous attention to the fire, and Dick did so, too. They kept it chiefly a great bed of coals, never allowing the flames to rise as high as the buffalo meat, and they watched over it twenty-four hours. In order to keep this watch, they deserted the cabin for a night, sleeping by turns before the fire under the frame of poles, which was no hardship to them.

The fierce timber wolves came again in the night, attracted by the savory odor of buffalo meat; and once they crept near and were so threatening that Albert, whose turn it was at the watch, became alarmed. He awakened Dick, and, in order to teach these dangerous marauders a lesson, they shot two of them. Then the shrewd animals, perceiving that the two-legged beasts by the fire carried something very deadly with which they slew at a distance, kept for a while to the forest and out of sight.

After the twenty-four hours of fire drying, the buffalo meat was greatly reduced in weight and bulk, though it was packed as full as ever with sustenance. It was now cured, that is, jerked, and would keep any length of time. While the frame was ready they jerked an elk, two mule deer, a big silver-tip bear that Dick shot on the mountain side, and many fish that they caught in the lake and the little river. They would scale the fish, cut them open down the back, and then remove the bone. After that the flesh was jerked on the scaffold in the same way that the meat of the buffalo and deer was treated.

Before these operations were finished, the big timber wolves began to be troublesome again. Neither boy dared to be anywhere near the jerking stage without a rifle or revolver, and Dick finally invented a spring pole upon which they could put the fresh meat that was waiting its turn to be prepared—they did not want to carry the heavy weight to the house for safety, and then have to bring it back again.

While Dick's spring pole was his own invention, as far as he was concerned, it was the same as that used by thousands of other trappers and hunters. He chose a big strong sapling which Albert and he with a great effort bent down. Then he cut off a number of the boughs high up, and in each crotch fastened a big piece of meat. The sapling was then allowed to spring back into place and the meat was beyond the reach of wolf.

But the wolves tried for it, nevertheless. Dick awakened Albert the first night after this invention was tried and asked him if he wished to see a ghost dance. Albert, wrapped to his eyes in the great buffalo robe, promptly sat up and looked.

They had filled four neighboring saplings with meat, and at least twenty wolves were gathered under them, looking skyward, but not at the sky—it was the flesh of elk and buffalo that they gazed at so longingly, and delicious odors that they knew assailed their nostrils.

But the wolf is an enterprising animal. He does not merely sit and look at what he wants, expecting it to come to him. Every wolf in the band knew that no matter how hard and long he might look that splendid food in the tree would not drop down into his waiting mouth. So they began to jump for it, and it was this midnight and wilderness ballet that Albert opened his eyes to watch.

One wolf, the biggest of the lot, leaped. It was a fine leap, and might have won him a championship among his kind, but he did not reach the prize. His teeth snapped together, touching only one another, and he fell. Albert imagined that he could hear a disappointed growl. Another wolf leaped, the chief leaped again, a third, a fourth, and a fifth leaped, and then all began to leap together.

The air was full of flying wolfish forms, going up or coming down. They went up, hearts full of hope, and came down, mouths empty of everything but disappointed foam. Teeth savagely hit teeth, and growls of wrath were abundant. Albert felt a ridiculous inclination to laugh. The whole affair presented its ludicrous aspect to him.

"Did you ever see so much jumping for so little reward? " he whispered to Dick.

"No, not unless they're taking exercise to keep themselves thin, although I never heard of a fat wolf. "

But a wolf does not give up easily. They continued to leap faster and faster, and now and then a little higher than before, although empty tooth still struck empty tooth. Now and then a wolf more prone to complaint than the others lifted up his voice and howled his rage and chagrin to the moon. It was a genuine moan, a long, whining cry that echoed far through the forest and along the slopes, and whenever Albert heard it he felt more strongly than ever the inclination to laugh.

"I suppose that a wolf's woes are as real as our own, " he whispered, "but they do look funny and act funny. "

"Strikes me the same way, " replied Dick with a grin. "But they're robbers, or would be if they could. That meat's ours, and they're trying to get it. "

It was in truth a hard case for the wolves. They were very big and very strong. Doubtless, the selfsame wolf that had been driven away from the Annex by the mountain lion was among them, and all of them were atrociously hungry. It was not merely an odor now, they could also see the splendid food hanging just above their heads. Never before had they leaped so persistently, so ardently, and so high, but there was no reward, absolutely none. Not a tooth felt the touch of flesh. The wolves looked around at one another jealously, but the record was as clean as their teeth. There had been no surreptitious captures.

"Will they keep it up all night? " whispered Albert.

"Can't say, " replied Dick. "We'll just watch. "

All the wolves presently stopped leaping and crouched on the earth, staring straight up at the prizes which hung, as ever, most tantalizingly out of reach. The moonlight fell full upon them, a score or more, and Albert fancied that he could see their hungry, disappointed eyes. The spectacle was at once weird and ludicrous. Albert felt again that temptation to laugh, but he restrained it.

Suddenly the wolves, as if it were a preconcerted matter, uttered one long, simultaneous howl, full, alike in its rising and falling note, of pain, anguish, and despair, then they were gone in such swiftness and silence that it was like the instant melting of ghosts into thin air. It took a little effort of will to persuade Albert that they had really been there.

"They've given it up, " he said. "The demon dancers have gone. "

"Demon dancers fits them, " said Dick. "It's a good name. Yes, they've gone, and I don't think they'll come back. Wolves are smart, they know when they're wasting time. "

When they finished jerking their buffalo meat and venison, Dick took the fine double-barreled shotgun which they had used but little hitherto, and went down to the lake in search of succulent waterfowl. The far shore of the lake was generally very high, but on the side of the cabin there were low places, little shallow bays, the bottoms covered with grass, which were much frequented by wild geese and wild ducks, many of which, owing to the open character of the winter, had not yet gone southward. The ducks, in particular, muscovy, mallard, teal, widgeon, and other kinds, the names of which Dick did not know, were numerous. They had been molested so little that they were quite tame, and it was so easy to kill them in quantities that the element of sport was entirely lacking.

Dick did not fancy shooting at a range of a dozen yards or so into a dense flock of wild ducks that would not go away, and he wished also to save as many as he could of their shot cartridges, for he had an idea that he and his brother would remain in the valley a long time. But both he and Albert wanted good supplies of duck and geese, which were certainly toothsome and succulent, and they were taking a pride, too, in filling the Annex with the best things that the mountains could afford. Hence Dick did some deep thinking and finally evolved a plan, being aided in his thoughts by earlier experience in Illinois marshes.

He would trap the ducks and geese instead of shooting them, and he and Albert at once set about the task of making the trap. This idea was not original with Dick. As so many others have been, he was, in part, and unconscious imitator. He planted in the shallow water a series of hoops, graded in height, the largest being in the deepest water, while they diminished steadily in size as they came nearer to the land. They made the hoops of split saplings, and planted them about four feet apart.

Then the covered all these hoops with a netting, the total length of which was about twenty-five feet. They also faced each hoop with a netting, leaving an aperture large enough for the ducts to enter. It was long and tedious work to make the netting, as this was done by cutting the hide of an elk and the hide of a mule deer into strips and plaiting the strips on the hoops. They then had a network tunnel, at the smaller end of which they constructed an inclosure five or six feet square by means of stout poles which they thrust into the mud, and the same network covering which they used on the tunnel.

"It's like going in at the big end of a horn and coming out at the little one into a cell, " said Albert. "Will it work? "

"Work? " replied Dick. "Of course, it will. You just wait and you'll see. "

Albert looked out upon the lake, where many ducks were swimming about placidly, and he raised his hand.

"Oh, foolish birds! " he apostrophized. "Here is your enemy, man, making before your very eyes the snare that will lead you to destruction, and you go on taking no notice, thinking that the sunshine will last forever for you. "

"Shut up, Al, " said Dick, "you'll make me feel sorry for those ducks. Besides, you're not much of a poet, anyway. "

When the trap was finished they put around the mouth and all along the tunnel quantities of the grass and herbs that the ducks seemed to like, and then Dick announced that the enterprise was finished.

"We have nothing further to do about it, " he said, "but to take out our ducks. "

It was toward twilight when they finished the trap, and both had been in the cold water up to their knees. Dick had long since become hardened to such things, but he looked at Albert rather anxiously. The younger boy, however, did not begin to cough. He merely hurried back to the fire, took off his wet leggings, and toasted his feet and legs. Then he ate voraciously and slept like a log the night through. But both he and Dick went down to the lake the next morning with much eagerness to see what the trap contained, if anything.

It was a fresh winter morning, not cold enough to freeze the surface of the lake, but extremely crisp. The air contained the extraordinary exhilarating quality which Dick had noticed when they first came into the mountains, but which he had never breathed anywhere else. It seemed to him to make everything sparkle, even his blood, and suddenly he leaped up, cracked his heels together, and shouted.

"Why, Dick, " exclaimed Albert, "what on earth is the matter with you? "

"Nothing is the matter with me. Instead, all's right. I'm so glad I'm alive, Al, old man, that I wanted to shout out the fact to all creation. "

"Feel that way myself, " said Albert, "and since you've given such a good example, think I'll do as you did. "

He leaped up, cracked his heels together, and let out a yell that the mountains sent back in twenty echoes. Then both boys laughed with sheer pleasure in life, the golden morning, and their happy valley. So engrossed were they in the many things that they were doing that they did not yet find time to miss human faces.

As they approached the trap, they heard a great squawking and cackling and found that the cell, as Albert called the square inclosure, contained ten ducks and two geese swimming about in a great state of trepidation. They had come down the winding tunnel and through the apertures in the hoops, but they did not have sense enough to go back the same way. Instead they merely swam around the square and squawked.

"Now, aren't they silly? " exclaimed Albert. "With the door to freedom open, they won't take it. "

"I wonder, " said Dick philosophically, "if we human beings are not just the same. Perhaps there are easy paths out of our troubles lying right before us and superior creatures up in the air somewhere are always wondering why we are such fools that we don't see them. "

"Shut up, Dick, " said Albert, "your getting too deep. I've no doubt that in our net are some ducks that are rated as uncommonly intelligent ducks as ducks go. "

They forgot all about philosophy a few moments later when they began to dispose of their capture. They took them out, one by one, through a hole that they made in the cell and cut off their heads. The net was soon full up again, and they caught all the ducks and geese they wanted with such ridiculous ease that at the end of a week they took it down and stored it in the cabin.

They jerked the ducks and geese that they did not need for immediate use, and used the feathers to stuff beds and pillows for themselves. The coverings of these beds were furs which they stitched together with the tendons of the deer.

They began to be annoyed about this time by the depredations of mountain lions, which, attracted by the pleasant odors, came down from the slopes to the number of at least half a dozen, Dick surmised, and prowled incessantly about the cabin and Annex, taking the place of the timber wolves, and proving more troublesome and dangerous alike. One of them managed at night to seize the edge of an elk skin that hung on the roof of the cabin, and the next morning the skin was half chewed up and wholly ruined.

Both boys were full of rage, and they watched for the lions, but failed to get a shot at them. But Dick, out of the stores of his memory, either some suggestion from reading, or trappers' and hunters' tales, devised a gun trap. He put a large piece of fresh deer meat in the woods about a quarter of a mile from the cabin. It was gone the next morning, and the tracks about showed that the lions had been present.

Then Dick drove two stout forked sticks into the ground, the forks being about a yard above the earth. Upon these he lashed one of their rifles. Then he cut a two-foot section of a very small sapling, one end of which he inserted carefully between the ground that the trigger of the rifle. The other end was supported upon a small fork somewhat higher than those supporting the rifle. Then he procured another slender but long section of sapling that reached from the end of the short piece in the crotch some distance beyond the muzzle of the rifle. The end beyond the muzzle had the stub of a bough on it, but the end in the crotch was tied there with a strip of hide. Now, if anything should pull on the end of this stick, it would cause the shorter stick to spring the trigger of the rifle and discharge it. Dick tested everything, saw that all was firmly and properly in place, and the next thing to do was to bait the trap.

He selected a piece of most tempting deer meat and fastened it tightly on the hooked end of the long stick. It was obvious that any animal pulling at this bait would cause the short stick tied at the other end of it to press against the trigger of the rifle, and the rifle would be fired as certainly as if the trigger had been pulled by the hand of man. Moreover, the barrel of the rifle was parallel with the long stick, and the bullet would certainly be discharged into the animal pulling at the bait.

After the bait had been put on Dick put the cartridge in the rifle. He was careful to do this last, as he did not wish to take any chances with the trap while he was testing it. But he and Albert ran a little wall of brush off on either side in order that the cougar, if cougar it were, should be induced to approach the muzzle directly in front. When all the work was finished, the two boys inspected it critically.

"I believe that our timber wolves would be too smart to come up to that trap, " said Albert.

"Perhaps, " said Dick; "but the wolf has a fine intellect, and I've never heard that the cougar or puma was particularly noted for brain power. Anyhow, I know that traps are built for him in this manner, and we shall see whether it will work. "

"Are we going to hide somewhere near by and watch during the night? "

"There's no need to make ourselves uncomfortable. If the gun gets him, it'll get him whether we are or are not here. "

"That's so, " said Albert. "Well, I'm willing enough to take to the cabin. These nights are growing pretty cold, I can tell you. "

Taking a last look at the gun trap and assuring themselves that it was all right, they hurried away to Castle Howard. The night was coming on much colder than any that they had yet had, and both were glad to get inside. Albert stirred the coals from beneath the ashes, put on fresh wood, and soon they had a fine blaze. The light flickered over a cabin greatly improved in appearance and wonderfully snug.

The floor, except directly in front of the hearth, where sparks and coals would pop out, was covered with the well-tanned skins of buffalo, elk, mule deer, bear, and wolf. The walls were also thickly hung with furs, while their extra weapons, tools, and clothing hung there on hooks. It was warm, homelike, and showed all the tokens of prosperity. Dick looked around at it with an approving eye. It was not only a house, and a good house at that, but it was a place that one might make a base for a plan that he had in mind. Yes, circumstance had certainly favored them. Their own courage, skill, and energy had done the rest.

Albert soon fell asleep after supper, but Dick was more wakeful, although he did not wish to be so. It was the gun trap that kept his eyes open. He took a pride in doing things well, and he wanted the trap to work right. A fear that it might not do so worried him, but in turn he fell into a sound sleep from which he was awakened by a report. He thought at first that something had struck the house, but when his confused senses were gathered into a focus he knew that it was a rifle shot.

"Up, Al, up! " he cried, "I think a cougar has been fooling with our trap! "

Albert jumped up. They threw on their coats and went out into a dark and bitterly cold night. If they had not been so eager to see what had happened, they would have fled back to the refuge of the warm cabin, but they hurried on toward the snug little hollow in which the gun trap had been placed. At fifty yards they stopped and went much more slowly, as a terrific growling and snarling smote their ears.

"It's the cougar, and we've got him, " said Dick. "He's hit bad or he wouldn't be making such a terrible fuss. "

They approached cautiously and saw on the ground, almost in front of the gun, a large yellowish animal writhing about and tearing the earth. His snarls and rage increased as he scented the two boys drawing near.

"I think his shoulder is broken and his backbone injured, " said Dick. "That's probably the reason he can't get away. I don't like to see him suffer and I'll finish him now. "

He sent a bullet through the cougar's head and that was the end of him. In order to save it from the wolves, they took his hide from him where he lay, and spread it the next day on the roof of the cabin.

The gun trap was so successful that they baited it again and again, securing three more cougars, until the animals became too wary to try for the bait. The fourth cougar did not sustain a severe wound and fled up the mountain side, but Dick tracked him by the trail of blood that he left, overtook him far up the slope, and slew him with single shot. All these skins were added to their collection, and when the last was spread out to dry, Dick spoke of the plan that he had in mind.

"Al, " he said, "these mountains, or at least this corner of them, seem to be left to us. The Sioux, I suppose, are on the warpath elsewhere, and they don't like mountains much, anyhow. Our wonderful valley, the slopes, and all the ravines and canyons are full of game. The beaver must be abundant farther in, and I propose that we use our opportunity and turn fur hunters. There's wealth around us for the taking, and we were never sure of it in California. We've got enough ammunition to last us two years if we want to stay that long. Besides, Al, old boy, the valley has been the remaking of you. You know that. "

Albert laughed from sheer delight.

"Dick, " he said, "you won't have to get a gun and threaten me with death unless I stay. I'll be glad to be a fur hunter, and, Dick, I tell you, I'm in love with this valley. As you say, it's made me over again, and oh, it's fine to be well and strong, to do what you please, and not always to be thinking, 'how can I stand this? Will it hurt me?'"

"Then, " said Dick, "it's settled. We'll not think for a long time of getting back to civilization, but devote ourselves to gathering up furs and skins. "

Chapter IX The Timber Wolves

The cold increased, although snow fell but little, which Dick considered good luck, chiefly on Albert's account. He wanted the hardening process to continue and not to be checked by thaws and permeating dampness. Meanwhile, they plunged with all the energy and fire of youth into the task of fur hunting. They had already done much in that respect, but now it was undertaken as a vocation. They became less scrupulous about sparing the buffaloes, and they shot more than twenty in the defiles of the mountains, gathering a fine lot of robes. Several more skins of the bear, grizzly, and silver tip were added to their collection, and the elk also furnished an additional store. Many wolverines were taken in dead falls and snares, and their skins were added to the rapidly growing heap.

They baited the trap gun once more, hoping that a fifth cougar might prove rash enough to dare it. No cougar came, but on the third night a scornful grizzly swallowed the deer meat as a tidbit, and got a bullet in the neck for his carelessness. In his rage, he tore the trap to pieces and tossed the rifle to one side, but, fortunately, he did not injure the valuable weapon, his attention turning instantly to something else. Later on the boys dispatched him as he lay wounded upon the ground.

Their old clothing was now about worn out and it also became necessary to provide garments of another kind in order to guard against the great cold. Here their furs became invaluable; they made moccasins, leggings, caps, and coats alike of them, often crude in construction, but always warm.

They found the beaver father in the mountains, as Dick had surmised, and trapped them in great abundance. This was by far their most valuable discovery, and they soon had a pack of sixty skins, which Dick said would be worth more than a thousand dollars in any good market. They also made destructive inroads upon the timber wolves, the hides of which were more valuable than those of any other wolf. In fact, they made such havoc that the shrewd timber wolf deserted the valley almost entirely.

As the boys now made their fur hunting a business, they attended to every detail with the greatest care. They always removed the skin immediately after the death of the animal, or, if taken in a trap, as soon after as possible. Every particle of fat or flesh was removed from the inside of the skin, and they were careful at the same time never to cut into the skin itself, as they knew that the piercing of a fur with a knife would injure its value greatly. Then the skin was put to dry in a cold, airy place, free alike from the rays of the sun or the heat of a fire. They built near the cabin a high scaffold for such purposes, too high and strong for any wild beast to tear down or to reach the furs upon it. Then they built above this on additional poles a strongly thatched bark roof that would protect the skins from rain, and there they cured them in security.

"I've heard, " said Dick, "that some trappers put preparations or compounds on the skins in order to cure them, but since we don't have any preparations or compounds we won't use them. Besides, our furs seem to cure up well enough without them. "

Dick was right. The cold, dry air of the mountains cured them admirably. Two or three times they thought to help along the process by rubbing salt upon the inner sides. They could always get plenty of salt by boiling out water from the salt springs, but as they seemed to do as well without it, they ceased to take the trouble.

The boys were so absorbed now in their interesting and profitable tasks that they lost all count of the days. They knew they were far advanced into a splendid open winter, but it is probably that they could not have guessed within a week of the exact day. However, that was a question of which they thought little. Albert's health and strength continued to improve, and with the mental stimulus added to the physical, the tide of life was flowing very high for both.

They now undertook a new work in order to facilitate their trapping operations. The beaver stream, and another that they found a little later, ran far back into the mountains, and the best trapping place was about ten miles away. After a day's work around the beaver pond, they had to choose between a long journey in the night to the cabin or sleeping in the open, the latter not a pleasant thing since the nights had become so cold. Hence, they began the erection of a bark shanty in a well-sheltered cove near the most important of the beaver localities. This was a work of much labor, but, as in all other cases, they persisted until the result was achieved triumphantly.

They drove two stout, forked poles deep into the ground, leaving a projection of about eight feet above the earth. The poles themselves were about eight feet apart. From fork to fork they placed a strong ridgepole. Then they rested against the ridgepole from either side other and smaller poles at an angle of forty or fifty degrees. The sloping poles were about a foot and a half apart. These poles were like the scantling or inside framework of a wooden house and they covered it all with spruce and birch bark, beginning at the bottom and allowing each piece to overlap the one beneath it, after the fashion of a shingled roof. They secured pieces partly with wooden pegs and partly with other and heavier wooden poles leaned against them. One end of the shelter was closed up with bark wholly, secured with wooden pegs, and the other end was left open in order that its tenants might face the fire which would be built three or four feet in front of it. They packed the floor with dead leaves, and put on the top of the leaves a layer of thick bark with the smooth side upward.

The bark shanty was within a clump of trees, and its open side was not fifteen feet from the face of an abrupt cliff. Hence there was never any wind to drive the smoke from the fire back into their faces, and, wrapped in their furs, they slept as snugly in the shanty as if they had been in the cabin itself. But they were too wise to leave anything there in their absence, knowing that it was not sufficient protection against the larger wild animals. In fact, a big grizzly, one night when they were at the cabin, thrust his nose into the shanty and, lumbering about in an awkward and perhaps frightened manner, knocked off half of one of the bark sides. It took nearly a day's work to repair the damage, and it put Dick in an ill humor.

"I'd like to get a shot at that bear! " he exclaimed. "He had no business trying to come into a house when he was not invited. "

"But he is an older settler than we are, " said Albert, in a whimsical tone.

Dick did get a shot at a bear a few days later, and it was a grizzly, at that. The wound was not fatal, and the animal came on with great courage and ferocity. A second shot from Dick did not stop him and the boy was in great danger. But Albert, who was near, sent two heavy bullets, one after the other, into the beast, and he toppled over, dying. It was characteristic of the hardy life they were leading and its tendency toward the repression of words and emotion that Dick merely uttered a brief, "Thanks, Al, you were just in time, " and Albert nodded in reply.

The skin of old Ephraim went to join that of his brother who had been taken sometime before, and Dick himself shot a little later a third, which contributed a fine skin.

The boys did not know how hard they were really working, but their appetites would have bee a fine gauge. Toiling incessantly in a crisp, cold air, as pure as any that the world affords, they were nearly always hungry. Fortunately, the happy valley, their own skill and courage, and the supplies that Dick had brought from the last wagon train furnished them an unlimited larder. Game of great variety was their staple, but they had both flour and meal, from which, though they were sparing of their use, they made cakes now and then. They had several ways of preparing the Indian meal that Dick had taken from the wagon. They would boil it for about an hour, then, after it cooled, would mix it with the fat of game and fry it, after which the compound was eaten in slices. They also made mealcakes, johnnycakes and hoecakes.

Albert was fond of fish, especially of the fine trout that they caught in the little river, and soon he invented or discovered a way of cooking them that provided an uncommon delicacy for their table. He would slit the trout open, clean it, and the season it with salt and also with pepper, which they had among their stores. Then he would lay the fish in the hot ashes of a fire that had burned down to embers, cover it up thoroughly with the hot ashes and embers, and let it cook thirty or forty minutes—thirty minutes for the little fellows and forty minutes for the big ones. When he thought the fish was done to the proper turn, he would take it from the ashes, clean it, and then remove the skin, which would almost peel off of its own accord.

The fish was then ready for the eating, and neither Dick nor Albert could ever bear to wait. The flesh looked so tempting and the odor was so savory that hunger instantly became acute.

"They are so good, " said Albert, "because my method of cooking preserves all the juices and flavors of the fish. Nothing escapes. "

"Thanks, professor, " said Dick. "You must be right, so kindly pass me another of those trout, and be quick about it. "

It is a truth that both boys became epicures. Their valley furnished so much, and they had a seasoning of hard work and open mountain air that was beyond compare. They even imitated Indian and trapper ways of cooking geese, ducks, quail, sage hens, and other wild fowl that the region afforded. They could cook these in the ashes as they did the trout, and they also had other methods. Albert would take a duck, cut it open and clean it, but leave the feathers on. Then he would put it in water, until the feathers were soaked thoroughly, after which he would cover it up with ashes, and put hot coals on top of the ashes. When the bird was properly cooked and drawn from the ashes, the skin could be pulled off easily, taking the feathers, of course, with it. Then a duck, sweet, tender, and delicate, such as no restaurant could furnish, was ready for the hardy youngsters. At rare intervals they improve on this by stuffing the duck with seasoning and Indian meal. Now and then they served a fat goose the same way and found it equally good.

They cooked the smaller birds in a simpler manner, especially when they were at the bark shanty, which they nicknamed the "Suburban Villa. " The bird was plucked of its feathers, drawn and washed, and then they cut it down the back in order to spread it out. Nothing was left but to put the bird on the end of a sharp stick, hold it over the coals, and turn it around until it was thoroughly broiled or roasted. They also roasted slices of big game in the same way.

As Albert was cooking a partridge in this manner one evening at the Suburban Villa, Dick, who was sitting on his buffalo-robe blanket in the doorway, watched him and began to make comparisons. He recalled the boy who had left Omaha with the wagon train six or eight months before, a thin, spiritless fellow with a slender, weak neck, hollow, white cheeks, pale lips, and listless eyes. That boy drew coughs incessantly from a hollow chest, and the backs of his hands were ridged when the flesh had gone away, leaving the bones standing up. This boy whom Dick contemplated was quite a different being. His face was no longer white, it was instead a mixture of red and brown, and both tints were vivid. Across one cheek were some brier scratches which he had acquired the day before, but which he had never noticed. The red-brown cheeks were filled out with the effects of large quantities of good food digested well. As he bent over the fire, a chest of good width seemed to puff out with muscle and wind expansion. Despite the extreme cold, his sleeves were rolled up to the elbow, and the red wrists and hands were well covered with tough, seasoned flesh. The eyes that watched the roasting bird were intent, alert, keenly interested in that particular task, and in due course, in any other that might present itself.

Dick drew a long breath of satisfaction. Providence had treated them well. Then he called loudly for his share of the bird, saying that he was starving, and in a few moments both fell to work.

Their fur operations continued to extend. They had really found a pocket, and isolated corner in the high Rockies where the fur-bearing animals, not only abundant, were also increasing. It was, too, the dead of winter, the very best time for trapping, and so, as far as their own goings and comings were concerned, they were favored further by the lucky and unusual absence of snow. They increased the number of their traps—dead falls, box traps, snares, and other kinds, and most of them were successful.

They knew instinctively the quality of the furs that they obtained. They could tell at a glance whether they were prime, that is, thick and full, and as they cured them and baled them, they classified them.

Constant application bred new ideas. In their pursuit of furs, they found that they were not quite so sparing of the game as they had been at first. Some of their scruples melted away. Albert now recalled a device of trappers of which he had read. This was the use of a substance generally called barkstone, which they found to be of great help to them in the capture of that animal.

The barkstone or castoreum, as it is commercially known, was obtained principally from the beaver himself. The basis of it was an acrid secretion with a musky odor of great power, found in two glands just under the root of the beaver's tail. Each gland was from one and one half to two inches in length. The boys cut out these glands and squeezed the contents into an empty tin can. This at first was of a yellowish-red color, but after a while, when it dried, it became a light brown.

This substance formed the main ingredient of barkstone, and in their medicine chest they found a part of the remainder. The secretion was transferred to a bottle and the mixed with it essence of peppermint and ground cinnamon. As Albert remembered it, ground nutmeg also was needed, but as they had no nutmeg they were compelled to take their chances without it. Then they poured whisky on the compound until it looked like a paste.

Then the bottle was stopped up with the greatest care, and in about a week, when they stole a sniff or two at it, they found that the odor had increased ten or a dozen times in power.

They put eight or ten drops of the barkstone upon the bait for the beaver, or somewhere near the trap, and, despite some defects in the composition, it proved an extraordinary success. The wariest beaver of all would be drawn by it, and their beaver bales grew faster than any other.

Dick calculated one day that they had at least five thousand dollars worth of furs, which seemed a great sum to both boys. It certainly meant, at that time and in that region, a competence, and it could be increased greatly.

"Of course, " said Dick, "we'll have to think some day of the way in which we must get these furs out, and for that we will need horses or mules, but we won't bother our heads about it yet. "

After the long period of clear, open weather, the delayed snow came. It began to fall one evening at twilight, when both boys were snug in the cabin, and it came in a very gentle, soothing way, as if it meant no harm whatever. Big, soft flakes fell as softly as the touch of down, but every time the boys looked out they were still coming in the same gentle but persistent way. The next morning the big flakes still came down and all that day and all the next night. When the snow stopped it lay five feet deep on the level, and uncounted feet deep in the gullies and canyons.

"We're snowed in, " said Albert in some dismay, "and we can't go to our traps. Why, this is likely to last a month! "

"We can't walk through it, " said Dick meditatively, "but we can walk on it. We've got to make snowshoes. They're what we need. "

"Good! " said Albert with enthusiasm. "Let's get to work at once. "

Deep snows fall in Illinois, and both, in their earlier boyhood, had experimented for the sake of sport with a crude form of snowshoe. Now they were to build upon this slender knowledge, for the sake of an immediate necessity, and it was the hardest task that they had yet set for themselves. Nevertheless, it was achieved, like the others.

They made a framework of elastic stripes of ash bent in the well-known shape of the snowshoe, which bears some resemblance to the shape of the ordinary shoe, only many times larger and sharply pointed at the rear end. Its length was between five and six feet, and the ends were tightly wound with strips of hide. This frame was bent into the shoe shape after it had been soaked in boiling water.

Then they put two very strong strips of hide across the front part of the framework, and in addition passed at least a half dozen stout bands of hide from strip to strip.

Then came the hard task of attaching the shoe to the foot of the boy who was to wear it. The ball of the foot was set on the second crosspiece and the foot was then tied there with a broad strip of hide which passed over the instep and was secured behind the ankle. It required a good deal of practice to fasten the foot so it would not slip up and down; and also in such a manner that the weight of the shoe would be proportioned to it properly.

They had to exercise infinite patience before two pairs of snowshoes were finished. There was much hunting in deep snow for proper wood, many strips and some good hide were spoiled, but the shoes were made and then another equally as great confronted the two boys—to learn how to use them.

Each boy put on his pair at the same time and went forth on the snow, which was now packed and hard. Albert promptly caught one of his shoes on the other, toppled over, and went down through the crust of the snow, head first. Dick, although in an extremely awkward situation himself, managed to pull his brother out and put him in the proper position, with his head pointing toward the sky instead of the earth. Albert brushed the snow out of his eyes and ears, and laughed.

"Good start, bad ending, " he said. "This is certainly the biggest pair of shoes that I ever had on, Dick. They feel at least a mile long to me."

"I know that mine are a mile long, " said Dick, as he, too, brought the toe of one shoe down upon the heel of the other, staggered, fell over sideways, but managed to right himself in time.

"It seems to me, " said Albert, "that the proper thing to do is to step very high and very far, so you won't tangle up one shoe with the other. "

"That seems reasonable, " said Dick, "and we'll try it. "

They practiced this step for an hour, making their ankles ache badly. After a good rest they tried it for another hour, and then they began to make progress. They found that they got along over the snow at a fair rate of speed, although it remained an awkward and tiring gait. Nevertheless, one could travel an indefinite distance, when it was impossible to break one's way far through five or six feet of packed snow, and the shoes met a need.

"They'll do, " said Albert; "but it will never be like walking on the solid earth in common shoes. "

Albert was right. Their chief use for these objects, so laboriously constructed, was for the purpose of visiting their traps, some of which were set at least a dozen miles away. They wished also to go back to the shanty and see that it was all right. They found a number of valuable furs in the traps, but the bark shanty had been almost crushed in by the weight of the snow, and they spent sometime strengthening and repairing it.

In the course of these excursions their skill with the snowshoes increased and they were also able to improve upon the construction, correcting little errors in measurement and balance. The snow showed no signs of melting, but they made good progress, nevertheless, with their trapping, and all the furs taken were of the highest quality.

It would have been easy for them to kill enough game to feed a small army, as the valley now fairly swarmed with it, although nearly all of it was of large species, chiefly buffalo, elk, and bear. There was one immense herd of elk congregated in a great sheltered space at the northern end of the valley, where they fed chiefly upon twigs and lichens.

Hanging always upon the flanks of this herd was a band of timber wolves of great size and ferocity, which never neglected an opportunity to pull down a cripple or a straying yearling.

"I thought we had killed off all these timber wolves, " said Albert when he first caught sight of the band.

"We did kill off most of those that were here when we came, " said Dick, "but others, I suppose, have followed the game from the mountains into the valley. "

Albert went alone a few days later to one of their traps up the valley, walking at a good pace on his snowshoes. A small colony of beavers had been discovered on a stream that came down between two high cliffs, and the trap contained a beaver of unusually fine fur. Albert removed the skin, put it on his shoulder, and, tightening his snowshoes, started back to Castle Howard.

The snow had melted a little recently, and in many places among the trees it was not deep, but Albert and Dick had made it a point to wear their snowshoes whenever they could, for the sake of the skill resulting from practice.

Albert was in a very happy frame of mind. He felt always now a physical elation, which, of course, became mental also. It is likely, too, that the rebound from long and despairing ill health still made itself felt. None so well as those who have been ill and are cured! He drew great draughts of the frosty air into his strong, sound lungs, and the emitted it slowly and with ease. It was a fine mechanism, complex, but working beautifully. Moreover, he had an uncommonly large and rich beaver fur over his shoulder. Such a skin as that would bring twenty-five dollars in any decent market.

Albert kept to the deep snow on account of his shoes, and was making pretty good time, when he heard a long howl, varied by a kind of snappy, growling bark.

"One of those timber wolves, " said Albert to himself, "and he has scented the blood of the beaver. "

He thought no more about the wolf until two or three minutes later when he heard another howl and then two or three more. Moreover, they were much nearer.

"Now, I wonder what they're after? " thought Albert.

But he went on, maintaining his good pace, and then he heard behind him a cry that was a long, ferocious whine rather than a howl. Albert looked back and saw under the trees, where the snow was lighter, a dozen leaping forms. He recognized at once the old pests, the timber wolves.

"Now, I wonder what they're after? " he repeated, and then as the whole pack suddenly gave tongue in a fierce, murderous howl, he saw that it was himself. Albert, armed though he was—neither boy ever went forth without gun or revolver—felt the blood grow cold in every vein. These were not the common wolves of the prairie, nor yet the ordinary wolf of the East and Middle West, but the great timber wolf of the Northwest, the largest and fiercest of the dog tribe. He had grown used to the presence of timber wolves hovering somewhere near, but now they presented themselves in a new aspect, bearing down straight upon him, and pushed by hunger. He understood why they were about to attack him. They had been able to secure but little of the large game in the valley, and they were drawn on by starvation.

He looked again and looked fearfully. They seemed to him monstrous in size for wolves, and their long, yellowish-gray bodies were instinct with power. Teeth and eyes alike were gleaming. Albert scarcely knew what to do first. Should he run, taking to the deepest snow, where the wolves might sink to their bodies and thus fail to overtake him? But in his own haste he might trip himself with the long, ungainly snowshoes, and then everything would quickly be over. Yet it must be tried. He could see no other way.

Albert, almost unconsciously prayed for coolness and judgment, and it was well for him that his life in recent months had taught him hardihood and resource. He turned at once into the open space, away from the trees, where the snow lay several feet deep, and he took long, flying leaps on his snowshoes. Behind him came the pack of great, fierce brutes, snapping and snarling, howling and whining, a horrible chorus that made shivers chase one another up and down the boy's spine. But as he reckoned, the deep snow made them flounder, and checked their speed.

Before him the open ground and the deep snow stretched straight away beside the lake until it reached the opening between the mountains in which stood Castle Howard. As Albert saw the good track lie before him, his hopes rose, but presently, when he looked back again, they fell with cruel speed. The wolves, despite the depth of the snow, had gained upon him. Sometimes, perhaps, it proved hard enough to sustain the weight of their bodies, and then they more than made up lost ground.

Albert noted a wolf which he took at once to be the leader, not only because he led all the others, but because also of his monstrous size. Even in that moment of danger he wondered that a wolf could grow so large, and that he should have such long teeth. But the boy, despite his great danger, retained his presence of mind. If the wolves were gaining, then he must inflict a check upon them. He whirled about, steadied himself a moment on his snowshoes, and fired directly at the huge leader. The wolf had swung aside when he saw the barrel of the rifle raised, but the bullet struck down another just behind him. Instantly, some of the rest fell upon the wounded brute and began to devour him, while the remainder, after a little hesitation, continued to pursue Albert.

But the boy had gained, and he felt that the repeating rifle would be for a while like a circle of steel to him. He could hold them back for a time with bullet after bullet, although it would not suffice to stop the final rush when it came, if it came.

Albert looked longingly ahead. He saw a feather of blue smoke against the dazzling white and silver of the sky, and he knew that it came from their cabin. If he were only there behind those stout log walls! A hundred wolves, bigger than the big leader, might tear at them in vain! And perhaps Dick, too, would come! He felt that the two together would have little to fear.

The wolves set up their fierce, whining howl again, and once more it showed that they had gained upon the fleeing boy. He turned and fired once, twice, three times, four times, as fast as he could pull the trigger, directly into the mass of the pack. He could not tell what he had slain and what he had wounded, but there was a hideous snapping and snarling, and the sight of wolf teeth flashing into wolf flesh.

Albert ran on and that feather of blue smoke was larger and nearer. But was it near enough? He could hear the wolves behind him again. All these diversions were only temporary. No matter how many of their number were slain or wounded, no matter how many paused to devour the dead and hurt, enough were always left to follow him. The pursuit, too, had brought reinforcements from the lurking coverts of the woods and bushes.

Albert saw that none of his bullets had struck the leader. The yellowish-gray monster still hung close upon him, and he was to Albert like a demon wolf, one that could not be slain. He would try again. He wheeled and fired. The leader, as before, swerved to one side and a less fortunate wolf behind him received the bullet. Albert fired two more bullets, and then he turned to continue his flight. But the long run, the excitement, and his weakened nerves caused the fatal misstep. The toe of one snowshoe caught on the heel of the other, and as a shout pierced the air, he went down.

The huge gray leader leaped at the fallen boy, and as his body paused a fleeting moment in midair before it began the descent, a rifle cracked, a bullet struck him in the throat, cutting the jugular vein and coming out behind. His body fell lifeless on the snow, and he who had fired the shot came on swiftly, shouting and firing again.

It was well that Dick, sometime after Albert's departure, had concluded to go forth for a little hunt, and it was well also that in addition to his rifle he had taken the double-barreled shotgun thinking that he might find some winter wild fowl flying over the snow and ice-covered surface of the lake. His first shot slew the master wolf, his second struck down another, his third was as fortunate, his fourth likewise, and then, still running forward, he bethought himself of the shotgun that was strapped over his shoulder. He leveled it in an instant and fairly sprayed the pack of wolves with stinging shot. Before that it had been each bullet for a wolf and the rest untouched, but now there was a perfect shower of those hot little pellets. It was more than they could stand, big, fierce, and hungry timber wolves though they were. They turned and fled with beaten howls into the woods.

Albert was painfully righting himself, when Dick gave him his hand and sped the task. Albert had thought himself lost, and it was yet hard to realize that he had not disappeared down the throat of the master wolf. His nerves were overtaxed, and he was near collapse.

"Thank you, Dick, old boy, " he said. "If you hadn't come when you did, I shouldn't be here. "

"No, you wouldn't, " replied Dick grimly. "Those wolves eat fast. But look, Al, what a monster this fellow is! Did you ever see such a wolf? "

The great leader lay on his side upon the snow, and a full seven feet he stretched from the tip of his nose to the root of his stumpy tail. No such wolf as he had ever been put inside a cage, and it was rare, indeed, to find one so large, even in the mountains south of the very Far North.

"That's a skin that will be worth something, " said Dick, "and here are more, but before we begin the work of taking them off, you'll have to be braced up, Al. You need a stimulant. "

He hurried back to Castle Howard and brought one of the bottles of whisky, a little store that they had never touched except in the compounding of the barkstone for the capture of beaver. He gave Albert a good stiff drink of it, after which the boy felt better, well enough, in fact, to help Dick skin the monster wolf.

"It gives me pleasure to do this, " said Albert, as he wielded the knife. "You thought, Mr. Wolf, that I was going to adorn your inside; instead, your outside will be used as an adornment trodden on by the foot of my kind. "

They secured four other fine and unimpaired skins among the slain, and after dressing and curing, they were sent to join the stores in the Annex.

Chapter X
Dick Goes Scouting

Dick did not believe that the timber wolves, after suffering so much in the pursuit of Albert, would venture again to attack either his brother or himself. He knew that the wolf was one of the shrewdest of all animals, and that, unless the circumstances were very unusual indeed, the sight of a gun would be sufficient to warn them off. Nevertheless, he decided to begin a campaign against them, though he had to wait a day or two until Albert's shaken nerves were restored.

They wished to save their ammunition as much as possible, and they built three large dead falls, in which they caught six or seven great wolves, despite their cunning. In addition they hunted them with rifles with great patience and care, never risking a shot until they felt quite sure that it would find a vital spot. In this manner they slew about fifteen more, and by that time the wolves were thoroughly terrified. The scent of the beings carrying sticks which poured forth death and destruction at almost any distance, was sufficient to send the boldest band of timber wolves scurrying into the shadows of the deepest forest in search of hiding and safety.

The snow melted and poured in a thousand streams from the mountains. The river and all the creeks and brooks roared in torrents, the earth soaked in water, and the two boys spent much of the time indoors making new clothing, repairing traps and nets, and fashioning all kinds of little implements that were of use in their daily life. They could realize, only because they now had to make them, how numerous such implements were. Yet they made toasting sticks of hard wood, carved out wooden platters, constructed a rude but serviceable dining table, added to their supply of traps of various kinds, and finally made two large baskets of split willow. The last task was not as difficult as some others, as both had seen and taken a part in basket making in Illinois. The cabin was now crowded to inconvenience. Over their beds, from side to side, and up under the sloping roof, they had fastened poles, and from all of these hung furs and skins, buffalo, deer, wolf, wild cat, beaver, wolverine, and others, and also stores of jerked game. The Annex was in the same crowded condition. The boys had carried the hollow somewhat higher up with their axes, but the extension gave them far less room than they needed.

"It's just this, Dick, " said Albert, "we getting so rich that we don't know what to do with all our property. I used to think it a joke that the rich were unhappy, but now I see where their trouble comes in. "

"I know that the trappers cache their furs, that is, bury them or hide them until they can take them away, " said Dick, "but we don't know how to bury furs so they'll keep all right. Still, we've got to find a new place of some kind. Besides, it would be better to have them hidden where only you and I could find them, Al. Maybe we can find such a place. "

Albert agreed, and they began a search along the cliffs. Dick knew that extensive rocky formations must mean a cave or an opening of some kind, if they only looked long enough for it, at last they found in the side of a slope a place that he thought could be made to suit. It was a rocky hollow running back about fifteen feet, and with a height and width of perhaps ten feet. It was approached by an opening about four feet in height and two feet in width. Dick wondered at first that it had not been used as a den by some wild animal, but surmised that the steepness of the ascent and the extreme roughness of the rocky floor had kept them out.

But these very qualities recommended the hollow to the boys for the use that they intended it. Its position in the side of the cliff made it a hard place to find, and the solid rock of its floor, walls, and roof insured the dryness that was necessary for the storage of their furs.

"We'll call this the Cliff House, " said Albert, "and we'll take possession at once. "

They broke off the sharper of the stone projections with their ax heads, and then began the transfer of the furs. It was no light task to carry them up the step slope to the Cliff House, but, forced to do all things for themselves, they had learned perseverance, and they carried all their stock of beaver furs and all the buffalo robes and bearskins, except those in actual use, together with a goodly portion of the wolfskins, elk hides, and others.

Dick made a rude but heavy door which fitted well enough into the opening to keep out any wild animal, no matter how small, and in front of it, in a little patch of soft soil, they set out two transplanted pine bushes which seemed to take root, and which Dick was sure would grow in the spring.

When the boys looked up from the bottom of the slope, they saw no trace of the Cliff House, only an expanse of rock, save a little patch of earth where two tiny pines were growing.

"Nobody but ourselves will ever find our furs! " exclaimed Dick exultingly. "The most cunning Indian would not dream that anything was hidden up there behind those little pines, and the furs will keep as well inside as if they were in the best storehouse ever built. "

The discovery and use of the rock cache was a great relief to both. Their cabin had become so crowded with furs and stores, that the air was often thick and heavy, and they did not have what Dick called elbow room. Now they used the cabin almost exclusively for living purposes. Most of the stores were in the Annex, while the dry and solid Cliff House held the furs.

"Have you thought, Dick, what you and I are? " asked Albert.

"I don't catch your meaning. "

"We're aristocrats of the first water, Mr. Richard Howard and Mr. Albert Howard, the Mountain Kings. We can't get along with less than four residences. We live in Castle Howard, the main mansion, superior to anything of its kind in a vast region; then we have the Annex, a tower used chiefly as a supply room and treasure chest; then the Suburban Villa, a light, airy place of graceful architecture, very suitable as a summer residence, and now we have the Cliff House, in a lofty and commanding position noted for its wonderful view. We are really a fortunate pair, Dick. "

"I've been thinking that for sometime, " replied Dick rather gravely.

Hitherto they had confined their operations chiefly to their own side of the lake, but as they ranged farther and farther in search of furs they began to prowl among the canyons and narrow valleys in the mountains on the other side. They made, rather far up the northern side, some valuable catches of beaver, but in order to return with them, they were compelled to come around either the northern or southern end of the lake, and the round trip was tremendously long and tiring.

"It's part of a man's business to economize time and strength, " said Dick, "and we must do it. You and I, Al, are going to make a canoe. "

"How? "

"I don't know just yet, but I'm studying it out. The idea will jump out of my head in two or three days. "

It was four days before it jumped, but when it did, it jumped to some purpose.

"First, we'll make a dugout, " he said. "We've got the tools—axes, knives, saws, and augers—and we'd better start with that. "

They cut down a big and perfectly straight pine and chose a length of about twelve feet from the largest part of the trunk. Both boys had seen dugouts, and they knew, in a general way, how to proceed. Their native intelligence supplied the rest.

They cut off one side of the log until it was flat, thus making the bottom for the future canoe. They cut the opposite side away in the well-known curve that a boat makes, low in the middle and high at each end. This part of the work was done with great caution, but Dick had an artistic eye, and they made a fairly good curve. Next they began the tedious and laborious work of digging out, using axes, hatchets, and chisel.

This was a genuine test of Albert's new strength, but he stood it nobly. They chipped away for a long time, until the wood on the sides and bottom was thin but strong enough to stand any pressure. Then they made the proper angle and curve of bow and stern, cut and made two stout broad paddles, and their dugout was ready—a long canoe with a fairly good width, as the original log had been more than two feet in diameter. It was both light and strong, and, raising it on their shoulders, they carried it down to the lake where they put it in the water.

Albert, full of enthusiasm, sprang into the canoe and made a mighty sweep with his paddle. The light dugout shot away, tipped on one side, and as Albert made another sweep with his paddle to right it, it turned over, bottom side up, casting the rash young paddler into ten feet of pure cold water. Albert came up with a mighty splash and sputter. He was a good swimmer, and he had also retained hold of the paddle unconsciously, perhaps. Dick regarded him contemplatively from the land. He had no idea of jumping in. One wet and cold boy was enough. Beside, rashness deserved its punishment.

"Get the canoe before it floats farther away, " he called out, "and tow it to land. It has cost us too much work to be lost out on the lake. "

Albert swam to the canoe, which was now a dozen yards away, and quickly towed it and the paddle to land. There, shivering, the water running from him in streams, he stepped upon the solid earth.

"Run to the cabin as fast as you can, " said Dick. "Take off those wet things, rub yourself down before the fire; then put on dry clothes and come back here and help me. "

Albert needed no urging, but it seemed to him that he would freeze before he reached the cabin, short as the distance was. Fortunately, there was a good fire on the hearth, and, after he had rubbed down and put on his dry, warm suit of deerskin, he never felt finer in his life. He returned to the lake, but he felt sheepish on the way. That had been a rash movement of his, overenthusiastic, but he had been properly punished. His chagrin was increased when he saw Dick a considerable distance out on the lake in the canoe, driving it about in graceful curves with long sweeps of his paddle.

"This is the way it ought to be done, " called out Dick cheerily. "Behold me, Richard Howard, the king of canoe men! "

"You've been practicing while I was gone! " exclaimed Albert.

"No doubt of it, my young friend, and that is why you see me showing such skill, grace, and knowledge. I give you the same recipe without charge: Look before you leap, especially if you're going to leap into a canoe. Now we'll try it together. "

He brought the canoe back to land, Albert got in cautiously, and for the rest of the day they practiced paddling, both together and alone. Albert got another ducking, and Dick, in a moment of overconfidence, got one, too, somewhat to Albert's pleasure and relief, as it has been truly said that misery loves company, but in two or three days they learned to use the canoe with ease. Then, either together or alone, they would paddle boldly the full length of the lake, and soon acquired dexterity enough to use it for freight, too; that is, they would bring back in it across the lake anything that they had shot or trapped on the other side.

So completely had they lost count of time that Dick had an idea spring was coming, but winter suddenly shut down upon them again. It did not arrive with wind and snow this time, but in the night a wave of cold came down from the north so intense that the sheltered valley even did not repel it.

Dick and Albert did not appreciate how really cold it was until they went from the cabin into the clear morning air, when they were warned by the numbing sensation that assailed their ears and noses. They hurried into the house and thawed out their faces, which stung greatly as they were exposed to the fire. Remembering the experiences of their early boyhood, they applied cold water freely, which allayed the stinging. After that they were very careful to wrap up fingers, ears, and noses when they went forth.

Now, the channel that Albert had made from the water of the hot spring proved of great use. The water that came boiling from the earth cooled off rapidly, but it was not yet frozen when it reached the side of Castle Howard, and they could make use of it.

The very first morning they found their new boat, of which they were so proud, hard and fast with ten inches of solid ice all around it. Albert suggested leaving it there.

"We have no need of it so long as the lake is covered with ice, " he said, "and when the ice melts it will be released. "

But Dick looked a little farther. The ice might press in on it and crush it, and hence Albert and he cut it out with axes, after which they put it in the lee of the cabin. Meanwhile, when they wished to reach the traps on the farther side of the lake, they crossed it on the ice, and, presuming that the cold might last long, they easily made a rude sledge which they used in place of the canoe.

"If we can't go through the water, we can at least go over it, " said Albert.

While the great cold lasted, a period of about two weeks, the boys went on no errands except to their traps. The cold was so intense that often they could hear the logs of Castle Howard contracting with a sound like pistol shots. Then they would build the fire high and sit comfortably before it. Fortunately, the valley afforded plenty of fuel. Both boys wished now that they had a few books, but books were out of the question, and they sought always to keep themselves busy with the tasks that their life in the valley entailed upon them. Both knew that this was best.

The cold was so great that even the wild animals suffered from it. The timber wolves, despite their terrible lessons, were driven by it down the valley, and at night a stray one now and then would howl mournfully near the cabin.

"He's a robber and would like to be a murderer, " Albert would say, "but he probably smells this jerked buffalo meat that I'm cooking and I'm sorry for him. "

But the wolves were careful to keep out of rifle shot.

Dick made one trip up the valley and found about fifty buffaloes sheltered in a deep ravine and clustering close together for warmth. They were quite thin, as the grass, although it had been protected by the snow, was very scanty at that period of the year. Dick could have obtained a number of good robes, but he spared them.

"Maybe I won't be so soft-hearted when the spring comes and you are fatter, " he said.

The two, about this time, took stock of their ammunition, which was the most vital of all things to them. For sometime they had used both the shot and ball cartridges only in cases of necessity, and they were relying more and more on traps, continually devising new kinds, their skill and ingenuity increasing with practice.

Dick had brought a great store of cartridges from the last train, especially from the unrifled wagon in the gully, and both boys were surprised to see how many they had left. They had enough to last a long time, according to their present mode of life.

"If you are willing, that settles it, " said Dick.

"If I am willing for what? " asked Albert.

"Willing to stay over another year. You see, Al, we've wandered into a happy hunting ground. There are more furs, by the hundreds, for the taking, and it seems that this is a lost valley. Nobody else comes here. Besides, you are doing wonderfully. All that old trouble is gone, and we want it to stay gone. If we stay here another year, and you continue to eat the way you do and grow the way you do, you'll be able to take a buffalo by the horns and wring its neck. "

Albert grinned pleasantly at his brother.

"You don't have to beg me to stay, " he said. "I like this valley. It has given me life and what is to be our fortune, our furs. Why not do all we can while we can? I'm in favor of the extra year, Dick. "

"Then no more need be said about it. The Cliff House isn't half full of furs yet, but in another year we can fill it. "

The great cold began to break up, the ice on the lake grew thinner and thinner and then disappeared, much of the big game left the valley, the winds from the north ceased to blow, and in their stead came breezes from the south, tipped with warmth. Dick knew that spring was near. It was no guess, he could feel it in every bone of him, and he rejoiced. He had had enough of winter, and it gave him the keenest pleasure when he saw tiny blades of new grass peeping up in sheltered places here and there.

Dick, although he was not conscious of it, had changed almost as much as Albert in the last eight or nine months. He had had no weak chest and throat to cure, but his vigorous young frame had responded nobly to the stimulus of self-reliant life. The physical experience, as well as the mental, of those eight or nine months, had been equal to five times their number spent under ordinary conditions, and he had grown greatly in every respect. Few men were as strong, as agile, and as alert as he.

He and Albert, throughout that long winter, had been sufficient unto each other. They had a great sense of ownership, the valley and all its manifold treasurers belonged to them—a feeling that was true, as no one else came to claim it—and they believed that in their furs they were acquiring and ample provision for a start in life.

When the first tender shades of green began to appear in the valley and on the slopes, Dick decided upon a journey.

"Do you know, Al, how long we have been in this valley? " he asked.

"Eight or ten months, I suppose, " replied Albert.

"It must be something like that, and we've been entirely away from our race. If we had anybody to think about us—although we haven't—they'd be sure that we are dead. We're just as ignorant of what is happening in the world, and I want to go on a skirmishing trip over the mountains. You keep house while I'm gone. "

Albert offered mild objections, which he soon withdrew, as at heart he thought his brother right, and the next day, early in the morning, Dick started on his journey. He carried jerked buffalo meat in a deerskin pouch that he had made for himself, his customary repeating rifle, revolver, and a serviceable hatchet.

"Look after things closely, Al, " said Dick, "and don't bother about setting the traps. Furs are not good in the spring. "

"All right, " responded Albert. "How long do you think you'll be gone? "

"Can't say, precisely. Three or four days, I presume, but don't you worry unless it's a full week. "

It was characteristic of the strength and self-restraint acquired by the two that they parted with these words and a hand clasp only, yet both had deep feeling. Dick looked back from the mouth of the cleft toward Castle Howard and saw a boy in front of it waving a cap. He waved his own in reply and then went forward more swiftly down the valley.

It did not take him long to reach the first slope, and, when he had ascended a little, he paused for rest and inspection. Spring had really made considerable progress. All the trees except the evergreens had put forth young leaves and, as he looked toward the north, the mountains unrolled like a vast green blanket that swept away in ascending folds until it ended, and then the peaks and ridges, white with snow, began.

Dick climbed father, and their valley was wholly lost to sight. It was not so wonderful after all that nobody came to it. Trappers who knew of it long ago never returned, believing that the beaver were all gone forever, and it was too near to the warlike Sioux of the plains for mountain Indians to make a home there.

Dick did not stop long for the look backward—he was too intent upon his mission—but resumed the ascent with light foot and light heart. He remembered very well the way in which he and Albert had come, and he followed it on the return. All night, with his buffalo robe about him, he slept in the pine alcove that had been the temporary home of Albert and himself. He could see no change in it in all the months, except traces to show that some wild animal had slept there.

"Maybe you'll come to-night, Mr. Bear or Mr. Mountain Lion, to sleep in your little bed. " said Dick as he lay down in his buffalo robe, "but you'll find me here before you. "

He was wise enough to know that neither bear nor mountain lion would ever molest him, and he slept soundly. He descended the last slopes and came in sight of the plains on the afternoon of the next day. Everything seemed familiar. The events of that fatal time had made too deep an impression upon him and Albert ever to be forgotten. He knew the very rocks and trees and so went straight to the valley in which he had found the wagon filled with supplies. It lay there yet, crumpled somewhat by time and the weight of snow that had fallen upon it during the winter, but a strong man with good tools might put it in shape for future service.

"Now, if Al and I only had horses, we might get it out and take away our furs in it, " said Dick, "but I suppose I might as well wish for a railroad as for horses. "

He descended into the gully and found the tracks of wolves and other wild beasts about the wagon. In their hunger, they had chewed up every fragment of leather or cloth, and had clawed and scratched among the lockers. Dick had searched those pretty well before, but now he looked for gleanings. He found little of value until he discovered, jammed down in a corner, an old history and geography of the United States combined in one volume with many maps and illustrations. It was a big octavo book, and Dick seized it with the same delight with which a miner snatches up his nugget of gold. He opened it, took a rapid look through flying pages, murmured, "Just the thing, " closed it again, and buttoned it securely inside his deerskin coat. He had not expected anything; nevertheless, he had gleaned to some purpose.

Dick left the wagon and went into the pass where the massacre had occurred. Time had not dimmed the horror of the place for him and he shuddered as he approached the scene of ambush, but he forced himself to go on.

The wagons were scattered about, but little changed, although, as in the case of the one in the gully, all the remaining cloth and leather had been chewed by wild animals. Here and there were the skeletons of the fallen, and Dick knew that the wild beasts had not been content with leather and cloth alone. He went through the wagons one by one, but found nothing of value left except a paper of needles, some spools of thread, and a large pair of scissors, all of which he put in the package with the history.

It was nightfall when he finished the task, and retiring to the slope, he made his bed among some pines. He heard wolves howling twice in the night, but he merely settled himself more easily in his warm buffalo robe and went to sleep again. Replenishing his canteen with water the next morning, he started out upon the plains, intending to make some explorations.

Dick had thought at first that they were in the Black Hills, but he concluded later that they were further west. The mountains about them were altogether too high for the Black Hills, and he wished to gain some idea of their position upon the map. The thought reminded him that he had a book with maps in his pocket, and he took out the precious volume.

He found a map of the Rocky Mountain territory, but most of the space upon it was vague, often blank, and he could not exactly locate himself and Albert, although he knew that they were very far west of any settled country.

"I can learn from that book all about the world except ourselves, " he said, as he put it back in his pocket. But he was not sulky over it. His was a bold and adventurous spirit and he was not afraid, nor was his present trip merely to satisfy curiosity. He and Albert must leave the valley some day, and it was well to know the best way in which it could be done.

He started across the plain in a general southwesterly direction, intending to travel for about a day perhaps, camp for the night, and return on the following day to his mountains. He walked along with a bold, swinging step and did not look back for an hour, but when he turned at last he felt as if he had ventured upon the open ocean in a treacherous canoe. There were the mountains, high, sheltered, and friendly, while off to the south and west the plains rolled away in swell after swell as long and desolate as an untraveled sea, and as hopeless.

Dick saw toward noon some antelope grazing on the horizon, but he was not a hunter now, and he did not trouble himself to seek a shot. An hour or two later he saw a considerable herd of buffaloes scattered about over the plain, nibbling the short bunch grass that had lived under the snow. They were rather an inspiring sight, and Dick felt as if, in a sense, they were furnishing him company. They drove away the desolation and loneliness of the plains, and his inclinations toward them were those of genuine friendliness. They were in danger of no bullet from him.

While he was looking at them, he saw new figures coming over the distant swell. At first he thought they were antelope, but when they reached the crest of the swell and their figures were thrown into relief against the brilliant sky, he saw that they were horsemen.

They came on with such regularity and precision, that, for a moment or two, Dick believed them to be a troop of cavalry, but he learned better when they scattered with a shout and began to chase the buffaloes. Then he knew that they were a band of Sioux Indians hunting.

The full extent of his danger dawned upon him instantly. He was alone and on foot. The hunt might bring them down upon him in five minutes. He was about to run, but his figure would certainly be exposed upon the crest of one of the swells, as theirs had been, and he dropped instead into one of a number of little gullies that intersected the plain.

It was an abrupt little gully, and Dick was well hidden from any eyes not within ten yards of him. He lay at first so he could not see, but soon he began to hear shots and the trampling of mighty hoofs. He knew now that the Sioux were in among the buffaloes, dealing out death, and he began to have a fear of being trodden upon either by horsemen or huge hoofs. He could not bear to lie there and he warned only by sound, so he turned a little further on one side and peeped over the edge of the gully.

The hunters and hunter were not as near as he thought; he had been deceived by sound, the earth being such a good conductor. Yet they were near enough for him to see that he was in great danger and should remain well hidden. He could observe, however, that the hunt was attended with great success. Over a dozen buffaloes had fallen and the others were running about singly or in little groups, closely pursued by the exultant Sioux. Some were on one side of him and some on the other. There was no chance for him, no matter how careful he might be, to rise from the gully and sneak away over the plain. Instead, he crouched more closely and contracted himself into the narrowest possible space, while the hunt wheeled and thundered about him.

It is not to be denied that Dick felt many tremors. He had seen what the Sioux could do. He knew that they were the most merciless of all the northwestern Indians, and he expected only torture and death if he fell into their hands, and there was his brother alone now in the valley. Once the hunt swung away to the westward and the sounds of it grew faint. Dick hoped it would continue in that direction, but by and by it came back again and he crouched down anew in his narrow quarters. He felt that every bone in him was stiffening with cramp and needlelike pains shot through his nerves. Yet he dared not move. And upon top of his painful position came the knowledge that the Sioux would stay there to cut up the slain buffaloes. He was tempted more than once to jump up, run for it and take his chances.

He noticed presently a gray quality in the air, and as he glanced off toward the west, he saw that the red sun was burning very low. Dick's heart sprang up in gladness; it was the twilight, and the blessed darkness would bring chance of escape. Seldom has anyone watched the coming of night with keener pleasure. The sun dropped down behind the swells, the gray twilight passed over all the sky, and after it came the night, on black wings.

Fires sprang up on the plain, fires of buffalo chips lighted by the Sioux, who were now busy skinning and cutting up the slain buffaloes. Dick saw the fires all about him, but none was nearer than a hundred yards, and, despite them, he decided that now was his best time to attempt escape before the moon should come out and lighten up the night.

He pulled himself painfully from the kind gully. He had lain there hours, and he tested every joint as he crept a few feet on the plain. They creaked for a while, but presently the circulation was restored, and, rising to a stooping position, with his rifle ready, he slipped off toward the westward.

Dick knew that great caution was necessary, but he had confidence in the veiling darkness. Off to the eastward he could see one fire, around which a half dozen warriors were gathered, busy with a slain buffalo, working and feasting. He fancied that he could trace their savage features against the red firelight, but he himself was in the darkness.

Another fire rose up, and this was straight before him. Like the others, warriors were around it, and Dick turned off abruptly to the south. Then he heard ponies stamping and he shifted his course again. When he had gone about a dozen yards he lay flat upon the plain and listened. He was hardy and bold, but, for a little while, he was almost in despair. It seemed to him that he was ringed around by a circle of savage warriors and that he could not break through it.

His courage returned, and, rising to his knees, he resumed his slow progress. His course was now southwesterly, and soon he heard again the stamping of hoofs. It was then that a daring idea came into Dick's head.

That stamping of hoofs was obviously made by the ponies of the Sioux. Either the ponies were tethered to short sticks, or they had only a small guard, perhaps a single man. But as they were with the buffaloes, and unsuspecting of a strange presence, they would not detail more than one man to watch their horses. It was wisdom for him to slip away one of the horses, mount it when at a safe distance, and then gallop toward the mountains.

Dick sank down a little lower and crept very slowly toward the point from which the stamping of hoofs proceeded. When he had gone about a dozen yards he heard another stamping of hoofs to his right and then a faint whinny. This encouraged him. It showed him that the ponies were tethered in groups, and the group toward which he was going might be without a guard. He continued his progress another dozen yards, and then lay flat upon the plain. He had seen two vague forms in the darkness, and he wished to make himself a blur with the earth. They were warriors passing from one camp fire to another, and Dick saw them plainly, tall men with blankets folded about them like togas, long hair in which eagle feathers were braided after the Sioux style, and strong aquiline features. They looked like chiefs, men of courage, dignity, and mind, and Dick contrasted them with the ruffians of the wagon train. The contrast was not favorable to the white faces that he remembered so well.

But the boy saw nothing of mercy or pity in these red countenances. Bold and able they might be, but it was no part of theirs to spare their enemies. He fairly crowded himself against the earth, but they went on, absorbed in their own talk, and he was not seen. He raised up again and began to crawl. The group of ponies came into view, and he saw with delight that they had no watchman. A half dozen in number and well hobbled, they cropped the buffalo grass. They were bare of back, but they wore their Indian bridles, which hung from their heads.

Dick knew a good deal about horses, and he was aware that the approach would be critical. The Indian ponies might take alarm or they might not, but the venture must be made. He did not believe that he could get beyond the ring of the Sioux fires without being discovered, and only a dash was left.

Dick marked the pony nearest to him. It seemed a strong animal, somewhat larger than the others, and, pulling up a handful of bunch grass, he approached it, whistling very softly. He held the grass in his left hand and his hunting knife in the right, his rifle being fastened to his back. The pony raised his head, looked at him in a friendly manner, then seemed to change his mind and backed away. But Dick came on, still holding out the grass and emitting that soft, almost inaudible whistle. The pony stopped and wavered between belief and suspicion. Dick was not more than a dozen feet away now, and he began to calculate when he might make a leap and seize the bridle.

The boy and the pony were intently watching the eyes of each other. Dick, in that extreme moment, was gifted with preternatural acuteness of mind and vision, and he saw that the pony still wavered. He took another step forward, and the eyes of the pony inclined distinctly from belief to suspicion; another short and cautious step, and they were all suspicion. But it was too late for the pony. The agile youth sprang, and dropping the grass, seized him with his left hand by the bridle. A sweep or two of the hunting knife and the hobbles were cut through.

The pony reared and gave forth an alarmed neigh, but Dick, quickly replacing the knife in his belt, now held the bridle with both hands, and those two hands were very strong. He pulled the pony back to its four feet and sprang, with one bound, upon his back. Then kicking him vigorously in the side, he dashed away, with rifle shots spattering behind him.

Chapter XI
The Terrible Pursuit

Dick knew enough to bend low down on the neck of the flying mustang, and he was untouched, although he heard the bullets whistling about him. The neigh of the pony had betrayed him, but he was aided by his quickness and the friendly darkness, and he felt a surge of exultation that he could not control, boy that he was. The Sioux, jumping upon their ponies, sent forth a savage war whoop that the desolate prairie returned in moaning echoes, and Dick could not refrain from a reply. He uttered one shout, swung his rifle defiantly over his head, then bending down again, urged his pony to increased speed.

Dick heard the hoofs of his pursuers thundering behind him, and more rifle shots came, but they ceased quickly. He knew that the Sioux would not fire again soon, because of the distance and the uncertain darkness. It was his object to increase that distance, trusting that the darkness would continue free from moonlight. He took one swift look backward and saw the Sioux, a dozen or more, following steadily after. He knew that they would hang on as long as any chance of capturing him remained, and he resolved to make use of the next swell that he crossed. He would swerve when he passed the crest, and while it was yet between him and his pursuers, perhaps he could find some friendly covert that would hide him. Meanwhile he clung tightly to his rifle, something that one always needed in this wild and dangerous region.

He crossed a swell, but there was no friendly increase of the darkness and he was afraid to swerve, knowing that the Sioux would thereby gain upon him, since he would make himself the curve of the bow, while they remained the string.

In fact, the hasty glance back showed that the Sioux had gained, and Dick felt tremors. He was tempted for a moment to fire upon his pursuers, but it would certainly cause a loss of speed, and he did not believe that he could hit anything under such circumstances. No, he would save his bullets for a last stand, if they ran him to earth.

The Sioux raised their war whoop again and fired three or four shots. Dick felt a slight jarring movement run through his pony, and then the animal swerved. He was afraid that he had trodden in a prairie-dog hole or perhaps a little gully, but in an instant or two he was running steadily again, and Dick forgot the incident in the excitement of the flight.

He was in constant fear lest the coming out of the moon should lighten up the prairie and make him a good target for the Sioux bullets, but he noted instead, and with great joy, that it was growing darker. Heavy clouds drifted across the sky, and a cold wind arose and began to whistle out of the northwest. It was a friendly black robe that was settling down over the earth. It had never before seemed to him that thick night could be so welcome.

Dick's pony rose again on a swell higher than the others, and was poised there for the fraction of a second, a dark silhouette against the darker sky. Several of the Sioux fired. Dick felt once more that momentary jar of his horse's mechanism, but it disappeared quickly and his hopes rose, because he saw that the darkness lay thickly between this swell and the next, and he believed that he now could lose his pursuers.

He urged his horse vigorously. He had made no mistake when he chose this pony as strong and true. The response was instant and emphatic. He flew down the slope, but instead of ascending the next swell he turned at an angle and went down the depression that lay between them. There the darkness was thickest, and the burst of speed by the pony was so great that the shapes of his pursuers became vague and then were lost. Nevertheless, he heard the thudding of their hoofs and knew that they could also hear the beat of his. That would guide them for a while yet. He thought he might turn again and cross the next swell, thus throwing them entirely off his track, but he was afraid that he would be cast into relief again when he reached the crest, and so continued down the depression.

He heard shouts behind him, and it seemed to him that they were not now the shouts of triumph, but the shouts of chagrin. Clearly, he was gaining because after the cries ceased, the sound of hoof beats came but faintly. He urged his horse to the last ounce of his speed and soon the sound of the pursuing hoofs ceased entirely.

The depression ended and he was on the flat plain. It was still cloudy, with no moon, but his eyes were used enough to the dark to tell him that the appearance of the country had changed. It now lay before him almost as smooth as the surface of a table, and never relaxing the swift gallop, he turned at another angle.

He was confident now that the Sioux could not overtake or find him. A lone object in the vast darkness, there was not a chance in a hundred for them to blunder upon him. But the farther away the better, and he went on for an hour. He would not have stopped then, but the good pony suddenly began to quiver, and then halted so abruptly that Dick, rifle and all, shot over his shoulder. He felt a stunning blow, a beautiful set of stars flashed before his eyes, and he was gone, for the time, to another land.

When Dick awoke he felt very cold and his head ached. He was lying flat upon his back, and, with involuntary motion, he put his hand to his head. He felt a bump there and the hand came back damp and stained. He could see that the fingers were red—there was light enough for that ominous sight, although the night had no yet passed.

Then the flight, the danger, and his fall all came back in a rush to Dick. He leaped to his feet, and the act gave him pain, but not enough to show that any bone was broken. His rifle, the plainsman's staff and defense, lay at his feet. He quickly picked it up and found that it, too, was unbroken. In fact, it was not bent in the slightest, and here his luck had stood him well. But ten feet away lay a horse, the pony that had been a good friend to him in need.

Dick walked over to the pony. It was dead and cold. It must have been dead two to three hours at least, and he had lain that long unconscious. There was a bullet hole in its side and Dick understood now the cause of those two shivers, like the momentary stopping of a clock's mechanism. The gallant horse had galloped on until he was stopped only by death. Dick felt sadness and pity.

"I hope you've gone to the horse heaven, " he murmured.

Then he turned to thoughts of his own position. Alone and afoot upon the prairie, with hostile and mounted Sioux somewhere about, he was still in bad case. He longed now for his mountains, the lost valley, the warm cabin, and his brother.

It was quite dark and a wind, sharp with cold, was blowing. It came over vast wastes, and as it swept across the swells kept up a bitter moaning sound. Dick shivered and fastened his deerskin tunic a little tighter. He looked up at the sky. Not a star was there, and sullen black clouds rolled very near to the earth. The cold had a raw damp in it, and Dick feared those clouds.

Had it been day he could have seen his mountains, and he would have made for them at once, but now his eyes did not reach a hundred yards, and that bitter, moaning wind told him nothing save that he must fight hard against many things if he would keep the life that was in him. He had lost all idea of direction. North and south, east and west were the same to him, but one must go even if one went wrong.

He tried all his limbs again and found that they were sound. The wound on his head had ceased to bleed and the ache was easier. He put his rifle on his shoulder, waved, almost unconsciously, a farewell to the horse, as one leaves the grave of a friend, and walked swiftly away, in what course he knew not.

He felt much better with motion. The blood began to circulate more warmly, and hope sprang up. If only that bitter, moaning wind would cease. It was inexpressibly weird and dismal. It seemed to Dick a song of desolation, it seemed to tell him at times that it was not worth while to try, that, struggle as he would, his doom was only waiting.

Dick looked up. The black clouds had sunk lower and they must open before long. If only day were near at hand, then he might choose the right course. Hark! Did he not hear hoof beats? He paused in doubt, and then lay down with his ear to the earth. Then he distinctly heard the sound, the regular tread of a horse, urged forward in a straight course, and he knew that it could be made only by the Sioux. But the sound indicated only one horse, or not more than two or three at the most.

Dick's courage sprang up. Here was a real danger and not the mysterious chill that the moaning of the wind brought to him. If the Sioux had found him, they had divided, and it was only a few of their number that he would have to face. He hugged his repeating rifle. It was a fine weapon, and just then he was in love with it. There was no ferocity in Dick's nature, but the Sioux were seeking the life that he wished to keep.

He rose from the earth and walked slowly on in his original course. He had no doubt that the Sioux, guided by some demon instinct, would overtake him. He looked around for a good place of defense, but saw none. Just the same low swells, just the same bare earth, and not even a gully like that in which he had lain while the hunt of the buffalo wheeled about him.

He heard the hoof beats distinctly now, and he became quite sure that they were made by only a single horseman. His own senses had become preternaturally acute, and, with the conviction that he was followed by but one, came a rush of shame. Why should he, strong and armed, seek to evade a lone pursuer? He stopped, holding his rifle ready, and waited, a vague, shadowy figure, black on the black prairie.

Dick saw the phantom horseman rise on a swell, the faint figure of an Indian and his pony, and there was no other. He was glad now that he had waited. The horse, trained for such work as this, gave the Sioux warrior a great advantage, but he would fight it out with him.

Dick sank down on one knee in order to offer a smaller target, and thrust his rifle forward for an instant shot. But the Sioux had stopped and was looking intently at the boy. For fully two minutes neither he nor his horse moved, and Dick almost began to believe that he was the victim of an illusion, the creation of the desolate plains, the night, the floating black vapors, his tense nerves, and heated imagination. He was tempted to try a shot to see if it were real, but the distance and the darkness were too great. He strengthened his will and remained crouched and still, his finger ready for the trigger of his rifle.

The Sioux and his horse moved at last, but they did not come forward; they rode slowly toward the right, curving in a circle about the kneeling boy, but coming no nearer. They were still vague and indistinct, but they seemed blended into one, and the supernatural aspect of the misty form of horse and rider increased. The horse trod lightly now, and Dick no longer heard the sound of footsteps, only the bitter moaning of the wind over the vast dark spaces.

The rider rode silently on his circle about the boy, and Dick turned slowly with him, always facing the eyes that faced him. He could dimly make out the shape of a rifle at the saddlebow, but the Sioux did not raise it, he merely rode on in that ceaseless treadmill tramp, and Dick wondered what he meant to do. Was he waiting for the others to come up?

Time passed and there was no sign of a second horseman. The single warrior still rode around him, and Dick still turned with him. He might be coming nearer in his ceaseless curves, but Dick could not tell. Although he was the hub of the circle, he began to have a dizzy sensation, as if the world were swimming about him. He became benumbed, as if his head were that of a whirling dervish.

Dick became quite sure now that the warrior and his horse were unreal, a creation of the vapors and the mists, and that he himself was dreaming. He saw, too, at last that they were coming nearer, and he felt horror, as if something demonic were about to seize him and drag him down. He crouched so long that he felt pain in his knees, and all things were becoming a blur before his eyes. Yet there had not been a sound but that of the bitter, moaning wind.

There was a flash, a shot, the sigh of a bullet rushing past, and Dick came out of his dream. The Sioux had raised the rifle from his saddlebow and fired. But he had been too soon. The shifting and deceptive quality of the darkness caused him to miss. Dick promptly raised his own rifle and fired in return. He also missed, but a second bullet from the warrior cut a lock from his temple.

Dick was now alert in every nerve. He had not wanted the life of this savage, but the savage wanted his; it seemed also that everything was in favor of the savage getting it, but his own spirit rose to meet the emergency; he, too, became the hunter.

He sank a little lower and saved his fire until the warrior galloped nearer. Then he sent a bullet so close that he saw one of the long eagle feathers drop from the hair of the warrior. The sight gave him a savage exultation that he would have believed a few hours before impossible to him. The next bullet might not merely clip a feather!

The Sioux, contrary to the custom of the Indian, did not utter a sound, nor did Dick say a word. The combat, save for the reports of the rifle shots, went on in absolute silence. It lasted a full ten minutes, when the Indian urged his horse to a gallop, threw himself behind the body and began firing under the neck. A bullet struck Dick in the left arm and wounded him slightly, but it did not take any of his strength and spirit.

Dick sought in vain for a sight of the face of his fleeting foe. He could catch only a glimpse of long, trailing hair beneath the horse's mane, and then would come the flash of a rifle shot. Another bullet clipped his side, but only cut the skin. Nevertheless, it stung, and while it stung the body it stung Dick's wits also into keener action. He knew that the Sioux warrior was steadily coming closer and closer in his deadly circle, and in time one of his bullets must strike a vital spot, despite the clouds and darkness.

Dick steadied himself, calming every nerve and muscle. Then he lay down on his stomach on the plain, resting slightly on his elbow, and took careful aim at the flying pony. He felt some regret as he looked down the sights. This horse might be as faithful and true as the one that had carried him to temporary safety, but he must do the deed. He marked the brown patch of hair that lay over the heart and pulled the trigger.

Dick's aim was true—the vapors and clouds had not disturbed it—and when the rifle flashed, the pony bounded into the and fell dead. But the agile Sioux leaped clear and darted away. Dick marked his brown body, and then was his opportunity to send a mortal bullet, but a feeling of which he was almost ashamed held his hand. His foe was running, and he was no longer hunted. The feeling lasted but a moment, and when it passed, the Sioux was out of range. A moment later and his misty foe had become a part of the solid darkness.

Dick stood upright once more. He had been the victor in a combat that still had for him all the elements of the ghostly. He had triumphed, but just in time. His nerves were relaxed and unstrung, and his hands were damp. He carefully reloaded all the empty chambers of his repeating rifle, and without looking at the falling horse, which he felt had suffered for the wickedness of another, strode away again over the plain, abandoning the rifle of the fallen Sioux as a useless burden.

It took Dick sometime after his fight with the phantom horseman to come back to real earth. Then he noticed that both the clouds and the dampness had increased, and presently something cold and wet settled upon his face. It was a flake of snow, and a troop came at its heels, gentle but insistent, chilling his hands and gradually whitening the earth, until it was a gleaming floor under a pall of darkness.

Dick was in dismay. Here was a foe that he could not fight with rifle balls. He knew that the heavy clouds would continue to pour forth snow, and the day, which he thought was not far away, would disclose as little as the night. The white pall would hide the mountains as well as the black pall had done, and he might be going farther and father from his valley.

He felt that he had been released from one danger and then another, only to encounter a third. It seemed to him, in his minute of despair, that Fate had resolved to defeat all his efforts, but, the minute over, he renewed his courage and trudged bravely on, he knew not whither. It was fortunate for him that he wore a pair of the heavy shoes saved from the wagon, and put on for just such a journey as this. The wet from the snow would have soon soaked though his moccasins, but, as his thick deerskin leggings fitted well over his shoes, he kept dry, and that was a comfort.

The snow came down without wind and fuss, but more heavily than ever, persistent, unceasing, and sure of victory. It was not particularly cold, and the walking kept up a warm and pleasant circulation in Dick's veins. But he knew that he must not stop. Whether he was going on in a straight line he had no way to determine. He had often heard that men, lost on the plains, soon begin to travel in a circle, and he watched awhile for his own tracks; but if they were there, they were covered up by snow too soon for him to see, and, after all, what did it matter?

He saw after a while a pallid yellowish light showing dimly through the snow, and he knew that it was the sunrise. But it illuminated nothing. The white gloom began to replace the black one. It was soon full day, but the snow was so thick that he could not see more than two or three hundred yards in any direction. He longed now for shelter, some kind of hollow, or perhaps a lone tree. The incessant fall of the snow upon his head and its incessant clogging under his feet were tiring him, but he only trod a plain, naked save for its blanket of snow.

Dick had been careful to keep his rifle dry, putting the barrel of it under his long deerskin coat. Once as he shifted it, he felt a lump over his chest, and for an instant or two did not know what caused it. Then he remember the history and geography of the United States. He laughed with grim humor.

"I am lost to history, " he murmured, "and geography will not tell me where I am. "

He crossed a swell—he knew them now more by feeling than by sight—and before beginning the slight assent of the next one he stopped to eat. He had been enough of a frontiersman, before starting upon such a trip, to store jerked buffalo in the skin knapsack that he had saved for himself. The jerked meat offered the largest possible amount of sustenance in the smallest possible space, and Dick ate eagerly. Then he felt a great renewal of courage and strength. He also drank of the snow water, that is, he dissolved the snow in his mouth, but he did not like it much.

He stood there for a while resting, and resolved only to walk enough to keep himself warm. Certainly, nothing was to be gained by exhausting himself and the snow which was now a foot deep showed no signs of abating. The white gloom hung all about him and he could not see the sky overhead.

Just as he took this resolution, Dick saw a shadow in the circling white. The shadow was like that of a man, but before he could see farther there was a little flash of red, a sharp, stinging report, and a bullet clipped the skin of his cheek, burning like fire. Dick was startled, and for full cause—but he recognized the Sioux warrior who had fought him on horseback. He had stared too long at that man and at a time too deadly not to know that head and face and the set of his figure. He had followed Dick through all the hours and falling snow, bent upon taking his life. A second shot, quickly following the first, showed that he meant to miss no chance.

The second bullet, like the first, just grazed Dick, and mild of temper though he habitually was, he was instantly seized with the fiercest rage. He could not understand such hatred, such ferocity, such an eagerness to take human life. And this was the man whom he had spared, whom he could easily have slain when he was running! The Sioux was raising his rifle for a third bullet, when Dick shot him through the chest. There was no doubt about his aim now. It was not disturbed by the whitish mist and the falling snow.

The Sioux fell full length, without noise and without struggle, and his gun flew from his hand. His body lay half buried in the snow, some of the long eagle feathers in his hair thrusting up like the wing of a slain bird. Dick looked at him with shuddering horror. All the anger was gone from him now, and it is true that in his heart he felt pity for this man, who had striven so hard and without cause to take his life. He would have been glad to go away now, but forced himself to approach and look down at the Indian.

The warrior lay partly on his side with one arm beneath his body. The blood from the bullet hole in his chest dyed the snow, and Dick believed that he had been killed instantly. But Dick would not touch him. He could not bring himself to do that. Nor would he take any of his arms. Instead, he turned away, after the single look, and, bending his head a little to the snow, walked rapidly toward the yellowish glare that told where the sun was rising. He did not know just why he went in that direction, but it seemed to him the proper thing to walk toward the morning.

Two hours, perhaps, passed and the fall of snow began to lighten. The flakes still came down steadily, but not in such a torrent. The area of vision widened. He saw dimly, as through a mist, three or four hundred yards, perhaps, but beyond was only the white blur, and there was nothing yet to tell him whether he was going toward the mountains or away from them.

He rested and ate again. Then he recovered somewhat, mentally as well as physically. Part of the horror of the Indian, his deadly pursuit, and the deadly ending passed. He ached with weariness and his nerves were quite unstrung, but the snow would cease, the skies would clear, and then he could tell which way lay the mountains and his brother.

He rested here longer than usual and studied the plain as far as he could see it. He concluded that its character had changed somewhat, that the swells were high than they had been, and he was hopeful that he might find shelter soon, a deep gully, perhaps, or a shallow prairie stream with sheltering cottonwoods along its course.

Another hour passed, but he did not make much progress. The snow was now up to his knees, and it became an effort to walk. The area of vision had widened, but no mountains yet showed through the white mist. He was becoming tired with a tiredness that was scarcely to be born. If he stood still long enough to rest he became cold, a deadly chill that he knew to be the precursor of death's benumbing sleep would creep over him, and then he would force himself to resume the monotonous, aching walk.

Dick's strength waned. His eyesight, affected by the glare of the snow, became short and unsteady, and he felt a dizziness of the brain. Things seemed to dance about, but his will was so strong that he could still reason clearly, and he knew that he was in desperate case. It was his will that resisted the impulse of his flesh to throw his rifle away as a useless burden, but he laughed aloud when he thought of the map of the United States in the inside pocket of his coat.

"They'll find me, if they ever find me, with that upon me, " he said aloud, "and they, too, will laugh. "

He stumbled against something and doubled his fist angrily as if he would strike a man who had maliciously got in his way. It was the solid bark of a big cottonwood that had stopped him, and his anger vanished in joy. Where one cottonwood was, others were likely to be, and their presence betokened a stream, a valley, and a shelter of some kind.

He was still dazed, suffering partially from snow blindness, but now he saw a line of sturdy cottonwoods and beyond it another line. The stream, he knew, flowed between. He went down the line a few hundred yards and came, as he had hoped, into more broken ground.

The creek ran between banks six or seven feet high, with a margin between stream and bank, and the cottonwoods on these banks were reinforced by some thick clumps of willows. Between the largest clump and the line of cottonwoods, with the bank as a shelter for the third side, was a comparatively clear space. The snow was only a few inches deep there, and Dick believed that he could make a shelter. He had, of course, brought his blanket with him in a tight roll on his back, and he was hopeful enough to have some thought of building a fire.

He stooped down to feel in the snow at a likely spot, and the act saved his life. A bullet, intended for his head, was buried in the snow beyond him, and a body falling down the bank lay quite still at his feet. It was the long Sioux. Wounded mortally, he had followed Dick, nevertheless, with mortal intent, crawling, perhaps most of the time, and with his last breath he had fired what he intended to be the fatal shot.

He was quite dead now, his power for evil gone forever. There could be no doubt about it. Dick at length forced himself to touch the face. It had grown cold and the pulse in the wrist was still. It yet gave him a feeling of horror to touch the Sioux, but his own struggle for life would be bitter and he could spare nothing. The dead warrior wore a good blanket, which Dick now took, together with his rifle and ammunition, but he left all the rest. Then he dragged the warrior from the sheltered space to a deep snow bank, where he sank him out of sight. He even took the trouble to heap more snow upon him in the form of a burial, and he felt a great relief when he could no longer see the savage brown features.

He went back to his sheltered space, and, upon the single unprotected side threw up a high wall of snow, so high that it would serve as a wind-break. Then he began to search for fallen brushwood. Meanwhile, it was turning colder, and a bitter wind began to moan across the plain.

Chapter XII
The Fight with Nature

Dick realized suddenly that he was very cold. The terrible pursuit was over, ending mortally for the pursuer, but he was menaced by a new danger. Sheltered though his little valley was, he could, nevertheless, freeze to death in it with great ease. In fact, he had begun already to shiver, and he noticed that while his feet were dry, the snow at last had soaked through his deerskin leggings and he was wet from knee to ankle. The snow had ceased, although a white mist hovered in a great circle and the chill of the wind was increasing steadily. He must have a fire or die.

He resumed his search, plunging into the snow banks under the cottonwoods and other trees, and at last he brought out dead boughs, which he broke into short pieces and piled in a heap in the center of the open space. The wood was damp on the outside, of course, but he expected nothing better and was not discouraged. Selecting a large, well-seasoned piece, he carefully cut away all the wet outside with his strong hunting knife. Then he whittled off large quantities of dry shavings, put them under the heap of boughs, and took from his inside a pocket a small package of lucifer matches.

Dick struck one of the matches across the heel of his shoe. No spark leaped up. Instead, his heart sank down, sank further, perhaps, than it had ever done before in his life. The match was wet. He took another from the pocket; it, too, was wet, and the next and the next and all. The damp from the snow, melted by the heat of his body, had penetrated his buckskin coat, although in the excitement of pursuit and combat he had not noticed it.

Dick was in despair. He turned to the snow a face no less white. Had he escaped all the dangers of the Sioux for this? To freeze to death merely because he did not have a dry lucifer match? The wind was still rising and it cut to his very marrow. Reality and imagination were allied, and Dick was almost overpowered. He angrily thrust the wet little package of matches back into the inside pocket of his coat — his border training in economy had become so strong that even in the moment of despair he would throw away nothing — and his hand in the pocket came into contact with something else, small, hard, and polished. Dick instantly felt a violent revulsion from despair to hope.

The small object was a sunglass. That wagon train was well equipped. Dick had made salvage of two sunglasses, and in a moment of forethought had given one to Albert, keeping the other for himself, each agreeing then and there to carry his always for the moment of need that might come.

Dick drew out the sunglass and fingered it as one would a diamond of great size. Then he looked up. A brilliant sun was shining beyond white, misty clouds, but its rays came through them dim and weak. The mists or, rather, cloudy vapor might lift or thin, and in that chance lay the result of his fight for life. While he waited a little, he stamped up and down violently, and threw his arms about with energy. It did not have much effect. The wet, cold, the raw kind that goes through, was in him and, despite all the power of his will, he shivered almost continually. But he persisted for a half hour and then became conscious of an increasing brightness about him. The white mist was not gone, but it was thinning greatly, and the rays of the sun fell on the snow brilliant and strong.

Dick took the dry stick again and scraped off particles of wood so fine that they were almost a power. He did not stop until he had a little heap more than an inch high. Meanwhile, the sun's rays, pouring through the whitish mist, continued to grow fuller and stronger.

Dick carefully polished the glass and held it at the right angle between the touchwood, that is, the scrapings, and the sun. The rays passing through the glass increased many times in power and struck directly upon the touchwood. Dick crouched over the wood in order to protect it from the wind, and watched, his breath constricted, while his life waited on the chance.

A minute, two minutes, three minutes, five passed and then a spark appeared in the touchwood, and following it came a tiny flame. Dick shouted with joy and shifted his body a little to put shavings on the touchwood. An ill wind struck the feeble blaze, which was not yet strong enough to stand fanning into greater life, and it went out, leaving a little black ash to mark where the touchwood had been.

Dick's nerves were so much overwrought that he cried aloud again, and now it was a cry of despair, not of joy. He looked at the little black ash as if his last chance were gone, but his despair did not last long. He seized the dry stick again and scraped off another little pile of touchwood. Once more the sunglass and once more the dreadful waiting, now longer than five minutes and nearer ten, while Dick waited in terrible fear, lest the sun itself should fail him, and go behind impenetrable clouds.

But the second spark came and after it, as before, followed the little flame. No turning aside now to allow a cruel chance to an ill wind. Instead, he bent down his body more closely than ever to protect the vital blaze, and, reaching out one cautious arm, fed it first with the smallest of the splinters, and then with the larger in an ascending scale.

Up leaped the flames, red and strong. Dick's body could not wholly protect them now, but they fought for themselves. When the wind shrieked and whipped against them, they waved back defiance, and the more the wind whipped them, the higher and stronger they grew.

The victory was with the flames, and Dick fed them with wood, almost with his body and soul, and all the time as the wind bent them over they crackled and ate deeper and deeper into the wood. He could put on damp wood now. The flames merely leaped out, licked up the melted snow with a hiss and a sputter, and developed the stick in a mass of glowing red.

Dick fed his fire a full half hour, hunting continually in the snow under the trees for brushwood and finding much of it, enough to start a second fire at the far end of the sheltered place, with more left in reserve. He spent another half hour heaping up the snow as a bulwark about his den, and then sat down between the two fires to dry and warm, almost to roast himself.

It was the first time that Dick understood how much pleasure could be drawn from a fire alone. What beautiful red and yellow flames! What magnificent glowing coals! What a glorious thing to be there, while the wind above was howling over the snowy and forlorn plain! His clothes dried rapidly. He no longer shivered. The grateful warmth penetrated every fiber of him and it seemed strange now that he should have been in despair only an hour ago. Life was a wonderful and brilliant thing. There was no ache in his bones, and the first tingling of his hands, ears, and nose he had relieved with the application of wet snow. Now he felt only comfort.

After a while Dick ate again of his jerked buffalo meat, and with the food, warmth, and rest, he began to feel sleepy. He plunged into the snow, hunted out more wood to add to his reserve, and then, with the two blankets, the Indian's and his own, wrapped about him, sat down where the heat of the two fires could reach him from either side, and with a heap of the wood as a rest for his back.

Dick did not really intend to go to sleep, but he had been through great labors and dangers and had been awake long. He drew up one of the blankets until it covered all of his head and most of his face, and began to gaze into the coals of the larger fire. The wind—and it was now so cold that the surface of the snow was freezing—still whistled over him, but the blanket protected his head from its touch. The whistle instead increased his comfort like the patter of rain on a roof to him who is dry inside.

The fire had now burned down considerable and the beds of coals were large and beautiful. They enveloped Dick in their warmth and cheer and began to pain splendid words of hope for him. He could read what they said in glowing letters, but the singular feeling of peace and rest deepened all the while. He wondered vaguely that one could be so happy.

The white snow became less white, the red fire less red, and a great gray mist came floating down over Dick's eyes. Up rose a shadowy world in which all things were vague and wavering. Then the tired lids dropped down, the gray mist gave way to a soft blackness, and Dick sank peacefully into the valley of sleep.

The boy slept heavily hour after hour, with his hooded head sunk upon his knees, and his rifle lying across his lap, while over him shrieked the coldest wind of the great northwestern plains. The surface of the frozen ground presented a gleaming sheet like ice, over which the wind acquired new strength and a sharper edge, but the boy in his alcove remained safe and warm. Now and then a drift of fine snowy particles that would have stung like small shot was blown over the barrier, but they only stuck upon the thick folds of the blankets and the boy slept on. The white mist dissolved. The sun poured down beams brilliantly cold and hard, and over them was the loom of the mountains, but the boy knew nothing of them, nor cared.

The fires ceased to flame and became great masses of glowing coals that would endure long. The alcove was filled with the grateful warmth, and when the sun was in the zenith, Dick still slept, drawing long, regular breaths from a deep strong chest. The afternoon grew and waned, twilight came over the desolate snow fields, the loom of the mountains was gone, and the twilight gave way to an icy night.

When Dick awoke it was quite dark, save for the heaps of coals which still glowed and threw out warmth. He felt at first a little wonderment that he had slept so long, but he was not alarmed. His forethought and energy had provided plenty of wood and he threw on fresh billets. Once more the flames leaped up to brighten and to cheer, and Dick, walking to the edge of his snow bank, looked over. The wind had piled up the snow there somewhat higher before the surface froze, and across the barrier he gazed upon some such scene as one might behold near the North Pole. He seemed to be looking over ice fields that stretched away to infinity, and the wind certainly had a voice that was a compound of chill and desolation.

It was so solemn and weird that Dick was glad to duck down again into his den, and resume the seat where he had slept so long. He ate a little and then tried to slumber again, but he had already slept so much that he remained wide awake. He opened his eyes and let them stay open, after several vain efforts.

The moonlight now came out with uncommon brilliancy and the plain glittered. But it was the coldest moon that Dick had ever seen. He began to feel desolate and lonely again, and, since he could not sleep, he longed for something to do. Then the knowledge came to him. He put on fresh wood, and between firelight and moonlight he could see everything clearly.

Satisfied with his light, Dick took from his pocket the History of the United States that was accompanying him so strangely in his adventures, and began to study it. He looked once more at the map of the Rocky Mountain territories, and judged that he was in Southern Montana. Although his curiosity as to the exact spot in which he lay haunted him, there was no way to tell, and turning the leaves away from the map, he began to read.

It was chance, perhaps, that made him open at the story that never grows old to American youth—Valley Forge. It was not a great history, it had no brilliant and vivid style, but the simple facts were enough for Dick. He read once more of the last hope of the great man, never greater than then, praying in the snow, and his own soul leaped at the sting of example. He was only a boy, obscure, unknown, and the fate of but two rested with him, yet he, too, would persevere, and in the end his triumph also would be complete. He read no further, but closed the book and returned it carefully to his pocket. Then he stared into the fire, which he built up higher that the cheerful light might shine before him.

Dick did not hide from himself even now the dangers of his position. He was warm and sheltered for the present, he had enough of the jerked buffalo to last several days, but sooner or later he must leave his den and invade the snowy plain with its top crust of ice. This snow might last two or three weeks or a month. It was true that spring had come, but it was equally true, as so often happens in the great Northwest, that spring had refused to stay.

Dick tried now to see the mountains. The night was full of brilliant moonlight, but the horizon was too limited; it ended everywhere, a black wall against the snow, and still speculating and pondering, Dick at last fell asleep again.

When the boy awoke it was another clear, cold day, with the wind still blowing, and there in the northwest he joyously saw the white line of the mountains. He believed that he could recognize the shape of certain peaks and ridges, and he fixed on a spot in the blue sky which he was sure overhung Castle Howard.

Dick saw now that he had been going away from the mountains. He was certainly farther than he had been when he first met the Sioux, and it was probable that he had been wandering then in an irregular course, with its general drift toward the southwest. The mountains in the thin, high air looked near, but his experience of the West told him that they were far, forty miles perhaps, and the tramp that lay before him was a mighty undertaking. He prepared for it at once.

He cut a stout stick that would serve as a cane, looked carefully to the security of his precious sun glass, and bidding his little den, which already had begun to wear some of the aspects of a home, a regretful farewell, started through the deep snow.

He had wrapped his head in the Indian's blanket, covering everything but eyes, nose, and mouth, and he did not suffer greatly from the bitter wind. But it was weary work breaking the way through the snow, rendered all the more difficult by the icy crust on top. The snow rose to his waist and he broke it at first with his body, but by and by he used the stick, and thus he plodded on, not making much more than a mile an hour.

Dick longed now for the shelter of the warm den. The cold wind, despite the protection of the blanket, began to seek out the crannies in it and sting his face. He knew that he was wet again from ankle to knee, but he struggled resolutely on, alike for the sake of keeping warm and for the sake of shortening the distance. Yet there were other difficulties than those of the snow. The ground became rough. Now and then he would go suddenly through the treacherous snow into an old buffalo wallow or a deep gully, and no agility could keep him from falling on his face or side. This not only made him weary and sore, but it was a great trial to his temper also, and the climax came when he went through the snow into a prairie brook and came out with his shoes full of water.

Dick shivered, stamped his feet violently, and went on painfully breaking his way through the snow. He began to have that dull stupor of mind and body again. He could see nothing on the surface of the white plain save himself. The world was entirely desolate. But if the Sioux were coming a second time he did not care. He was amused at the thought of the Sioux coming. There were hidden away somewhere in some snug valley, and were too sensible to venture upon the plain.

Late in the afternoon the wind became so fierce, and Dick was so tired, that he dug a hole in the deepest snow bank he could find, wrapped the blankets tightly around him, and crouched there for warmth and shelter. Then, when the muscles were at rest, he began to feel the cold all through his wet feet and legs. He took off his shoes and leggings inside the shelter of his blankets, and chafed feet and legs with vigorous hands. This restored warmth and circulation, but he was compelled after a while to put on his wet garments again. He had gained a rest, however, and as he did not fear the damp so much while he was moving, he resumed the painful march.

The mountains seemed as far away as ever, but Dick knew that he had come five or six miles. He could look back and see his own path through the deep snow, winding and zigzagging toward the northwest. It would wind and zigzag no matter how hard he tried to go in a straight line, and finally he refused to look back any more at the disclosure of his weakness.

He sought more trees before the sun went down, as his glass could no longer be of use without them, but found none. There could be no fire for him that night, and digging another deep hole in the snow he slept the darkness through, nevertheless, warmly and comfortably, like an Eskimo in his ice hut. He did not suffer as much as he had thought he would from his wet shoes and leggings, and in the night, wrapped within the blankets they dried on him.

Dick spent the second day in alternate tramps of an hour and rests of half an hour. He was conscious that he was growing weaker from this prodigious exertion, but he was not willing to acknowledge it. In the afternoon he came upon a grove of cottonwoods and some undergrowth and he tried to kindle a fire, but the sun was not strong enough for his glass, and, after an hour's wasted effort, he gave it up, discouraged greatly. Before night the wind, which had been from the northwest, shifted to the southwest and became much warmer. By and by it snowed again heavily and Dick, who could no longer see his mountains, being afraid that he would wander in the wrong direction, dug another burrow and went to sleep.

He was awakened by the patter of something warm upon his face, and found that the day and rain had come together. Dick once more was struck to the heart with dismay. How could he stand this and the snow together? The plain would now run rivers of water and he must trudge through a terrible mire, worse even than the snow.

He imagined that he could see his mountains through the rain sheets, and he resumed his march, making no effort now to keep anything but his rifle and ammunition dry. He crossed more than one brook, either permanent or made by the rain and melting snow, and sloshed though the water, ankle deep, but paid no attention to it. He walked with intervals of rest all through the day and the night, and the warm rain never ceased. The snow melted at a prodigious rate, and Dick thought several times in the night that he heard the sound of plunging waters. These must be cataracts from the snow and rain, and he was convinced that he was near the mountains.

The day came again, the rain ceased, the sun sprang out, the warm winds blew, and there were the mountains. Perhaps the snow had not been so heavy on them as on the plain, but most of it was gone from the peaks and slopes and they stood up, sheltering and beautiful, with a shade of green that the snow had not been able to take away.

The sight put fresh courage in Dick's heart, but he was very weak. He staggered as he plowed through the mixed snow and mud, and plains and mountains alike were rocking about in a most uncertain fashion.

In a ravine at the foot of the mountains he saw a herd of about twenty buffaloes which had probably taken refuge there from the snowstorm, but he did not molest them. Instead, he shook his rifle at them and called out:

"I'm too glad to escape with my own life to take any of yours. "

Dick's brain was in a feverish state and he was not wholly responsible for what he said or did, but he began the ascent with a fairly good supply of strength and toiled on all the day. He never knew where he slept that night, but he thinks it was in a clump of pines, and the next morning when he continued, he felt that he had made a wonderful improvement. His feet were light and so was his head, but he had never before seen slopes and peaks and pines and ash doing a daylight dance. They whirled about in the most eccentric manner, yet it was all exhilarating, in thorough accord with his own spirits, and Dick laughed aloud with glee. What a merry, funny world it was! Feet and head both grew lighter. He shouted aloud and began to sing. Then he felt so strong and exuberant that he ran down one of the slopes, waving his cap. An elk sprang out of a pine thicket, stared a moment or two with startled eyes at the boy, and then dashed away over the mountain.

Dick continued to sing, and waved his fur cap at the fleeing elk. It was the funniest thing he had ever seen in his life. The whirling dance of mountain and forest became bewildering in its speed and violence. He was unable to keep his feet, and plunged forward into the arms of his brother, Albert. Then everything sank away from him.

Chapter XIII
Albert's Victory

When Dick opened his eyes again he raised his hand once more to wave it at the fleeing elk and then he stopped in astonishment. The hand was singularly weak. He had made a great effort, but it did not go up very far. Nor did his eyes, which had opened slowly and heavily, see any elk. They saw instead rows and rows of furs and then other rows hanging above one another. His eyes traveled downward and they saw log walls almost covered with furs and skins, but with rifles, axes, and other weapons and implements on hooks between. A heavy oaken window shutter was thrown back and a glorious golden sunlight poured into the room.

The sunlight happened to fall upon Dick's own hand, and that was the next object at which he looked. His amazement increased. Could such a thin white hand as that belong to him who had lately owned such a big red one? He surveyed it critically, in particular, the bones showing so prominently in the back of it, and then he was interrupted by a full, cheerful voice which called out:

"Enough of that stargazing and hand examination! Here, drink this soup, and while you're doing it, I'll tell you how glad I am to see you back in your right mind! I tell you you've been whooping out some tall yarns about an Indian following you for a year or two through snow a mile or so deep! How you fought him for a month without stopping! And how you then waded for another year through snow two or three times as deep as the first! "

It was his brother Albert, and he lay on his own bed of furs and skins in their own cabin, commonly called by them Castle Howard, snugly situated in the lost or enchanted valley. And here was Albert, healthy, strong, and dictatorial, while he, stretched weakly upon a bed, held our a hand through which the sun could almost shine. Truly, there had been great changes!

He raised his head as commanded by Albert—the thin, pallid, drooping Albert of last summer, the lusty, red-faced Albert of to-day—and drank the soup, which tasted very good indeed. He felt stronger and held up the thin, white hand to see if it had not grown fatter and redder in the last ten seconds. Albert laughed, and it seemed to Dick such a full, loud laugh, as if it were drawn up from a deep, iron-walled chest, inclosing lungs made of leather, with an uncommon expansion. It jarred upon Dick. It seemed too loud for so small a room.

"I see you enjoyed that soup, Dick, old fellow, " continued Albert in the same thundering tones. "Well, you ought to like it. It was chicken soup, and it was made by an artist—myself. I shot a fat and tender prairie hen down the valley, and here she is in soup. It's only a step from grass to pot and I did it all myself. Have another. "

"Think I will, " said Dick.

He drank a second tin plate of the soup, and he could feel life and strength flowing into every vein.

"How did I get here, Al? " he asked.

"That's a pretty hard question to answer, " replied Albert, smiling and still filling the room with his big voice. "You were partly brought, partly led, partly pushed, you partly walked, partly jumped, and partly crawled, and there were even little stretches of the march when you were carried on somebody's shoulder, big and heavy as you are. Dick, I don't know any name for such a mixed gait. Words fail me. "

Dick smiled, too.

"Well, no matter how I got here, it's certain that I'm here, " he said, looking around contentedly.

"Absolutely sure, and it's equally as sure that you've been here five days. I, the nurse, I, the doctor, and I, the spectator, can vouch for that. There were times when I had to hold you in your bed, there were times when you were so hot with fever that I expected to see you burst into a mass of red and yellow flames, and most all the while you talked with a vividness and imagination that I've never known before outside of the Arabian Nights. Dick, where did you get the idea about a Sioux Indian following you all the way from the Atlantic to the Pacific, with stops every half hour for you and him to fight? "

"It's true, " said Dick, and then he told the eager boy the story of his escape from the Sioux band, the terrible pursuit, the storm, and his dreadful wandering.

"It was wonderful luck that I met you, Al, old fellow, " he said devoutly.

"Not luck exactly, " said Albert. "You were coming back to the valley on our old trail, and, as I had grown very anxious about you, I was out on the same path to see if I could see any sign of you. It was natural that we should meet, but I think that, after all, Dick, Providence had the biggest hand in it. "

"No doubt, " said Dick, and after a moment's pause he added, "Did it snow much up here? "

"But lightly. The clouds seem to have avoided these mountains. It was only from your delirium that I gathered the news of the great storm on the plains. Now, I think you've talked enough for an invalid. Drop you head back on that buffalo robe and go to sleep again. "

It seemed so amazing to Dick ever to receive orders from Albert that he obeyed promptly, closed his eyes, and in five minutes was in sound slumber.

Albert hovered about the room, until he saw that Dick was asleep and breathing strongly and regularly. Then he put his hand on Dick's brow, and when he felt the temperature his own eyes were lighted up by a fine smile. That forehead, hot so long, was cool now, and it would be only a matter of a few days until Dick was his old, strong and buoyant self again. Albert never told his brother how he had gone two days and nights without sleep, watching every moment by the delirious bedside, how, taking the chances, he had dosed him with quinine from their medical stores, and how, later, he had cooked for him the tenderest and most delicate food. Nor did he speak of those awful hours—so many of them—when Dick's life might go at any time.

Albert knew now that the great crisis was over, and rejoicing, he went forth from Castle Howard. It was his intention to kill another prairie chicken and make more of the soup that Dick liked so much. As he walked, his manner was expansive, indicating a deep satisfaction. Dick had saved his life and he had saved Dick's. But Dick was still an invalid and it was his duty, meanwhile to carry on the business of the valley. He was sole workman, watchman, and defender, and his spirit rose to meet the responsibility. He would certainly look after his brother as well as anyone could do it.

Albert whistled as he went along, and swung his gun in debonair fashion. It would not take him, an expert borderer and woodsman, long to get that prairie chicken, and after that, as he had said before, it was only a step from grass to pot.

It was perhaps the greatest hour of Albert Howard's life. He, the helped, was now the helper; he, the defended, was now the defender. His chest could scarcely contain the mighty surge of exultation that heart and lungs together accomplished. He was far from having any rejoicings over Dick's prostration; he rejoiced instead that he was able, since the prostration had come, to care for both. He had had the forethought and courage to go forth and seek for Dick, and the strength to save him when found.

Albert broke into a rollicking whistle and he still swung his shotgun somewhat carelessly for a hunter and marksman. He passed by one of the geysers just as it was sending up its high column of hot water and its high column of steam. "That's the way I feel, old fellow, " he said. "I could erupt with just as much force. "

He resumed his caution farther on and shot two fine, fat prairie hens, returning with them to Castle Howard before Dick awoke. When Dick did awake, the second installment of the soup was ready for him and he ate it hungrily. He was naturally so strong and vigorous and had lived such a wholesome life that he recovered, now that the crisis was past, with astonishing rapidity. But Albert played the benevolent tyrant for a few days yet, insisting that Dick should sleep a great number of hours out of every twenty-four, and making him eat four times a day of the tenderest and most succulent things. He allowed him to walk but a little at first, and, though the walks were extended from day to day, made him keep inside when the weather was bad.

Dick took it all, this alternate spoiling and overlordship, with amazing mildness. He had some dim perception of the true state of affairs, and was willing that his brother should enjoy his triumph to the full. But in a week he was entirely well again, thin and pale yet, but with a pulsing tide in his veins as strong as ever. Then he and Albert took counsel with each other. All trace of snow was gone, even far up on the highest slope, and the valley was a wonderful symphony in green and gold, gold on the lake and green on the new grass and the new leaves of the trees.

"It's quite settled, " said Albert, "that we're to stay another year in the valley. "

"Oh, yes, " said Dick, "we had already resolved on that, and my excursion on the plains shows that we were wise in doing so. But you know, Al, we can't do fur hunting in the spring and summer. Furs are not in good condition now. "

"No, " said Albert, "but we can get ready for the fall and winter, and I propose that we undertake right away a birchbark canoe. The dugout is a little bit heavy and awkward, hard to control in a high wind, and we'll really need the birch bark. "

"Good enough, " said Dick. "We'll do it. "

With the habits of promptness and precision they had learned from old Mother Necessity, they went to work at once, planning and toiling on equal terms, a full half-and-half partnership. Both were in great spirits.

In this task they fell back partly on talk that they had heard from some of the men with whom they had started across the plains, and partly on old reading, and it took quite a lot of time. They looked first for large specimens of the white birch, and finally found several on one of the lower slopes. This was the first and, in fact, the absolutely vital requisite. Without it they could do nothing, but, having located their bark supply, they left the trees and began at the lake edge the upper framework of their canoe, consisting of four strips of cedar, two for either side of the boat, every one of the four having a length of about fifteen feet. These strips had a width of about an inch, with a thickness a third as great.

The strips were tied together in pairs at the ends, and the two pairs were joined together at the same place after the general fashion in use for the construction of such canoes.

The frame being ready, they went to their white birch trees for the bark. They marked off the utmost possible length on the largest and finest tree, made a straight cut through the bark at either end, and triumphantly peeled off a splendid piece, large enough for the entire canoe. Then they laid it on the ground in a nice smooth place and marked off a distance two feet less than their framework or gunwales. They drove into the ground at each end of this space two tall stakes, three inches apart. The bark was then laid upon the ground inside up and folded evenly throughout its entire length. After that it was lifted and set between the stakes with the edges up. The foot of bark projecting beyond each stake was covered in each case with another piece of bark folded firmly over it and sewed to the sides by means of an awl and deer tendon.

This sewing done, they put a large stone under each end of the bark construction, causing it to sag from the middle in either direction into the curve suitable for a canoe. The gunwale which they had constructed previously was now fitted into the bark, and the bark was stitched tightly to it, both at top and bottom, with a further use of awl and tendon, the winding stitch being used.

They now had the outside of the canoe, but they had drawn many a long breath and perspired many a big drop before it was done. They felt, however, that the most serious part of the task was over, and after a short rest they began on the inside, which they lined with long strips of cedar running the full length of the boat. The pieces were about an inch and a half in width and about a third of an inch in thickness and were fitted very closely together. Over these they put the ribs of touch ash, which was very abundant in the valley and on the slopes. Strips two inches wide and a half inch thick were bent crosswise across the interior of the curve, close together, and were firmly fastened under the gunwales with a loop stitch of the strong tendon through the bark.

To make their canoe firm and steady, they securely lashed three string pieces across it and then smeared deeply all the seams with pitch, which they were fortunate enough to secure from one of the many strange springs and exudations in the valley. They now had a strong, light canoe, fifteen feet long and a little over two feet wide at the center. They had been compelled to exercise great patience and endurance in this task, particularly in the work with the awl and tendons. Skillful as they had become with their hands, they acquired several sore fingers in the task, but their pride was great when it was done. They launched the canoe, tried it several times near the shore in order to detect invisible seams, and then, when all such were stopped up tightly with pitch, they paddled boldly out into deep and far waters.

The practice they had acquired already with the dugout helped them greatly with the birch bark, and after one or two duckings they handled it with great ease. As amateurs sometimes do, they had achieved either by plan or accident a perfect design and found that they had a splendid canoe. This was demonstrated when the two boys rowed a race, after Dick had recovered his full strength—Dick in the dugout and Albert in the birch bark. The race was the full length of the lake, and the younger and smaller boy won an easy triumph.

"Well paddled, Al! " said Dick.

"It wasn't the paddling, Dick, " replied Albert, "it was light bark against heavy wood that did it. "

They were very proud of their two canoes and made a little landing for them in a convenient cove. Here, tied to trees with skin lariats, they were safe from wind and wave.

An evening or two after the landing was made secure, Dick, who had been out alone, came home in the dark and found Albert reading a book by the firelight.

"What's this? " he exclaimed.

"I took it out of the inside pocket of your coat, when I help you here in the snow, " replied Albert. "I put it on a shelf and in the strain of your illness forgot all about it until to-day. "

"That's my History and Map of the United States, " said Dick, smiling. "I took it from the wagon which yielded up so much to us. It wouldn't tell me where I was in the storm; but, do you know, Al, it helped me when I read in there about that greatest of all men praying in the snow. "

"I know who it is whom you mean, " said Albert earnestly, "and I intend to read about him and all the others. It's likely, Dick, before another year is past, that you and I will become about the finest historians of our country to be found anywhere between the Atlantic and Pacific. Maybe this is the greatest treasure of all that the wagon has yielded up to us. "

Albert was right. A single volume, where no other could be obtained, was a precious treasure to them, and it made many an evening pass pleasantly that would otherwise have been dull. They liked especially to linger over the hardships of the borderers and of their countrymen in war, because they found so many parallels to their own case, and the reading always brought them new courage and energy.

They spent the next month after the completion of the canoe in making all kinds of traps, including some huge dead falls for grizzly bear and silver tip.

They intended as soon as the autumn opened to begin their fur operations on a much larger scale than those of the year before. Numerous excursions into the surrounding mountains showed abundant signs of game and no signs of an invader, and they calculated that if all went well they would have stored safely by next spring at least twenty thousand dollars' worth of furs.

The summer passed pleasantly for both, being filled with work in which they took a great interest, and hence a great pleasure. They found another rock cavity, which they fitted up like the first in anticipation of an auspicious trapping season.

"They say, 'don't put all your eggs in one basket,'" said Albert, "and so we won't put all our furs in one cave. The Sioux may come sometime or other, and even if they should get our three residences, Castle Howard, the Annex, and the Suburban Villa, and all that is in them, they are pretty sure to miss our caves and our furs. "

"Of course some Indians must know of this valley, " said Dick, "and most likely it's the Sioux. Perhaps none ever wander in here now, because they're at war with our people and are using all their forces on the plains. "

Albert thought it likely, and both Dick and he had moments when they wondered greatly what was occurring in the world without. But, on the whole, they were not troubled much by the affairs of the rest of the universe.

Traps, house building, and curing food occupied them throughout the summer. Once the days were very hot in the valley, which served as a focus for the rays of the sun, but it was invariably cool, often cold, at night. They slept usually under a tent, or sometimes, on their longer expeditions in that direction, at the bark hut. Dick made a point of this, as he resolved that Albert should have no relapse. He could not see any danger of such a catastrophe, but he felt that another year of absolutely fresh and pure mountain air, breathed both night and day, would put his brother beyond all possible danger.

The life that both led even in the summer was thoroughly hardening. They bathed every morning, if in the tent by Castle Howard, in the torrent, the waters of which were always icy, flowing as they did from melting snows on the highest peaks. They swam often in the lake, which was also cold always, and at one of the hot springs they hollowed out a pool, where they could take a hot bath whenever they needed it.

The game increased in the valley as usual toward autumn, and they replenished their stores of jerked meat. They had spared their ammunition entirely throughout the summer and now they used it only on buffalo, elk, and mule deer. They were fortunate enough to catch several big bears in their huge dead falls, and, with very little expenditure of cartridges, they felt that they could open their second winter as well equipped with food as they had been when they began the first. They also put a new bark thatching on the roof of Castle Howard, and then felt ready for anything that might come.

"Rain, hail, sleet, snow, and ice, it's all the same to us, " said Dick.

They did not resume their trapping until October came, as they knew that the furs would not be in good condition until then. They merely made a good guess that it was October. They had long since lost all count of days and months, and took their reckoning from the change of the foliage into beautiful reds and yellows and the increasing coldness of the air.

It proved to be a cold but not rainy autumn, a circumstance that favored greatly their trapping operations. They had learned much in the preceding winter from observation and experience, and now they put it to practice. They knew many of the runways or paths frequented by the animals, and now they would place their traps in these, concealing them as carefully as possible, and, acting on an idea of Albert's, they made buckskin gloves for themselves, with which they handled the traps, in order to leave, if possible, no human odor to warn the wary game. Such devices as this and the more skillful making of their traps caused the second season to be a greater success than the first, good as the latter had been. They shot an additional number of buffaloes and elk, but what they sought in particular was the beaver, and they were lucky enough to find two or three new and secluded little streams, on which he had built his dams.

The valuable furs now accumulated rapidly, and it was wise forethought that had made them fit up the second cave or hollow. They were glad to have two places for them, in case one was discovered by an enemy stronger than themselves.

Autumn turned into winter, with snow, slush, and ice-cold rain. The preceding winter had been mild, but this bade fair to break some records for severe and variegated weather. Now came the true test for Albert. To trudge all day long in snow, icy rain or deep slush, to paddle across the lake in a nipping wind, with the chilly spray all over him, to go for hours soaking wet on every inch of his skin— these were the things that would have surely tried the dwellers in the houses of men, even those with healthy bodies.

Albert coughed a little after his first big soaking, but after a hot bath, a big supper, and a long night's sleep, it left, not to return. He became so thoroughly inured now to exposure that nothing seemed to affect him. Late in December—so they reckoned the time—when, going farther than usual into a long crevice of the mountains, they were overtaken by a heavy snowstorm. They might have reached the Suburban Villa by night, or they might not, but in any event the going would have been full of danger, and they decided to camp in the broadest part of the canyon in which they now were, not far from the little brook that flowed down it.

They had matches with them—they were always careful to keep them dry now—and after securing their dry shavings they lighted a good fire. Then they are their food, and looked up without fear at the dark mountains and the thick, driving snow. They were partially sheltered by the bank and some great ash trees, and, for further protection, they wrapped about themselves the blankets, without which they never went on any long journey.

Having each other for company, the adventure was like a picnic to both. It was no such desperate affair as that of Dick's when he was alone on the plain. They further increased their shelter from the snow by an artful contrivance of brush and fallen boughs, and although enough still fell upon them to make miserable the house-bred, they did not care. Both fell asleep after a while, with flurries of snow still striking upon their faces, and were awakened far in the night by the roar of an avalanche farther up the canyon; but they soon went to sleep again and arose the next day with injury.

Thus the winter passed, one of storm and cold, but the trapping was wonderful, and each boy grew in a remarkable manner in strength, endurance, and skill. When signs of spring appeared again, they decided that it was time for them to go. Had it not been for Dick's misadventure on the plain, and their belief that a great war was now in progress between the Sioux and the white people, one might have gone out to return with horses and mules for furs, while the other remained behind to guard them. But in view of all the dangers, they resolved to keep together. The furs would be secreted and the rest of their property must take its chances.

So they made ready.

Chapter XIV
Prisoners

It gave both Dick and Albert a severe wrench to leave their beautiful valley. They had lived in it now nearly two years, and it had brought strength and abounding life to Albert, infinite variety, content, and gratitude to Dick, and what seemed a fortune—their furs—to both. It was a beautiful valley, in which Nature had done for them many strange and wonderful things, and they loved it, the splendid lake, the grassy levels, the rushing streams, the noble groves, and the great mountains all about.

"I'd like to live here, Dick, " said Albert, "for some years, anyway. After we take out our furs and sell 'em, we can come back and use it as a base for more trapping. "

"If the Indians will let up, " said Dick.

"Do you think we'll meet 'em? "

"I don't know, but I believe the plains are alive with hostile Sioux. "

But Albert could not foresee any trouble. He was too young, to sanguine, too full now of the joy of life to think of difficulties.

They chose their weapons for the march with great care, each taking a repeating rifle, a revolver, a hunting knife, and a hatchet, the latter chiefly for camping purposes. They also divided equally among themselves what was left of the ball cartridges, and each took his sunglass and half of the remaining matches. The extra weapons, including the shotguns and shot cartridges, they hid with their furs. They also put in the caves many more of their most valuable possessions, especially the tools and remnants of medical supplies. They left everything else in the houses, just as they were when they were using them, except the bark hut, from which they took away all furnishings, as it was too light to resist the invasion of a large wild beast like a grizzly bear. But they fastened up Castle Howard and the Annex so securely that no wandering beast could possibly break in. They sunk their canoes in shallow water among reeds, and then, when each had provided himself with a large supply of jerked buffalo and deer meat and a skin water bag, they were ready to depart.

"We may find our houses and what is in them all right when we come back, or we may not, " said Dick.

"But we take the chance, " said Albert cheerfully.

Early on a spring morning they started down the valley by the same way in which they had first entered it. They walked along in silence for some minutes, and then, as if by the same impulse, the two turned and looked back. There was their house, which had sheltered them so snugly and so safely for so long, almost hidden now in the foliage of the new spring. There was a bit of moisture in the eyes of Albert, the younger and more sentimental.

"Good-by, " he said, waving his hand. "I've found life here. "

Dick said nothing, and they turned into the main valley. They walked with long and springy steps, left the valley behind them, and began to climb the slopes. Presently the valley itself became invisible, the mountains seeming to close in and blot it out.

"A stranger would have to blunder on it to find it, " said Dick.

"I hope no one will make any such blunder, " said Albert.

The passage over the mountains was easy, the weather continuing favorable, and on another sunshiny morning they reached the plains, which flowed out boundlessly before them. These, too, were touched with green, but the boys were perplexed. The space was so vast, and it was all so much alike, that it did not look as if they could ever arrive anywhere.

"I think we'd better make for Cheyenne in Wyoming Territory, " said Dick.

"But we don't know how far away it is, nor in what direction, " said Albert.

"No; but if we keep on going we're bound to get somewhere. We've got lots of time before us, and we'll take it easy. "

They had filled their skin water bags, made in the winter, at the last spring, and they set out at a moderate pace over the plain. Dick had thought once of visiting again the scene of the train's destruction in the pass, but Albert opposed it.

"No, " he said, "I don't want to see that place. "

This journey, they knew not whither, continued easy and pleasant throughout the day. The grass was growing fast on the plains, and all the little steams that wound now and then between the swells were full of water, and, although they still carried the filled water bags, Dick inferred that they were not likely to suffer from thirst. Late in the afternoon they saw a small herd of antelope and a lone buffalo grazing at a considerable distance, and Dick drew the second and comforting inference that game would prove to be abundant. He was so pleased with these inferences that he stated them to Albert, who promptly drew a third.

"Wouldn't the presence of buffalo and antelope indicate that there are not many Indians hereabouts? " he asked.

"It looks likely, " replied Dick.

They continued southward until twilight came, when they built in a hollow a fire of buffalo chips, which were abundant all over the plain, and watched their friendly mountains sink away in the dark.

"Gives me a sort of homesick feeling, " said Albert. "They've been good mountains to us. Shelter and home are there, but out here I feel as if I were stripped to the wind. "

"That describes it, " said Dick.

They did not keep any watch, but put out their fire and slept snugly in their blankets. They were awakened in the morning by the whine of a coyote that did not dare to come too near, and resumed their leisurely march, to continue in this manner for several days, meeting no human being either white or red.

They saw the mountains sink behind the sky line and then they felt entirely without a rudder. There was nothing to go by now except the sun, but they kept to their southern course. They were not greatly troubled. They found plenty of game, as Dick had surmised, and killed an antelope and a fat young buffalo cow.

"We may travel a long journey, Al, " said Dick with some satisfaction, "but it's not hard on us. It's more like loafing along on an easy holiday. "

On the fifth day they ran into a large buffalo herd, but did not molest any of its members, as they did not need fresh meat.

"Seems to me, " said Dick, "that Sioux would be after this herd if they weren't busy elsewhere. It looks like more proof that the Sioux are on the warpath and are to the eastward of us, fighting our own people. "

"The Sioux are a great and warlike tribe, are they not? " asked Albert.

"The greatest and most warlike west of the Mississippi, " replied Dick. "I understand that they are really a group of closely related tribes and can put thousands of warriors in the field. "

"Bright Sun, I suppose, is with them? "

"Yes, I suppose so. He is an Indian, a Sioux, no matter if he was at white schools and for years with white people. He must feel for his own, just as you and I, Al, feel for our own race. "

They wandered three or four more days across the plains, and were still without sign of white man or red. They experienced no hardship. Water was plentiful. Game was to be had for the stalking and life, had they been hunting or exploring, would have been pleasant; but both felt a sense of disappointment—they never came to anything. The expanse of plains was boundless, the loneliness became overpowering. They had not the remotest idea whether they were traveling toward any white settlement. Human life seemed to shun them.

"Dick, " said Albert one day, "do you remember the story of the Flying Dutchman, how he kept trying for years to round the Cape of Storms, and couldn't do it? I wonder if some such penalty is put on us, and if so, what for? "

The thought lodged in the minds of both. Oppressed by long and fruitless wanderings, they began to have a superstition that they were to continue them forever. They knew that it was unreasonable, but it clung, nevertheless. There were the rolling plains, the high, brassy sky, and the clear line of the horizon on all sides, with nothing that savored of human life between.

They had hoped for an emigrant train, or a wandering band of hunters, or possibly a troop of cavalry, but days passed and they met none. Still the same high, brassy sky, still the same unbroken horizons. The plains increased in beauty. There was a fine, delicate shade of green on the buffalo grass, and wonderful little flowers peeped shy heads just above the earth, but Dick and Albert took little notice of either. They had sunk into an uncommon depression. The terrible superstition that they were to wander forever was strengthening its hold upon them, despite every effort of will and reason. In the hope of better success they changed their course two or three times, continuing in each case several days in that direction before the next change was made.

"We've traveled around so much now, " said Albert despondently, "that we couldn't go back to our mountains if we wanted to do it. We don't know any longer in what direction they lie. "

"That's so, " said Dick, with equal despondency showing in his tone.

His comment was brief, because they talked but little now, and every day were talking less. Their spirits were affected too much to permit any excess of words. But they came finally to rougher, much more broken country, and they saw a line of trees on the crest of hills just under the sunset horizon. The sight, the break in the monotony, the cheerful trees made them lift up their drooping heads.

"Well, at any rate, here's something new, " said Dick. "Let's consider it an omen of good luck, Al. "

They reached the slope, a long one, with many depressions and hollows, containing thick groves of large trees, the heights beyond being crowned with trees of much taller growth. They would have gone to the summit, but they were tired with a long day's tramp and they had not yet fully aroused themselves from the lethargy that had overtaken them in their weary wanderings.

"Night's coming, " said Albert, "so let's take to that hollow over there with the scrub ash in it. "

"All right, " said Dick. "Suits me. "

It was a cozy little hollow, deeply shaded by the ash trees, but too rocky to be damp, and they did not take the trouble to light a fire. They had been living for some time on fresh buffalo and antelope, and had saved their jerked meat, on which they now drew for supper.

It was now quite dark, and each, throwing his blanket lightly around his shoulders, propped himself in a comfortable position. Then, for the first time in days, they began to talk in the easy, idle fashion of those who feel some degree of contentment, a change made merely by the difference in scene, the presence of hills, trees, and rocks after the monotonous world of the plains.

"We'll explore that country to-morrow, " said Dick, nodding his head toward the crest of the hills. "Must be something over there, a river, a lake, and maybe trappers. "

"Hope it won't make me homesick again for our valley, " said Albert sleepily. "I've been thinking too much of it, anyway, in the last few days. Dick, wasn't that the most beautiful lake of ours that you ever saw? Did you ever see another house as snug as Castle Howard? And how about the Annex and the Suburban Villa? And all those beautiful streams that came jumping down between the mountains?"

"If you don't shut up, Al, " said Dick, "I'll thrash you with this good handy stick that I've found here. "

"All right, " replied Albert, laughing; "I didn't mean to harrow up your feelings any more than I did my own. "

Albert was tired, and the measure of content that he now felt was soothing. Hence, his drowsiness increased, and in ten minutes he went comfortably to sleep. Dick's eyes were yet open, and he felt within himself such new supplies of energy and strength that he resolved to explore a little. The task that had seemed so hard two or three hours before was quite easy now. Albert would remain sleeping safely where he was, and, acting promptly, Dick left the hollow, rifle on shoulder.

It was an easy slope, but a long one. As he ascended, the trees grew more thickly and near the ascent were comparatively free from undergrowth. Just over the hill shone a magnificent full moon, touching the crest with a line of molten silver.

Dick soon reached the summit and looked down the far slope into a valley three or four hundred yards deep. The moon shed its full glory into the valley and filled it with rays of light.

The valley was at least two miles wide, and down its center flowed a fine young river, which Dick could see here and there in stretches, while the rest was hidden by forest. In fact, the whole valley seemed to be well clothed with mountain forest, except in one wide space where Dick's gaze remained after it had alighted once.

Here was human life, and plenty of it. He looked down upon a circle of at least two hundred lodges, tent-shaped structures of saplings covered with bark, and he had heard quite enough about such things to know these were the winter homes of the Sioux. The moonlight was so clear and his position so good that he was able to see figures moving about the lodges.

The sight thrilled Dick. Here he had truly come upon human life, but not the kind he wished to see. But it was vastly interesting, and he sought a closer look. His daring told him to go down the slope toward them, and he obeyed. The descent was not difficult, and there was cover in abundance—pines, ash, and oak.

As he was very careful, taking time not to break a twig or set a stone rolling, and stopping at intervals to look and listen, he was a half hour in reaching the valley, where, through the trees, he saw the Indian village. He felt that he was rash, but wishing to see, he crept closer, the cover still holding good. He was, in a way, fascinated by what he saw. It had the quality of a dream, and its very unreality made him think less of the danger. But he really did not know how expert he had become as a woodsman and trailer through his long training as a trapper, where delicacy of movement and craft were required.

He believed that the Indians, in such a secure location, would not be stirring beyond the village at this late hour, and he had little fear of anything except the sharp-nosed dogs that are always prowling about an Indian village. He was within three hundred yards of the lodges when he heard the faint sound of voices and footsteps. He instantly lay down among the bushes, but raised himself a little on his elbow in order to see.

Three Indians were walking slowly along a woodland path toward the village, and the presence of the path indicated the village had been here for many months, perhaps was permanent. The Indians were talking very earnestly and they made gestures. One raised his voice a little and turned toward one of his companions, as if he would emphasize his words. Then Dick saw his face clearly, and drew a long breath of surprise.

It was Bright Sun, but a Bright Sun greatly changed. He was wholly in native attire—moccasins, leggings, and a beautiful blue blanket draped about his shoulders. A row of eagle feathers adorned his long black hair, but it was the look and manner of the man that had so much significance. He towered above the other Indians, who were men of no mean height; but it was not his height either, it was his face, the fire of his eyes, the proud eagle beak which the Sioux had not less than the Roman, and the swift glance of command that could not be denied. Here was a great chief, a leader of men, and Dick was ready to admit it.

He could easily have shot Bright Sun dead as he passed, but he did not dream of doing such a thing. Yet Bright Sun, while seeming to play the part of a friend, had deliberately led the wagon train into a fatal ambush—of that Dick had no doubt. He felt, moreover, that Bright Sun was destined to cause great woe to the white people, his own people, but he could not fire; nor would he have fired even if the deed had been without danger to himself.

Dick, instead, gave Bright Sun a reluctant admiration. He looked well enough as the guide in white men's clothes, but in his own native dress he looked like one to be served, not to serve. The three paused for a full two minutes exactly opposite Dick, and he could have reached out and touched them with the barrel of his rifle; but they were thinking little of the presence of an enemy. Dick judged by the emphasis of their talk that it was on a matter of some great moment, and he saw all three of them point at times toward the east.

"It's surely war, " he thought, "and our army if somewhere off there in the east. "

Dick saw that Bright Sun remained the dominating figure throughout the discussion. Its whole effect was that of Bright Sun talking and the others listening. He seemed to communicate his fire and enthusiasm to his comrades, and soon they nodded a vigorous assent. Then the three walked silently away toward the village.

Dick rose from his covert, cast a single glance at the direction in which the three chiefs had disappeared, and then began to retrace his own steps. It was his purpose to arouse Albert and flee at once to a less dangerous region. But the fate of Dick and his brother rested at that moment with a mean, mangy, mongrel cur, such as have always been a part of Indian villages, a cur that had wandered farther from the village than usual that night upon some unknown errand.

Dick had gone about thirty yards when he became conscious of a light, almost faint, pattering sound behind him. He stepped swiftly into the heaviest shadow of trees and sought to see what pursued. He thought at first it was some base-born wolf of the humblest tribe, but, when he looked longer, he knew that it was one of the meanest of mean curs, a hideous, little yellowish animal, sneaking in his movements, a dog that one would gladly kick out of his way.

Dick felt considerable contempt for himself because he had been alarmed over such a miserable little beast, and resumed his swift walk. Thirty yards farther he threw a glance over his shoulder, and there was the wretched cur still following. Dick did not like it, considering it an insult to himself to be trailed by anything so ugly and insignificant. He picked up a stone, but hesitated a moment, and then put it down again. If he threw the stone the dog might bark or howl, and that was the last thing that he wanted. Already the cur, mean and miserable as he looked, had won a victory over him.

Dick turned into a course that he would not have taken otherwise, thinking to shake off his pursuer, but at the next open space he saw him still following, his malignant red eyes fixed upon the boy. The cur would not have weighed twenty cowardly pounds, but he became a horrible obsession to Dick. He picked up a stone again, put it down again, and for a mad instant seriously considered the question of shooting him.

The cur seemed to become alarmed at the second threat, and broke suddenly into a sharp, snarling, yapping bark, much like that of a coyote. It was terribly loud in the still night, and cold dread assailed

Dick in every nerve. He picked up the stone that he had dropped, and this time he threw it.

"You brute! " he exclaimed, as the stone whizzed by the cur's ear.

The cur returned the compliment of names with compounded many times over. His snarling bark became almost continuous, and although he did not come any nearer, he showed sharp white teeth. Dick paused in doubt, but when, from a point nearer the village, he heard a bark in reply, then another, and then a dozen, he ran with all speed up the slope. He knew without looking back that the cur was following, and it made him feel cold again.

Certainly Dick had good cause to run. All the world was up and listening now, and most of it was making a noise, too. He heard a tumult of barking, growling, and snapping toward the village, and then above it a long, mournful cry that ended in an ominous note. Dick knew that it was a Sioux war whoop, and that the mean, miserable little cur had done his work. The village would be at his heels. Seized with an unreasoning passion, he whirled about and shot the cur dead. It was a mad act, and he instantly repented it. Never had there been another rifle shot so loud. It crashed like the report of a cannon. Mountain and valley gave it back in a multitude of echoes, and on the last dying echo came, not a single war whoop, but the shout of many, the fierce, insistent, falsetto yell that has sounded the doom of many a borderer.

Dick shuddered. He had been pursued once before by a single man, but he was not afraid of a lone warrior. Now a score would be at his heels. He might shake them off in the dark, but the dogs would keep the scent, and his chief object was to go fast. He ran up the slope at his utmost speed for a hundred yards or more, and then remembering in time to nurse his strength, he slackened his footsteps.

He had thought of turning the pursuit away from the hollow in which Albert lay, but now that the alarm was out they would find him, anyway, and it was best for the two to stand or fall together. Hence, he went straight for the hollow.

It was bitter work running up a slope, but his two years of life in the open were a great help to him now. The strong heart and the powerful lungs responded nobly to the call. He ran lightly, holding his rifle in the hollow of his arm, ready for use if need be, and he watch warily lest he make an incautious footstep and fall. The moonlight was still full and clear, but when he took an occasional hurried glance backward he could not yet see his pursuers. He heard, now and then, however, the barking of a dog or the cry of a warrior.

Dick reached the crest of the hill, and there for an instant or two his figure stood, under the pines, a black silhouette against the moonlight. Four or five shots were fired at the living target. One bullet whizzed so near that it seemed to Dick to scorch his face.

He had gathered fresh strength, and that hot bullet gave a new impetus also. He ran down the slope at a great speed now, and he had calculated craftily. He could descend nearly twice as fast as they could ascend, and while they were reaching the crest he would put a wide gap between them.

He kept well in the shadow now as he made with long leaps straight toward the hollow, and he hoped with every heart beat that Albert, aroused by the shots, would be awake and ready. "Albert! " he cried, when he was within twenty feet of their camp, and his hope was rewarded. Albert was up, rifle in hand, crying:

"What is it, Dick? "

"The Sioux! " exclaimed Dick. "They're not far away! You heard the shots! Come! "

He turned off at an angle and ran in a parallel line along the slope, Albert by his side. He wished to keep to the forests and thickets, knowing they would have little chance of escape on the plain. As they ran he told Albert, in short, choppy sentences, what had happened.

"I don't hear anything, " said Albert, after ten minutes. "Maybe they've lost us. "

"No such good luck! Those curs of theirs would lead them. No, Al, we've got to keep straight on as long as we can! "

Albert stumbled on a rock, but, quickly recovering himself, put greater speed in every jump, when he heard the Indian shout behind him.

"We've got to shoot their dogs, " said Dick. "We'll have no other chance to shake them off. "

"If we get a chance, " replied Albert.

But they did not see any chance just yet. They heard the occasional howl of a cur, but both curs and Indians remained invisible. Yet Dick felt that the pursuers were gaining. They were numerous, and they could spread. Every time he and Albert diverged from a straight line—and they could not help doing so now and then—some portion of the pursuing body came nearer. It was the advantage that the many had over the few.

Dick prayed for darkness, a shading of the moon, but it did not come, and five minutes later he saw the yellow form of a cur emerge into an open space. He took a shot at it and heard a howl. He did not know whether he had killed the dog or not, but he hoped he had succeeded. The shot brought forth a cry to their right, and then another to the left. It was obvious that the Sioux, besides being behind them, were also on either side of them. They were gasping, too, from their long run, and knew that they could not continue much farther.

"We can't shake them off, Al, " said Dick, "and we'll have to fight. This is as good a place as any other. "

They dropped down into a rocky hollow, a depression not more than a foot deep, and lay on their faces, gasping for breath. Despite the deadly danger Dick felt a certain relief that he did not have to run any more—there comes a time when a moment's physical rest will overweigh any amount of mortal peril.

"If they've surrounded us, they're very quiet about it, " said Albert, when the fresh air had flowed back into his lungs. "I don't see or hear anything at all. "

"At least we don't hear those confounded dogs any more, " said Dick. "Maybe there was only one pursuing us, and that shot of mine got him. The howls of the cur upset my nerves more than the shouts of the Sioux. "

"Maybe so, " said Albert.

Then they were both quite still. The moonlight was silvery clear, and they could see pines, oaks, and cedars waving in a gentle wind, but they saw nothing else. Yet Dick was well aware that the Sioux had not abandoned the chase; they knew well where the boys lay, and were all about them in the woods.

"Keep close, Albert, " he said. "Indians are sly, and the Sioux are the slyest of them all. They're only waiting until one of us pops up his head, thinking they're gone. "

Albert took Dick's advice, but so long a time passed without sign from the Sioux that he began to believe that, in some mysterious manner, they had evaded the savages. The belief had grown almost into a certainty, when there was a flash and a report from a point higher up the slope. Albert felt something hot and stinging in his face. But it was only a tiny fragment of rock chipped off by the bullet as it passed.

Both Dick and Albert lay closer, as if they would press themselves into the earth, and soon two or three more shots were fired. All came from points higher up the slope, and none hit a living target, though they struck unpleasantly close.

"I wish I could see something, " exclaimed Albert impatiently. "It's not pleasant to be shot at and to get no shot in return. "

Dick did not answer. He was watching a point among some scrub pines higher up the slope, where the boughs seemed to him to be waving too much for the slight wind. Looking intently, he thought he saw a patch of brown through the evergreen, and he fired at it. A faint cry followed the shot, and Dick felt a strange satisfaction; they were hunting him—well, he had given a blow in return.

Silence settled down again after Dick's shot. The boys lay perfectly still, although they could hear each other's breathing. The silvery moonlight seemed to grow fuller and clearer all the time. It flooded the whole slope. Boughs and twigs were sheathed in it. Apparently, the moon looked down upon a scene that was all peace and without the presence of a human being.

"Do you think they'll rush us? " whispered Albert.

"No, " replied Dick. "I've always heard that the Indian takes as little risk as he possibly can. "

They waited a little longer, and then came a flare of rifle shots from a point farther up the slope. Brown forms appeared faintly, and Dick and Albert, intent and eager, began to fire in reply. Bullets sang by their ears and clipped the stones around them, but their blood rose the higher and they fired faster and faster.

"We'll drive 'em back! " exclaimed Dick.

They did not hear the rapid patter of soft, light footsteps coming from another direction, until a half dozen Sioux were upon them. Then the firing in front ceased abruptly, and Dick and Albert whirled to meet their new foes.

It was too late. Dick saw Albert struggling in the grasp of two big warriors, and then saw and heard nothing more. He had received a heavy blow on the head from the butt of a rifle and became unconscious.

Chapter XV
The Indian Village

When Dick awoke from his second period of unconsciousness it was to awake, as he did from the first, under a roof, but not, as in the case of the first, under his own roof. He saw above him an immense sloping thatch of bark on poles, and his eyes, wandering lower, saw walls of bark, also fastened to poles. He himself was lying on a large rush mat, and beside the door of the great tepee sat two Sioux warriors cleaning their rifles.

Dick's gaze rested upon the warriors. Curiously, he felt at that time neither hostility nor apprehension. He rather admired them. They were fine, tall men, and their bare arms and legs were sinewy and powerful. Then he thought of Albert. He was nowhere to be seen, but from the shadow of the wall on his right came a tall figure, full of dignity and majesty. It was Bright Sun, who looked down at Dick with a gaze that expressed inquiry rather than anger.

"Why have you come here? " he asked.

Although Dick's head ached and he was a captive, the question made a faint appeal to his sense of humor.

"I didn't come, " he replied; "I was brought. "

Bright Sun smiled.

"That is true, " he said, speaking the precise English of the schools, with every word enunciated distinctly. "You were brought, and by my warriors; but why were you upon these hills? "

"I give you the best answer I can, Bright Sun, " replied Dick frankly; "I don't know. My brother and I were lost upon the plains, and we wandered here. Nor have I the remotest idea now where I am. "

"You are in a village of the tribe of the Mendewahkanton Sioux, of the clan Queyata-oto-we, " replied Bright Sun gravely, "the clan and tribe to which I belong. The Mendewahkantons are one of the first tribes of the Seven Fireplaces, or the Great Sioux Nation. But all are great—Mendewahkanton, Wahpeton, Sisseton, Yankton, Teton, Ogalala, and Hunkpapa—down to the last clan of every tribe. "

He began with gravity and an even intonation, but his voice rose with pride at the last. Nothing of the white man's training was left to him but the slow, precise English. It was the Indian, the pride of his Indian race, that spoke. Dick recognized it and respected it.

"And this? " said Dick, looking around at the great house of bark and poles in which he lay.

"This, " replied Bright Sun, pride again showing in this tone, "is the house of the Akitcita, our soldiers and policemen, the men between twenty and forty, the warriors of the first rank, who live here in common, and into whose house women and children may not enter. I have read in the books at your schools how the Spartan young men lived together as soldiers in a common house, eating rough food and doing the severest duty, and the whole world has long applauded. The Sioux, who never heard of the Spartans, have been doing the same far back into the shadowy time. We, too, are a race of warriors."

Dick looked with renewed interest at the extraordinary man before him, and an amazing suggestion found lodgment in his mind. Perhaps the Sioux chief thought himself not merely as good as the white man, but better, better than any other man except those of his own race. It was so surprising that Dick forgot for a moment the question that he was eagerly awaiting a chance to ask—where was his brother Albert?

"I've always heard that the Sioux were brave, " said Dick vaguely, "and I know they are powerful. "

"We are the Seven Fireplaces. What the Six Nations once were in the East, we now are in the West, save that we are far more numerous and powerful, and we will not be divided. We have leaders who see the truth and who know what to do. "

The pride in his tone was tinged now with defiance, and Dick could but look at him in wonder. But his mind now came back to the anxious question:

"Where is my brother Albert, who was taken with me? You have not killed him? "

"He has not been hurt, although we are at war with your people, " replied Bright Sun. "He is here in the village, and he, like you, is safe for the present. Some of the warriors wished to kill both you and him, but I have learned wisdom in these matters from your people. Why throw away pawns that we hold? I keep your brother and you as hostages. "

Dick, who had raised himself up in his eagerness, sank back again, relieved. He could feel that Bright Sun told the truth, and he had faith, too, in the man's power as well as his word. Yet there was another question that he wished to ask.

"Bright Sun, " he said, "it was you, our guide, who led the train into the pass that all might be killed? "

Bright Sun shrugged his shoulders, but a spark leaped from his eyes.

"What would you ask of me? " he replied. "In your code it was cunning, but the few and small must fight with cunning. The little man, to confront the big man, needs the advantage of weapons. The Sioux make the last stand for the Indian race, and we strike when and where we can. "

The conscience of the chief was clear, so far as Dick could see, and there was nothing that he could say in reply. It was Bright Sun himself who resumed:

"But I spared you and your brother. I did that which caused you to be absent when the others were slain. "

"Why? "

"Because you were different. You were not like the others. It may be that I pitied you, and it may be also that I like you—a little—and— you were young. "

The man's face bore no more expression than carven oak, but Dick was grateful.

"I thank you, Bright Sun, " he said, "and I know that Albert thanks you, too. "

Bright sun nodded, and then fixed an intent gaze upon Dick.

"You and your brother escaped, " he said. "That was nearly two years ago, and you have not gone back to your people. Where have you been? "

Dick saw a deep curiosity lurking behind the intent gaze, but whatever he might owe to Bright Sun, he had no intention of gratifying it.

"Would you tell me where you have been in the last two years and all that you have done? " the chief asked.

"I cannot answer; but you see that we have lived, Albert and I, " Dick replied.

"And that you have learned the virtues of silence, " said Bright Sun. "I ask you no more about it to-day. Give me your word for the present that you will not try to escape, and your life and that of your brother will be the easier. It would be useless, anyhow, for you to make such an attempt. When you feel that you have a chance, you can withdraw your promise. "

Dick laughed, and the laugh was one of genuine good humor.

"That's certainly fair, " he said. "Since I can't escape, I might as well give my promise not to try it for the time being. Well, I give it. "

Bright Sun nodded gravely.

"Your brother will come in soon, " he said. "He has already given his promise, that is, a conditional one, good until he can confer with you. "

"I'll confirm it, " said Dick.

Bright Sun saluted and left the great lodge. Some warriors near the door moved aside with the greatest deference to let him pass. Dick lay on his rush mat, gazing after him, and deeply impressed.

When Bright Sun was gone he examined the lodge again. It was obvious that it was a great common hall or barracks for warriors, and Bright Sun's simile of the Spartans was correct. More warriors came in, all splendid, athletic young men of a high and confident bearing. A few were dressed in the white man's costume, but most of them were in blankets, leggings, and moccasins, and had magnificent rows of feathers in their hair. Every man carried a carbine, and most of them had revolvers also. Such were the Akitcita or chosen band, and in this village of about two hundred lodges they numbered sixty men. Dick did not know then that in times of peace all guests, whether white or red, were entertained in the lodge of the Akitcita.

Impressed as he had been by Bright Sun, he was impressed also by these warriors. Not one of them spoke to him or annoyed him in any manner. They went about their tasks, cleaning and polishing their weapons, or sitting on rough wooden benches, smoking pipes with a certain dignity that belonged to men of strength and courage. All around the lodge were rush mats, on which they slept, and near the door was a carved totem pole.

A form darkened the doorway, and Albert came in. He rushed to Dick when he saw that he was conscious again, and shook his hand with great fervor. The warriors went on with their tasks or their smoking, and still took no notice.

"This is a most wonderful place, Dick, " exclaimed the impressionable Albert, "and Bright Sun has treated us well. We can go about the village if we give a promise, for the time, that we'll not try to escape. "

"He's been here, " said Dick, "and I've given it. "

"Then, if you feel strong enough, let's go on and take a look. "

"Wait until I see if this head of mine swims around, " said Dick.

He rose slowly to his feet, and his bandaged head was dizzy at first, but as he steadied himself it became normal. Albert thrust out his hand to support him. It delighted him that he could be again of help to his older and bigger brother, and Dick, divining Albert's feeling, let it lie for a minute. Then they went to the door, Dick walking quite easily, as his strength came back fast.

The warriors of the Akitcita, of whom fully a dozen were now present in the great lodge, still paid no attention to the two youths, and Dick surmised that it was the orders of Bright Sun. But this absolute ignoring of their existence was uncanny, nevertheless. Dick studies some of the faces as he passed. Bold and fearless they were, and not without a certain nobility, but there was little touch of gentleness or pity, it was rather the strength of the wild animal, the flesh-eater, that seeks its prey. Sioux they were, and Sioux they would remain in heart, no matter what happened, wild warriors of the northwest. Dick perceived this fact in a lightening flash, but it was the lightening flash of conviction.

Outside the fresh air saluted Dick, mouth and nostrils, and the ache in his head went quite away. He had seen the valley by moonlight, when it was beautiful, but not as beautiful as their own valley, the one of which they would not tell to anybody. But it was full of interest. The village life, the life of the wild, was in progress all about him, and in the sunshine, amidst such picturesque surroundings, it had much that was attractive to the strong and brave.

Dick judged correctly that the village contained about two hundred winter lodges of bark and poles, and could therefore furnish about four hundred warriors. It was evident, too, that it was the scene of prosperity. The flesh of buffalo, elk, and deer was drying in the sun, hanging from trees or on little platforms of poles. Children played with the dogs or practiced with small bows and arrows. In the shadow of a tepee six old women sat gambling, and the two boys stopped to watch them.

The Indians are more inveterate gamblers than the whites, and the old women, wrinkled, hideous hags of vast age, played their games with an intent, almost breathless, interest.

They were playing Woskate Tanpan, or the game of dice, as it is known to the Sioux. Three women were on each side, and they played it with tanpan (the basket), kansu (the dice), and canyiwawa (the counting sticks). The tanpan, made of willow twigs, was a tiny basket, about three inches in diameter at the bottom, but broader at the top, and about two inches deep. Into this one woman would put the kansu or dice, a set of six plum stones, some carved and some not carved. She would put her hand over the tanpan, shake the kansu just as the white dice player does, and then throw them out. The value of the throw would be according to the kind and number of carvings that were turned up when the kansu fell.

The opposing sides, three each, sat facing each other, and the stakes for which they played—canyiwawa (the counting sticks)—lay between them. These were little round sticks about the thickness of a lead pencil, and the size of each heap went up or down, as fortune shifted back or forth. They could make the counting sticks represent whatever value they chose, this being agreed upon beforehand, and the old Sioux women had been known to play Woskate Tanpan two days and nights without ever rising from their seats.

"What old harpies they are! " said Dick. "Did you ever see anybody so eager over anything? "

"They are no worse than the men, " replied Albert. "A lot of warriors are gambling, too. "

A group of the men were gathered on a little green farther on, and the brothers joined them, beginning to share at once the interest that the spectators showed in several warriors who were playing Woskate Painyankapi, or the game of the Wands and the Hoop.

The warriors used in the sport canyleska (the hoop) and cansakala (the wands). The hoops were of ash, two or three feet in diameter, the ash itself being about an inch in diameter. Every hoop was carefully marked off into spaces, something like the face of a watch.

Cansakala (the wands) were of chokecherry, four feet long and three fourths of an inch in diameter. One end of every wand was squared for a distance of about a foot. The wands were in pairs, the two being fastened together with buckskin thongs about nine inches in length, and fastened at a point about one third of the length of the wands from the rounded ends.

A warrior would roll the hoop, and he was required to roll it straight and correctly. If he did not do so, the umpire made him roll it over, as in the white man's game of baseball the pitcher cannot get a strike until he pitches the ball right.

When the hoop was rolled correctly, the opposing player dropped his pair of wands somewhere in front of it. It was his object so to calculate the speed and course of the hoop when it fell it would lie upon his wands. If he succeeded, he secured his points according to the spaces on each wand within which the hoop lay—an exceedingly difficult game, requiring great skill of hand and judgment of eye. That if was absorbing was shown by the great interest with which all the spectators followed it and by their eager betting.

"I don't believe I could learn to do that in ten years, " said Albert; "you've got to combine too many things and to combine them fast. "

"They must begin on it while they're young, " said Dick; "but the Indian has a mind, and don't you forget it. "

"But they're not as we are, " rejoined Albert. "Nothing can ever make them so. "

Here, as in the house of the Akitcita, nobody paid any attention to the two boys, but Dick began to have a feeling that he was watched, not watched openly as man watches man, but in the furtive dangerous way of the great wild beasts, the man-eaters. The feeling grew into a conviction that, despite what they were doing, everybody in the camp—warrior, squaw, and child—was watching Albert and him. He knew that half of this was fancy, but he was sure that the other half was real.

"Albert, " he said, "I wouldn't make any break for liberty now, even if I hadn't given my promise. "

"Nor I, " said Albert. "By the time we had gone ten feet the whole village would be on top of us. Dick, while I'm here I'm going to make the best of it I can. "

In pursuance of this worthy intention Albert pressed forward and almost took the cansakala from the hands of a stalwart warrior. The man, amazed at first, yielded up the pair of wands with a grin. Albert signaled imperiously to the warrior with the hoop, and he, too, grinning, sent canyleska whirling.

Albert cast the wands, and the hoop fell many feet from them. A shout of laughter arose. The white youth was showing himself a poor match for the Sioux, and the women and children came running to see this proof of the superiority of their race.

The warrior from whom he had taken them gravely picked up the cansakala and handed them back to Albert, the other warrior again sent canyleska rolling, and again Albert threw the wands with the same ill fortune. A third and fourth time he tried, with but slight improvement, and the crowd, well pleased to see him fail, thickened all the time, until nearly the whole village was present.

"It's just as hard as we thought it was, Dick, and harder, " said Albert ruefully. "Here, you take it and see what you can do. "

He handed cansakala to Dick, who also tried in vain, while the crowd enjoyed the sport, laughing and chatting to one another, as they will in their own villages. Dick made a little more progress than Albert had achieved, but not enough to score any points worth mentioning, and he, too, retired discomfited, while the Sioux, especially the women, continued to laugh.

"I don't like to be beaten that way, " said Albert in a nettled tone.

"Never mind, Al, old fellow, " said Dick soothingly. "Remember it's their game, not ours, and as it makes them feel good, it's all the better for us. Since they've beaten us, they're apt to like us and treat us better. "

It was hard for Albert to take the more philosophical view, which was also the truthful one, but he did his best to reconcile himself, and he and Dick moved on to other sights.

Dick noticed that the village had been located with great judgment. On one side was the river, narrow but swift and deep; on the other, a broad open space that would not permit an enemy to approach through ambush, and beyond that the forest.

The tepees stood in a great circle, and, although Dick did not know it, their camps were always pitched according to rule, each gens or clan having its regular place in the circle. The tribe of the Mendewahkantons—a leading one of the Seven Fireplaces or Council Fires of the great Sioux nation—was subdivided into seven gentes or clans; the Kiyukas, or Breakers, so called because they disregarded the general marriage law and married outside their own clan; the Que-mini-tea, or Mountain Wood and Water people; the Kap'oja, or Light Travelers; the Maxa-yuta-cui, the People who Eat no Grease; the Queyata-oto-we, or the People of the Village Back from the River; the Oyata Citca, the Bad Nation, and the Tita-otowe, the People of the Village on the Prairie.

Each clan was composed of related families, and all this great tribe, as the boys learned later, had once dwelled around Spirit Lake, Minnesota, their name meaning Mysterious Lake Dwellers, but had been pushed westward years before by the advancing wave of white settlement. This was now a composite village, including parts of every gens of the Mendewahkantons, but there were other villages of the same tribe scattered over a large area.

When Dick and Albert reached the northern end of the village they saw a great number of Indian ponies, six or seven hundred perhaps, grazing in a wide grassy space and guarded by half-grown Indian boys.

"Dick, " said Albert, "if we only had a dozen of those we could go back and get our furs. "

"Yes, " said Dick, "if we had the ponies, if we knew where we are now, if we were free of the Sioux village, and if we could find the way to our valley, we might do what you say. "

"Yes, it does take a pile of 'ifs, '" said Albert, laughing, "and so I won't expect it. I'll try to be resigned. "

So free were they from any immediate restriction that it almost seemed to them that they could walk away as they chose, up the valley and over the hills and across the plains. How were the Sioux to know that these two would keep their promised word? But both became conscious again of those watchful eyes, ferocious, like the eyes of man-eating wild beasts, and both shivered a little as they turned back into the great circle of bark teepees.

Chapter XVI
The Gathering of the Sioux

Dick and Albert abode nearly two weeks in the great lodge of the Akitcita, that is, as guests, although they were prisoners, whose lives might be taken at any time, and they had splendid opportunities for observing what a genuine Spartan band the Akitcita were. Everyone had his appointed place for arms and his rush or fur mat for sleeping. There was no quarreling, no unseemly chatter, always a grave and dignified order and the sense of stern discipline. Not all the Akitcita were ever present in the daytime, but some always were. All tribal business was transacted here. The women had to bring wood and water to it daily, and the entire village supplied it every day with regular rations of tobacco, almost the only luxury of the Akitcita.

Both Dick and Albert were keenly observant, and they did not hesitate also to ask questions of Bright Sun whenever they had the chance. They learned from him that the different tribes of the Sioux had general councils at irregular intervals, that there was no hereditary rank among the chiefs, it being usually a question of energy and merit, although the rank was sometimes obtained by gifts, and ambitious man giving away all that he had for the prize. There were no women chiefs, and women were not admitted to the great council.

The boys perceived, too, that much in the life of the Sioux was governed by ancient ritual; nearly everything had its religious meaning, and both boys having an inherent respect for religion of any kind, were in constant fear lest they should violate unwillingly some honored law.

The two made friendly advances to the members of the Akitcita but they were received with a grave courtesy that did not invite a continuance. They felt daily a deepening sense of racial difference. They appreciated the humane treatment they had received, but they and the Sioux did not seem to come into touch anywhere. And this difference was accentuated in the case of Bright Sun. The very fact that he had been educated in their schools, that he spoke their language so well, and that he knew their customs seemed to widen the gulf between them into a sea. They felt that he had tasted of their life, and liked it not.

The two, although they could not like Bright Sun, began to have a certain deference for him. The old sense of power he had created in their minds increased greatly, and now it was not merely a matter of mind and manner; all the outward signs, the obvious respect in which he was held by everybody and the way in which the eyes of the warriors, as well as those of women and children, followed him, showed that he was a great leader.

After ten days or so in the great lodge of the Akitcita, Dick and Albert were removed to a small bark tepee of their own, to which they were content to go. They had no arms, not even a knife, but they were already used to their captivity, and however great their ultimate danger might be, it was far away for them to think much about it.

They observed, soon after their removal, that the life of the village changed greatly. The old women were not often to be found in the shadow of the lodges playing Woskate Tanpan, the men gave up wholly Woskate Painyankapi, and throughout the village, no matter how stoical the Sioux might be, there was a perceptible air of excitement and suspense. Often at night the boys heard the rolling of the Sioux war drums, and the medicine men made medicine incessantly inside their tepees. Dick chafed greatly.

"Big things are afoot, " he would say to Albert. "We know that the Sioux and our people are at war, but you and I, Al, don't know a single thing that has occurred. I wish we could get away from here. Our people are our own people, and I'd like to tell them to look out."

"I feel just as you do, Dick, " Albert would reply; "but we might recall our promise to Bright Sun. Besides, we wouldn't have the ghost of a chance to escape. I feel that a hundred eyes are looking at me all the time. "

"I feel that two hundred are looking at me, " said Dick, with a grim little laugh. "No, Al, you're right. We haven't a chance on earth to escape. "

Five days after their removal to the small lodge there was a sudden and great increase in the excitement in the village. In truth, it burst into a wild elation, and all the women and children, running toward the northern side of the village, began to shout cries of welcome. The warriors followed more sedately, and Dick and Albert, no one detaining them, joined in the throng.

"Somebody's coming, Al, that's sure, " said Dick.

"Yes, and that somebody's a lot of men, " said Albert. "Look! "

Three or four hundred warriors, a long line of them, were coming down the valley, tall, strong, silent men, with brilliant headdresses of feathers and bright blankets. Everyone carried a carbine or rifle, and they looked what they were—a truly formidable band, resolved upon some great attempt.

Dick and Albert inferred the character of the arrivals from the shouts that they heard the squaws and children utter: "Sisseton! " "Wahpeton! " "Ogalala! " "Yankton! " "Teton! " "Hunkpapa! "

The arriving warriors, many of whom were undoubtedly chiefs, gravely nodded to their welcome, and came silently on as the admiring crowd opened to receive them.

"It's my opinion, " said Dick, "that the Seven Fireplaces are about to hold a grand council in the lodge of the Akitcita. "

"I don't think there's any doubt about it, " replied Albert.

They also heard, amidst the names of the tribes, the names of great warriors or medicine men, names which they were destined to hear many times again, both in Indian and English—Sitting Bull, Rain-in-the-Face, Little Big Man, and others. Then they meant nothing to either Dick or Albert.

All the chiefs, led by Bright Sun, went directly to the lodge of the Akitcita, and the other warriors were taken into the lodges of their friends, the Mendewahkantons. Then the women ran to the lodges and returned with the best food that the village could furnish. It was given to the guests, and also many pounds of choice tobacco.

Dick and Albert had made no mistake in their surmise. The great council of the Seven Fireplaces of the Sioux was in session. All that day the chiefs remained in the lodge of the Akitcita, and when night was far advanced they were still there.

Dick and Albert shared the excitement of the village, although knowing far less of its nature, but they knew that a grand council of the Seven Fireplaces would not be held without great cause, and they feared much for their people. It was a warm, close night, with a thin moon and flashes of heat lightening on the hilly horizon. Through the heavy air came the monotonous rolling of a war drum, and the chant of a medicine man making medicine in a tepee near by went on without ceasing.

The boys did not try to sleep, and unable to stifle curiosity, they came from the little bark lodge. One or two Sioux warriors glanced at them, but none spoke. The Sioux knew that the village was guarded so closely by a ring of sentinels that a cat could not have crept through without being seen. The boys walked on undisturbed until they came near the great council lodge, where they stopped to look at the armed warriors standing by the door.

The dim light and the excited imaginations of the boys made the lodge grow in size and assume fantastic shapes. So many great chiefs had come together for a mighty purpose, and Dick was sure that Bright Sun, sitting in the ring of his equals, urged on the project, whatever it might be, and would be the dominating figure through all.

Although they saw nothing, they were fascinated by what they wished to see. The great lodge held them with a spell that they did not seek to break. Although it was past midnight, they stayed there, staring at the blank walls. Warriors passed and gave them sharp glances, but nothing was said to them. The air remained close and heavy. Heat lightening continued to flare on the distant hills, but no rain fell.

The chiefs finally came forth from the great council. There was no light for them save the cloudy skies and one smoking torch that a warrior held aloft, but the active imagination of the two boys were again impressed. Every chief seemed to show in his face and manner his pride of race and the savage strength that well became such a time and place. Some bore themselves more haughtily and were more brilliantly adorned than Bright Sun, but he was still the magnet from which power and influence streamed. Dick and Albert did not know why they knew it, but they knew it.

The chiefs did not go away to friendly lodges, but after they came forth remained in a group, talking. Dick surmised that they had come to an agreement upon whatever question they debated; now they were outside for fresh air, and soon would return to the lodge of the Akitcita, which, according to custom, would shelter them as guests.

Bright Sun noticed the brothers standing in the shadow of the lodge, and, leaving the group, he walked over to them. His manner did not express hostility, but he made upon both boys that old impression of power and confidence, tinged now with a certain exultation.

"You would know what we have been doing? " he said, speaking directly to Dick, the older.

"We don't ask, " replied Dick, "but I will say this, Bright Sun: we believe that the thing done was the thing you wished. "

Bright Sun permitted himself a little smile.

"You have learned to flatter, " he said.

"It was not meant as flattery, " said Dick; "but there is something more I have to say. We wish to withdraw our pledge not to attempt to escape. You remember it was in the agreement we could withdraw whenever we chose. "

"That is true, " said Bright Sun, giving Dick a penetrating look. "And so you think that it is time for you to go? "

"We will go, if we can, " said Dick boldly.

Bright Sun, who had permitted himself a smile a little while ago, now permitted himself a soft laugh.

"You put it well, " he said in his precise English, "'if we can. ' But the understanding is clear. The agreement is at an end. However, you will not escape. We need you as hostages, and I will tell you, too, that we leave this village and valley to-morrow. We begin a great march. "

"I am not surprised, " said Dick.

189

Bright Sun rejoined the other chiefs, and all of them went back into the lodge of the Akitcita, while Dick and Albert returned to their own little tepee. There, as each lay on his rush mat, they talked in whispers.

"What meaning do you give to it, Dick? " asked Albert.

"That all the Sioux tribes are going to make a mighty effort against our people, and they're going to make it soon. Why else are they holding this great council of the Seven Fireplaces? I tell you, Al, big things are afoot. Oh, if we could only find a chance to get away! "

Albert rolled over to the door of the lodge and peeped out. Several warriors were pacing up and down in front of the rows of tepees. He rolled back to his rush mat.

"They've got inside as well as outside guards now, " he whispered.

"I thought it likely, " Dick whispered back. "Al, the best thing that you and I can do now is to go to sleep. "

They finally achieved slumber, but were up early the next morning and saw Bright Sun's words come true. The village was dismantled with extraordinary rapidity. Most of the lighter lodges were taken down, but how much of the place was left, and what people were left with it, the boys did not know, because they departed with the warriors, each riding a bridleless pony. Although mounted, their chance of escape was not increased. Warriors were all about them, they were unarmed, and their ponies, uncontrolled by bridles, could not be made to leave their comrades.

Dick and Albert, nevertheless, found an interest in this journey, wondering to what mysterious destination it would lead them. They heard behind them the chant of the old women driving the ponies that drew the baggage on poles, but the warriors around them were silent. Bright Sun was not visible. Dick surmised that he was at the head of the column.

The clouds of the preceding night had gone away, and the day was cooler, although it was now summer, and both Dick and Albert found a certain pleasure in the journey. In their present of suspense any change was welcome.

They rode straight up the valley, a long and formidable procession, and as they went northward the depression became both shallower and narrower. Finally, they crossed the river at a rather deep ford and rode directly ahead. Soon the hills and the forest that clothed them sank out of sight, and Dick and Albert were once again in the midst of the rolling immensity of the plains. They could judge the point of the compass by the sun, but they knew nothing else of the country over which they traveled. They tried two or three times to open conversation with the warriors about them, trusting that the latter knew English, but they received no reply and gave up the attempt.

"At any rate, I can talk to you, Al, " said Dick after the last futile attempt.

"Yes, but you can't get any information out of me, " replied Albert with a laugh.

The procession moved on, straight as an arrow, over the swells, turning aside for nothing. Some buffaloes were seen on the horizon, but they were permitted to crop the bunch grass undisturbed. No Indian hunter left the ranks.

They camped that night on the open prairie, Dick and Albert sleeping in their blankets in the center of the savage group. It might have seemed to the ordinary observer that there was looseness and disorder about the camp, but Dick was experienced enough to know that all the Mendewahkantons were posted in the circle according to their clans, and that the delegates were distributed with them in places of honor.

Dick noticed, also, that no fires were built, and that the warriors had scrutinized the entire circle of the horizon with uncommon care. It could signify but one thing to him—white people, and perhaps white troops, were near. If so, he prayed that they were in sufficient force. He was awakened in the night by voices, and raising himself on his elbow he saw a group of men, at least a hundred in number, riding into the camp.

The latest arrivals were Sioux warriors, but of what tribe he could not tell. Yet it was always the Sioux who were coming, and it would have been obvious to the least observant that Dick's foreboding about a mighty movement was right. They were joined the next day by another detachment coming from the southwest, and rode on, full seven hundred warriors, every man armed with the white man's weapons, carbine or rifle and revolver.

"I pity any poor emigrants whom they may meet, " thought Dick; but, fortunately, they met none. The swelling host continued its march a second day, a third, and a fourth through sunshiny weather, increasing in warmth, and over country that changed but little. Dick and Albert saw Bright Sun only once or twice, but he had nothing to say to them. The others, too, maintained their impenetrable silence, although they never offered any ill treatment.

They were joined every day by bands of warriors, sometimes not more than two or three at a time, and again as many as twenty. They came from all points of the compass, but, so far as Dick and Albert could see, little was said on their arrival. Everything was understood. They came as if in answer to a call, took their places without ado in the savage army, and rode silently on. Dick saw a great will at work, and with it a great discipline. A master mind had provided for all things.

"Al, " he said to his brother, "you and I are not in the plan at all. We've been out of the world two years, and we're just that many years behind. "

"I know it's 1876, " said Albert, with some confidence, but he added in confession: "I've no idea what month it is, although it must be somewhere near summer. "

"About the beginning of June, I should think, " said Dick.

An hour after this little talk the country became more hilly, and presently they saw trees and high bluffs to their right. Both boys understood the signs. They were approaching a river, and possibly their destination.

"I've a feeling, " said Dick, "that we're going to stop now. The warriors look as if they were getting ready for a rest. "

He was quickly confirmed in his opinion by the appearance of mounted Indians galloping to meet them. These warriors showed no signs of fatigue or a long march, and it was now obvious that a village was near.

The new band greeted the force of Bright Sun with joy, and the stern silence was relaxed. There was much chattering and laughing, much asking and answering of questions, and soon Indian women and Indian boys, with little bows and arrows, came over the bluffs, and joining the great mounted force, followed on its flanks.

Dick and Albert were on ponies near the head of the column, and their troubles and dangers were forgotten in their eager interest in what they were about to see. The feeling that a first step in a great plan was accomplished was in the air. They could see it in the cessation of the Sioux reserve and in the joyous manner of the warriors, as well as the women. Even the ponies picked up their heads, as if they, too, saw rest.

The procession wound round the base of a hill, and then each boy uttered a little gasp. Before them lay a valley, about a mile wide, down the center of which flowed a shallow yellow river fringed with trees and also with undergrowth, very dense in places. But it was neither the river nor trees that had drawn the little gasps from the two boys, it was an Indian village, or rather a great town, extending as far as they could see—and they saw far—on either side of the stream. There were hundreds and hundreds of lodges, and a vast scene of animated and varied life. Warriors, squaws, children, and dogs moved about; smoke rose from scores and scores of fires, and on grassy meadows grazed ponies, thousands in number.

"Why, I didn't think there was so big an Indian town in all the West! " exclaimed Albert.

"Nor did I, " said Dick gravely, "and I'm thinking, Al, that it's gathered here for a purpose. It must be made up of all the Sioux tribes. "

Albert nodded. He knew the thought in Dick's mind, and he believed it to be correct.

Chance so had it that Bright Sun at this moment rode near them and heard their words. Dick of late had surmised shrewdly that Bright Sun treated them well, not alone for the sake of their value as hostages, but for a reason personal to himself. He had been associated long with white people in their schools, but he was at heart and in fact a great Sioux chief; he had felt the white man's assumption of racial superiority, and he would have these two with the white faces witness some great triumph that he intended to achieve over these same white people. This belief was growing on Dick, and it received more confirmation when Bright Sun said:

"You see that the Sioux nation has many warriors and is mighty. "

"I see that it is so, Bright Sun, " replied Dick frankly. "I did not know you were so numerous and so powerful; but bear in mind, Bright Sun, that no matter how many the Sioux may be, the white men are like the leaves of the tree—thousands, tens of thousands may fall, and yet only their own kin miss them. "

But Bright Sun shook his head.

"What you say is true, " he said, "because I have seen and I know; but they are not here. The mountains, the plains, the wilderness keep them back. "

Dick forebore a retort, because he felt that he owed Bright Sun something, and the chief seemed to take it for granted that he was silenced by logic.

"This is the Little Big Horn River, " Bright Sun said, "and you behold now in this village, which extends five miles on either side of it, the Seven Fireplaces of the Sioux. All tribes are gathered here. "

"And it is you who have gathered them, " said Dick. He was looking straight into Bright Sun's eyes as he spoke, and he saw the pupils of the Sioux expand, in fact dilate, with a sudden overwhelming sense of power and triumph. Dick knew he had guessed aright, but the Sioux replied with restraint:

"If I have had some small part in the doing of it, I feel proud. "

With that he left them, and Dick and Albert rode on into the valley of the river, in whatsoever direction their bridleless horses might carry them, although that direction was bound to be the one in which rode the group surrounding them.

Some of the squaws and boys, who caught sight of Dick and Albert among the warriors, began to shout and jeer, but a chief sternly bade them to be silent, and they slunk away, to the great relief of the two lads, who had little relish for such attention.

They were full in the valley now, and on one side of them was thick undergrowth that spread to the edge of the river. A few hundred yards father the undergrowth ceased, sand taking its place. All the warriors turned their ponies abruptly away from one particular stretch of sand, and Dick understood.

"It's a quicksand, Al, " he said; "it would suck up pony, rider, and all. "

They left the quicksand behind and entered the village, passing among the groups of lodges. Here they realized more fully than on the hills the great extent of the Indian town. Its inhabitants seemed a myriad to Dick and Albert, so long used to silence and the lack of numbers.

"How many warriors do you suppose this place could turn out, Dick? " asked Albert.

"Five thousand, but that's only a guess. It doesn't look much like our own valley, does it, Al? "

"No, it doesn't, " replied Albert with emphasis; "and I can tell you, Dick, I wish I was back there right now. I believe that's the finest valley the sun ever shone on. "

"But we had to leave sometime or other, " said Dick, "and how could we tell that we were going to run into anything like this? But it's surely a big change for us. "

"The biggest in the world. "

The group in which they rode continued along the river about two miles, and then stopped at a point where both valley and village were widest. A young warrior, speaking crude English, roughly bade them dismount, and gladly they sprang from the ponies. Albert fell over when he struck the ground, his legs were cramped so much by the long ride, but the circulation was soon restored, and he and Dick went without resistance to the lodge that was pointed out to them as their temporary home and prison.

It was a small lodge of poles leaning toward a common center at the top, there lashed together firmly with rawhide, and the whole covered with skins. It contained only two rude mats, two bowls of

Sioux pottery, and a drinking gourd, but it was welcome to Dick and Albert, who wanted rest and at the same time security from the fierce old squaws and the equally fierce young boys. They were glad enough to lie a while on the rush mats and rub their tired limbs. When they were fully rested they became very hungry.

"I wonder if they mean to starve us to death? " said Albert.

A negative answer was given in about ten minutes by two old squaws who appeared, bearing food, some venison, and more particularly wa-nsa, a favorite dish with the Sioux, a compound made of buffalo meat and wild cherries, which, after being dried, are pounded separately until they are very fine; then the two are pounded together for quite a while, after which the whole is stored in bladders, somewhat after the fashion of the white man's sausage.

"This isn't bad at all, " said Albert when he bit into his portion. "Now, if we only had something good to drink. "

Neither of the old squaws understood his words, but one of them answered his wish, nevertheless. She brought cherry-bark tea in abundance, which both found greatly to their liking and they ate and drank with deep content. A mental cheer was added also to their physical good feeling.

"Thanks, madam, " said Albert, when one of the old squaws refilled the little earthen bowl from which he drank the cherry-bark tea. "You are indeed kind. I did not expect to meet with such hospitality."

The Indian woman did not understand his words, but anybody could understand the boy's ingratiating smile. She smiled back at him.

"Be careful, Al, old man, " said Dick with the utmost gravity. "These old Indian women adopt children sometimes, or perhaps she will want to marry you. In fact, I think the latter is more likely, and you can't help yourself. "

"Don't, Dick, don't! " said Albert imploringly. "I am willing to pay a high price for hospitality, but not that. "

The women withdrew, and after a while, when the boys felt fully rested, they stepped outside the lodge, to find two tall young Sioux warriors on guard. Dick looked at them inquiringly, and one of them said in fair English:

"I am Lone Wolf, and this is Tall Pine. You can go in the village, but we go with you. Bright Sun has said so, and we obey. "

"All right, Mr. Lone Wolf, " said Dick cheerfully. "Four are company, two are none. We couldn't escape if we tried; but Bright Sun says that you and your friend Mr. Pine Tree are to be our comrades on our travels, well and good. I don't know any other couple in this camp that I'd choose before you two. "

Lone Wolf and Pine Tree were young, and maybe their youth caused them to smile slightly at Dick's pleasantry. Nor did they annoy the boys with excessive vigilance, and they answered many questions. It was, indeed, they said, the greatest village in the West that was now gathered on the banks of the Little Big Horn. Sioux from all tribes had come including those on reservations. All the clans of the Mendewahkantons, for instance, were represented on the reservations, but all of them were represented here, too.

It was a great war that was now going on, they said, and they had taken many white scalps, but they intimated that those they had taken were few in comparison with the number they would take. Dick asked them of their present purpose, but here they grew wary. The white soldiers might be near or they might be far, but the god of the Sioux was Wakantaka, the good spirit, and the god of the white man was Wakansica, the bad spirit.

Dick did not consider it worth while to argue with them. Indeed, he was in no position to do so. The history of the world in the last two years was a blank to him and Albert. But he observed throughout the vast encampment the same air of expectancy and excitement that had been noticeable in the smaller village. He also saw a group of warriors arrive, their ponies loaded with repeating rifles, carbines and revolvers. He surmised that they had been obtained from French-Canadian traders, and he knew well for what they were meant. Once again he made his silent prayer that if the white soldiers came they could come in great force.

Dick observed in the huge village all the signs of an abundant and easy life, according to Sioux standards. Throughout its confines kettles gave forth the odors pleasing to an Indian's nostrils. Boys broiled strips of venison on twigs before the fires. Squaws were jerking buffalo and deer meat in a hundred places, and strings of fish ready for the cooking hung before the lodges. Plenty showed everywhere.

Dick understood that if one were really a wild man, with all instincts of a wild man inherited through untold centuries of wild life, he could find no more pleasing sight than this great encampment abounding in the good things for wild men that the plains, hills, and water furnished. He saw it readily from the point of view of the Sioux and could appreciate their confidence.

Albert, who was a little ahead of Dick, peered between two lodges, and suddenly turned away with a ghastly face.

"What's the trouble, Al? " asked Dick.

"I saw a warrior passing on the other side of those lodges, " replied Albert, "and he had something at his belt—the yellow hair of a white man, and there was blood on it. "

"We have taken many scalps already, " interrupted the young Sioux, Lone Wolf, some pride showing in his tone.

Both Dick and Albert shuddered and were silent. The gulf between these men and themselves widened again into quite a sea. Their thoughts could not touch those of the Sioux at any point.

"I think we'd better go back to our own lodge, " said Dick.

"No, " said Lone Wolf. "The great chief, Bright Sun, has commanded us when we return to bring you into his presence, and it is time for us to go to him. "

"What does he want with us? " asked Albert.

"He knows, but I do not, " replied Lone Wolf sententiously.

"Lead on, " said Dick lightly. "Here, we go wherever we are invited."

They walked back a full mile, and Lone Wolf and Pine Tree led the way to a great lodge, evidently one used by the Akitcita, although Dick judged that in so great a village as this, which was certainly a fusion of many villages, there must be at least a dozen lodges of the Akitcita.

Lone Wolf and Pine Tree showed Dick and Albert into the door, but they themselves remained outside. The two boys paused just inside the door until their eyes became used to the half gloom of the place. Before them stood a dozen men, all great chiefs, and in the center was Bright Sun, the dominating presence.

Despite their natural courage and hardihood and the wild life to which they had grown used, Dick and Albert were somewhat awed by the appearance of these men, every one of whom was of stern presence, looking every inch a warrior. They had discarded the last particle of white man's attire, keeping only the white man's weapons, the repeating rifle and revolver. Every one wore, more or less loosely folded about him, a robe of the buffalo, and in all cases the inner side of this robe was painted throughout in the most vivid manner with scenes from the hunt or warpath, chiefly those that had occurred in the life of the wearer. Many colors were used in these paintings, but mostly those of cardinal dyes, red and blue being favorites.

"These, " said Bright Sun, speaking more directly to Dick, "are mighty chiefs of the Sioux Nation. This is Ta Sun Ke Ka-Kipapi-Hok'silan (Young-Man-Afraid-of-His-Horses). "

He nodded toward a tall warrior, who made a slight and grave inclination.

"I'd cut out at least half of that name, " said Dick under his breath.

"And this, " continued Bright Sun in his measured, precise English, "is Ite-Mogu'Ju (Rain-in-the-Face), and this Kun-Sun'ka (Crow Dog), and this Pizi (Gall), and this Peji (Grass)".

Thus he continued introducing them, giving to every one his long Indian appellation until all were named. The famous Sitting Bull (Tatanka Yotanka) was not present. Dick learned afterwards that he was at that very moment in his own tepee making medicine.

"What we wish to know, " said Bright Sun—"and we have ways to make you tell us—is whether you saw the white troops before we took you? "

Dick shivered a little. He knew what Bright Sun meant by the phrase "we have ways to make you tell, " and he knew also that Bright Sun would be merciless if mercy stood in the way of getting what he wished. No shred of the white man's training was now left about the Indian chief save the white man's speech.

"I have not seen a white man in two years, " replied Dick, "nor has my brother. We told you the truth when you took us. "

Bright Sun was silent for a space, regarding him with black eyes seeking to read every throb of his heart. Dick was conscious, too, that the similar gaze of all the others was upon him. But he did not flinch. Why should he? He had told the truth.

"Then I ask you again, " said Bright Sun, "where have you been all this time? "

"I cannot tell you, " replied Dick. "It is a place that we wish to keep secret. It is hidden far from here. But it is one to which no one else goes. I can say that much. "

Rain-in-the-Face made an impatient movement, and said some words in the Sioux tongue. Dick feared it was a suggestion that he be put to the torture, and he was glad when Bright Sun shook his head.

"There are such places, " said Bright Sun, "because the mountains are high and vast and but few people travel among them. It may be that he tells the truth. "

"It is the truth. I swear it! " said Dick earnestly.

"Then why do you refuse to tell of this place? " asked Bright Sun.

"Because we wish to keep it for ourselves, " replied Dick frankly.

The faintest trace of a smile was visible in Bright Sun's eyes.

"Wherever it may be it belongs to us, " said the chief; "but I believe that you are telling the truth. Nor do I hesitate to tell you that we have asked these questions because we wish to learn all that we can. The soldiers of your people are advancing under the yellow-haired general, Custer, Terry, Gibbon, and others. They come in great force, but the Sioux, in greater force and more cunning will destroy them. "

Dick was silent. He knew too little to make any reply to the statements of Bright Sun. Rain-in-the-Face and Crazy Horse spoke to Bright Sun, and they seemed to be urging something. But the chief again shook his head, and they, too, became silent. It was obvious to both boys that his influence was enormous.

"You can go, " he said to Dick and Albert, and they gladly left the lodge. Outside, Lone Wolf and Pine Tree fell in on either side of them and escorted them to their own tepee, in front of which they stood guard while the boys slept that night.

.

Chapter XVII
The Great Sun Dance

Dick and Albert remained in their tepee throughout the next morning, but in the afternoon they were allowed to go in the village a second time. Lone Wolf and Pine Tree, who had slept in the morning, were again their guards. Both saw at once that some great event was at hand. The excitement in the village had increased visibly, and a multitude was pouring toward a certain point, a wide, grassy plain beside the Little Big Horn. Lone Wolf and Pine Tree willingly took the captives with the crowd, and the two boys looked upon a sight which few white men have beheld in all its savage convulsions.

The wide, grassy space before them had been carefully chosen by the great medicine men of the nation, Sitting Bull at their head. Then the squaws had put up a great circular awning, like a circus tent, with part of the top cut out. This awning was over one hundred and fifty feet in diameter. After this, the medicine men had selected a small tree, which was cut down by a young, unmarried squaw. Then the tree, after it had been trimmed of all its branches and consecrated and prayed over by the medicine men, was erected in the center of the inclosed space, rising from the ground to a height of about twenty feet.

To the top of the pole were fastened many long thongs of rawhide reaching nearly to the ground, and as Dick and Albert looked a swarm of young men in strange array, or rather lack of array, came forth from among the lodges and entered the inclosed space. Dick had some dim perception of what was about to occur, but Lone Wolf informed him definitely.

"The sun dance, " he said. "Many youths are about to become great warriors. "

The greatest of sun dances, a sun dance of the mighty allied Sioux tribes, was about to begin. Forward went the neophytes, every one clad only in a breechclout ornamented with beads, colored horsehair and eagle feathers, and with horse tails attached to it, falling to the ground. But every square inch of the neophyte's skin was painted in vivid and fantastic colors. Even the nails on his fingers and toes were painted. Moreover, everyone had pushed two small sticks of tough wood under the skin on each side of the breast, and to those two sticks was fastened a rawhide cord, making a loop about ten inches long.

"What under the sun are those sticks and cords for? " asked Albert, shuddering.

"Wait and we'll see, " replied Dick, who guessed too well their purpose, although he could not help but look.

The neophytes advanced, and every one tied one of the long rawhide thongs depending from the top of the pole to the loop of cord that hung from his breast. When all were ready they formed a great circle, somewhat after the fashion of the dancers around a Maypole, and outside of those formed another and greater circle of those already initiated.

A medicine man began to blow a small whistle made from the wing bone of an eagle, the sacred bird of the Sioux, and he never stopped blowing it for an instant. It gave forth a shrill, penetrating sound, that began after a while to work upon the nerves in a way that was almost unendurable to Dick and Albert.

At the first sound of the whistle the warriors began to dance around the pole, keeping time to the weird music. It was a hideous and frightful dance, like some cruel rite of a far-off time. The object was to tear the peg from the body, breaking by violence through the skin and flesh that held it, and this proved that the neophyte by his endurance of excessive pain was fit to become a great warrior.

But the pegs held fast for a long time, while the terrible, wailing cry of the whistle went on and on. Dick and Albert wanted to turn away—in fact, they had a violent impulse more than once to run from it—but the eyes of the Sioux were upon them, and they knew that they would consider them cowards if they could not bear to look upon that which others no older than themselves endured. There was also the incessant, terrible wailing of the whistle, which seemed to charm them and hold them.

The youths by and by began to pull loose from the thongs, and in some cases where it was evident that they would not be able to do so a medicine man would seize them by the shoulders and help pull. In no case did a dancer give up, although they often fell in a faint when loosed. Then they were carried away to be revived, but for three days and three nights not a single neophyte could touch food, water, or any other kind of drink. They were also compelled, as soon as they recovered a measurable degree of strength, to join the larger group and dance three days and nights around the neophytes, who successively took their places.

The whole sight, with the wailing of the whistle, the shouts of the dancers, the beat of their feet, and the hard, excited breathing of the thousands about them, became weird and uncanny. Dick felt as if some strange, deadly odor had mounted to his brain, and while he struggled between going and staying a new shout arose.

A fresh group of neophytes sprang into the inclosed place. Every one of these had the little sticks thrust through the upper point of the shoulder blade instead of the breast, while from the loop dangled a buffalo head. They danced violently until the weight of the head pulled the sticks loose, and then, like their brethren of the pole, joined the great ring of outside dancers when they were able.

The crowd of neophytes increased, as they gave way in turn to one another, and the thong about them thickened. Hundreds and hundreds of dancers whirled and jumped to the shrill, incessant blowing of the eagle-bone whistle. It seemed at times to the excited imaginations of Dick and Albert that the earth rocked to the mighty tread of the greatest of all sun dances. Indian stoicism was gone, perspiration streamed from dark faces, eyes became bloodshot as their owners danced with feverish vigor, savage shouts burst forth, and the demon dance grew wilder and wilder.

The tread of thousands of feet caused a fine, impalpable dust to rise from the earth beneath the grass and to permeate all the air, filling the eyes and nostrils of the dancers, heating their brains and causing them to see through a red mist. Some fell exhausted. If they were in the way, they were dragged to one side; if not, they lay where they fell, but in either case others took their places and the whirling multitude always increased in numbers.

As far as Dick and Albert could see the Sioux were dancing. There was a sea of tossing heads and a multitude of brown bodies shining with perspiration. Never for a moment did the shrill, monotonous, unceasing rhythm of the whistle cease to dominate the dance. It always rose above the beat of the dancers, it penetrated everything, ruled everything—this single, shrill note, like the chant of a snake charmer. It even showed its power over Dick and Albert. They felt their nerves throbbing to it in an unwilling response, and the dust and the vivid electric excitement of the dancers began to heat their own brains.

"Don't forget that we're white, Al! Don't forget it! " cried Dick.

"I'm trying not to forget it! " gasped Albert.

The sun, a lurid, red sun, went down behind the hills, and a twilight that seemed to Dick and Albert phantasmagorial and shot with red crept over the earth. But the dance did not abate in either vigor or excitement; rather it increased. In the twilight and the darkness that followed it assumed new aspects of the weird and uncanny. Despite the torches that flared up, the darkness was mainly in control. Now the dancers, whirling about the pole and straining on the cords, were seen plainly, and now they were only shadows, phantoms in the dusk.

Dick and Albert had moved but little for a long time; the wailing of the demon whistle held them; and they felt that there was a singular attraction, too, in this sight, which was barbarism and superstition pure and simple, yet not without its power. They were still standing there when the moon came out, throwing a veil of silver gauze over the dancers, the lodges, the surface of the river, and the hills, but it took nothing away from the ferocious aspect of the dance; it was still savagery, the custom of a remote, fierce, old world. Dick and Albert at last recovered somewhat; they threw off the power of the flute and the excited air that they breathed and began to assume again the position of mere spectators.

It was then that Bright Sun came upon them, and they noticed with astonishment that he, the product of the white schools and of years of white civilization, had been dancing, too. There was perspiration on his face, his breath was short and quick, and his eyes were red with excitement. He marked their surprise, and said:

"You think it strange that I, too, dance. You think all this barbarism and superstition, but it is not. It is the custom of my people, a custom that has the sanction of many centuries, and that is bred into our bone and blood. Therefore it is of use to us, and it is more fit than anything else to arouse us for the great crisis that we are to meet. "

Neither Dick nor Albert made any reply. Both saw that the great deep of the Sioux chief's stoicism was for the moment broken up. He might never be so stirred again, but there was no doubt of it now, and they could see his side of it, too. It was his people and their customs against the white man, the stranger. The blood of a thousand years was speaking in him.

When he saw that they had no answer for him, Bright Sun left them and became engrossed once more with the dance, continually urging it forward, bringing on more neophytes, and increasing the excitement. Dick and Albert remained a while longer, looking on. Their guards, Lone Wolf and Pine Tree, still stood beside them. The two young warriors, true to their orders, had made no effort to join the dancers, but their nostrils were twitching and their eyes bloodshot. The revel called to them incessantly, but they could not go.

Dick felt at last that he had seen enough of so wild a scene. One could not longer endure the surcharged air, the wailing of the whistle, the shouts, the chants, and the beat of thousands of feet.

"Al, " he said, "let's go back to our lodge, if our guards will let us, and try to sleep. "

"The sooner the better, " said Albert.

Lone Wolf and Pine Tree were willing enough, and Dick suspected that they would join the dance later. After Albert had gone in, he stood a moment at the door of the lodge and looked again upon this, the wildest and most extraordinary scene that he had yet beheld. It was late in the night and the center of the sun dance was some distance from the lodge, but the shrill wailing of the whistle still reached him and the heavy tread of the dancers came in monotonous rhythm. "It's the greatest of all nightmares, " he said to himself.

It was a long time before either Dick or Albert could sleep, and when Dick awoke at some vague hour between midnight and morning he was troubled by a shrill, wailing note that the drum of his ear. Then he remembered. The whistle! And after it came the rhythmic, monotonous beat of many feet, as steady and persistent as ever. The sun dance had never ceased for a moment, and he fell asleep again with the sounds of it still in his ear.

The dance, which was begun at the ripening of the wild sage, continued three days and nights without the stop of an instant. No food and no drink passed the lips of the neophytes, who danced throughout that time—if they fell they rose to dance again. Then at the appointed hour it all ceased, although every warrior's brain was at white heat and he was ready to go forth at once against a myriad enemies. It was as if everyone had drunk of some powerful and exciting Eastern drug.

The dance ended, they began to eat, and neither Dick nor Albert had ever before seen such eating. The cooking fires of the squaws rose throughout the entire five miles of the village. They had buffalo, deer, bear, antelope, and smaller game in abundance, and the warriors ate until they fell upon the ground, where the lay in a long stupor. The boys thought that many of them would surely die, but they came from their stupor unharmed and were ready for instant battle. There were many new warriors, too, because none had failed at the test, and all were eager to show their valor.

"It's like baiting a wild beast, " said Dick. "There are five thousand ravening savages here, ready to fight anything, and to-night I'm going to try to escape. "

"If you try, I try, too, " said Albert.

"Of course, " said Dick.

The village was resting from its emotional orgy, and the guard upon the two boys was relaxed somewhat. In fact, it seemed wholly unnecessary, as they were rimmed around by the vigilance of many thousand eyes. But, spurred by the cruel need, Dick resolved that they should try. Fortunately, the very next night was quite dark, and only a single Indian, Pine Tree, was on guard.

"It's to-night or never, " whispered Dick to Albert within the shelter of the lodge. "They've never taken the trouble to bind us, and that gives us at least a fighting chance. "

"When shall we slip out? "

"Not before about three in the morning. That is the most nearly silent hour, and if the heathenish curs let us alone we may get away."

Fortune seemed to favor the two. The moon did not come out, and the promise of a dark night was fulfilled. An unusual stillness was over the village. It seemed that everybody slept. Dick and Albert waited through long, long hours. Dick had nothing by which to reckon time, but he believed that he could calculate fairly well by guess, and once, when he thought it was fully midnight, he peeped out at the door of the lodge. Pine Tree was there, leasing against a sapling, but his attitude showed laziness and a lack of vigilance. It might be that, feeling little need of watching, he slept on his feet. Dick devoutly hoped so. He waited at least two hours longer, and again peeped out. The attitude of Pine Tree had not changed. It must certainly be sleep that held him, and Dick and Albert prepared to go forth. They had no arms, and could trust only to silence and speed.

Dick was the first outside, and stood in the shadow of the lodge until Albert joined him. There they paused to choose a way among the lodges and to make a further inspection of sleeping Pine Tree.

The quiet of the village was not broken. The lodges stretched away in dusky rows and then were lost in darkness. This promised well, and their eyes came back to Pine Tree, who was still sleeping. Then Dick became conscious of a beam of light, or rather two beams. These beams shot straight from the open eyes of Pine Tree, who was not asleep at all. The next instant Pine Tree opened his mouth, uttered a yell that was amazingly loud and piercing, and leaped straight for the two boys.

As neither Dick nor Albert had arms, they could do nothing but run, and they fled between the lodges at great speed, Pine Tree hot upon their heels. It amazed Dick to find that the whole population of a big town could awake so quickly. Warriors, squaws, and children swarmed from the lodges and fell upon him and Albert in a mass. He could only see in the darkness that Albert had been seized and dragged away, but he knew that two uncommonly strong old squaws had him by the hair, three half-grown boys were clinging to his legs, and a powerful warrior laid hold of his right shoulder. He deemed it wisest in such a position to yield as quickly and gracefully as he could, in the hope that the two wiry old women would be detached speedily from his hair. This object was achieved as soon as the Sioux saw that he did not resist, and the vigilant Pine Tree stood before him, watching with an expression that Dick feared could be called a grin.

"The honors are yours, " said Dick as politely as he could, "but tell me what has become of my brother. "

"He is being taken to the other side of the river, " said the voice of Bright Sun over Pine Tree's shoulder, "and he and you will be kept apart until we decide what to do with you. It was foolish in you to attempt to escape. I had warned you. "

"I admit it, " said Dick, "but you in my place would have done the same. Once can only try. "

He tried to speak with philosophy, but he was sorely troubled over being separated from his brother. Their comradeship in captivity had been a support to each other.

There was no sympathy in the voice of Bright Sun. He spoke coldly, sternly, like a great war chief. Dick understood, and was too proud to make any appeal. Bright Sun said a few words to the warriors, and walked away.

Dick was taken to another and larger lodge, in which several warriors slept. There, after his arms were securely bound, he was allowed to lie down on a rush mat, with warriors on rush mats on either side of him. Dick was not certain whether the warriors slept, but he knew that he did not close his eyes again that night.

Although strong and courageous, Dick Howard suffered much mental torture. Bright Sun was a Sioux, wholly an Indian (he had seen that at the sun dance), and if Albert and he were no longer of any possible use as hostages, Bright Sun would not trouble himself to protect them. He deeply regretted their wild attempt at escape, which he had felt from the first was almost hopeless. Yet he believed, on second thought, that they had been justified in making the trial. The great sun dance, the immense gathering of warriors keyed for battle, showed the imminent need for warning to the white commanders, who would not dream that the Sioux were in such mighty force. Between this anxiety and that other one for Albert, thinking little of himself meanwhile, Dick writhed in his bonds. But he could do nothing else.

The warriors rose from their rush mats at dawn and ate flesh of the buffalo and deer and their favorite wa-nsa. Dick's arms were unbound, and he, too, was allowed to eat; but he had little appetite, and when the warriors saw that he had finished they bound him again.

"What are you going to do to me? " asked Dick in a kind of vague curiosity.

No one gave any answer. They did not seem to hear him. Dick fancied that some of them understood English, but chose to leave him in ignorance. He resolved to imitate their own stoicism and wait. When they bound his arms again, and his feet also, he made no resistance, but lay down quietly on the rush mat and gazed with an air of indifference at the skin wall of the lodge. All warriors went out, except one, who sat in the doorway with his rifle on his knee.

"They flatter me, " thought Dick. "They must think me of some importance or that I'm dangerous, since they bind and guard me so well. "

His thongs of soft deerskin, while secure, were not galling. They neither chafed nor prevented the circulation, and when he grew tired of lying in one position he could turn into another. But it was terribly hard waiting. He did not know what was before him. Torture or death? Both, most likely. He tried to be resigned, but how could one be resigned when one was so young and so strong? The hum of the village life came to him, the sound of voices, the tread of feet, the twang of a boyish bowstring, but the guard in the doorway never stirred. It seemed to Dick that the Sioux, who wore very little clothing, was carved out of reddish-brown stone. Dick wondered if he would ever move, and lying on his back he managed to raise his head a little on the doubled corner of the rush mat, and watch that he might see.

Bound, helpless, and shut off from the rest of the world, this question suddenly became vital to him: Would that Indian ever move, or would he not? He must have been sitting in that position at least two hours. Always he stared straight before him, the muscles on his bare arms never quivered in the slightest, and the rifle lay immovable across knees which also were bare. How could he do it? How could he have such control over his nerves and body? Dick's mind slowly filled with wonder, and then he began to have a suspicion that the Sioux was not real, merely some phantom of the fancy, or that he himself was dreaming. It made him angry—angry at himself, angry at the Sioux, angry at everything. He closed his eyes, held them tightly shut for five minutes, and then opened them again. The Sioux was still there. Dick was about to break through his assumed stoicism and shout at the warrior, but he checked himself, and with a great effort took control again of his wandering nerves.

He knew now that the warrior was real, and that he must have moved some time or other, but he did not find rest of spirit. A shaft of sunshine by and by entered the narrow door of the lodge and fell across Dick himself. He knew that it must be a fair day, but he was sorry for it. The sun ought not to shine when he was at such a pass.

Another interminable period passed, and an old squaw entered with a bowl of wa-nsa, and behind her came Lone Wolf, who unbound Dick.

"What's up now, Mr. Lone Wolf? " asked Dick with an attempt at levity. "Is it a fight or a foot race? "

"Eat, " replied Lone Wolf sententiously, pointing of the bowl wa-nsa. "You will need your strength. "

Dick's heart fell at these words despite all his self-command. "My time's come, " he thought. He tried to eat—in fact, he forced himself to eat—that Lone Wolf might not think that he quailed, and when he had eaten as much as his honor seemed to demand he stretched his muscles and said to Lone Wolf, with a good attempt at indifference:

"Lead on, my wolfish friend. I don't know what kind of a welcome mine is going to be, but I suppose it is just as well to find out now. "

The face of Lone Wolf did not relax. He seemed to have a full appreciation of what was to come and no time for idle jests. He merely pointed to the doorway, and Dick stepped into the sunshine. Lying so long in the dusky lodge, he was dazzled at first by the brilliancy of the day, but when his sight grew stronger he beheld a multitude about him. The women and children began to chatter, but the warriors were silent. Dick saw that he was the center of interest, and was quite sure that he was looking upon his last sun. "O Lord, let me die bravely! " was his silent prayer.

He resolved to imitate as nearly as he could the bearing of an Indian warrior in his position, and made no resistance as Lone Wolf led him on, with the great thong following. He glanced around once for

Bright Sun, but did not see him. The fierce chief whom they called Ite-Moga' Ju (Rain-in-the-Face) seemed to be in charge of Dick's fate, and he directed the proceedings.

But stoicism could not prevail entirely, and Dick looked about him again. He saw the yellow waters of the river with the sunlight playing upon them; the great village stretching away on either shore until it was hidden by the trees and undergrowth; the pleasant hills and all the pleasant world, so hard to leave. His eyes dwelt particularly upon the hill, a high one, overlooking the whole valley of the Little Big Horn, and the light was so clear that he could see every bush and shrub waving there.

His eyes came back from the hill to the throng about him. He had felt at times a sympathy for the Sioux because the white man was pressing upon them, driving them from their ancient hunting grounds that they loved; but they were now wholly savage and cruel—men, women, and children alike. He hated them all.

Dick was taken to the summit of one of the lower hills, on which he could be seen by everybody and from which he could see in a vast circle. He was tied in a peculiar manner. His hands remained bound behind him, but his feet were free. One end of a stout rawhide was secured around his waist and the other around a sapling, leaving him a play of about a half yard. He could not divine the purpose of this, but he was soon to learn.

Six half-grown boys, with bows and arrows, then seldom used by grown Sioux, formed a line at a little distance from him, and at a word from Rain-in-the-Face leveled their bows and fitted arrow to the string. Dick thought at first they were going to slay him at once, but he remembered that the Indian did not do things that way. He knew it was some kind of torture and although he shivered he steadied his mind to face it.

Rain-in-the-Face spoke again, and six bowstrings twanged. Six arrows whizzed by Dick, three on one side and three on the other, but all so close that, despite every effort of will, he shrank back against the sapling. A roar of laughter came from the crowd, and Dick flushed through all the tan of two years in the open air. Now he understood why the rawhide allowed him so much play. It was a torture of the nerves and of the mind. They would shoot their arrows by him, graze him perhaps if he stood steady, but if he sought to evade through fear, if he sprang either to one side or the other, they might strike in a vital spot.

He summoned up the last ounce of his courage, put his back against the sapling and resolved that he would not move, even if an arrow carried some of his skin with it. The bowstrings twanged again, and again six arrows whistled by. Dick quivered, but he did not move, and some applause came from the crowd. Although it was the applause of enemies, of barbarians, who wished to see him suffer, it encouraged Dick. He would endure everything and he would not look at these cruel faces; so he fixed his eyes on the high hill and did not look away when the bowstrings twanged a third time. As before, he heard the arrows whistle by him, and the shiver came into his blood, but his will did not let it extend to his body. He kept his eyes fixed upon the hill, and suddenly a speck appeared before them. No, it was not a speck, and, incredible as it seemed, Dick was sure that he saw a horseman come around the base of the hill and stop there, gazing into the valley upon the great village and the people thronging about the bound boy.

A second and third horseman appeared, and Dick could doubt no longer. They were white cavalrymen in the army uniform, scouts or the vanguard, he knew not what. Dick held his breath, and again that shiver came into his blood. Then he heard and saw an extraordinary thing. A singular deep, long-drawn cry came from the multitude in unison, a note of surprise and mingled threat. Then all whirled about at the same moment and gazed at the horsemen at the base of the hill.

The cavalrymen quickly turned back, rode around the hill and out of sight. Dozens of warriors rushed forward, hundreds ran to the lodges for more weapons and ammunition, the women poured in a stream down toward the river and away, the boys with the bows and arrows disappeared, and in a few minutes Dick was left alone.

Unnoticed, but bound and helpless, the boy stood there on the little hill, while the feverish life, bursting now into a turbulent stream, whirled and eddied around him.

Chapter XVIII
The Circle of Death

The quiver in Dick's blood did not cease now. He forgot for the time being that he was bound, and stood there staring at the hill where three horsemen had been for a few vivid moments. These men must be proof that a white army was near; but would this army know what an immense Sioux force was waiting for it in the valley of the Little Big Horn?

He tried to take his eyes away from the hill, but he could not. He seemed to know every tree and shrub on it. There at the base, in that slight depression, the three horsemen had stood, but none came to take their place. In the Indian village an immense activity was going on, both on Dick's side of the river and the other. A multitude of warriors plunged into the undergrowth on the far bank of the stream, where they lay hidden, while another multitude was gathering on this side in front of the lodges. The gullies and ravines were lined with hordes. The time was about two in the afternoon.

A chief appeared on the slope not far from Dick. It was Bright Sun in all the glory of battle array, and he glanced at the tethered youth. Dick's glance met his, and he saw the shadow of a faint, superior smile on the face of the chief. Bright Sun started to say something to a warrior, but checked himself. He seemed to think that Dick was secured well enough, and he did not look at him again. Instead, he gazed at the base of the hill where the horsemen had been, and while he stood there he was joined by the chiefs Rain-in-the-Face and Young-Man-Afraid-of-His-Horses.

Dick never knew how long a time passed while they all waited. The rattle of arms, the shouts, and the tread of feet in the village ceased. There was an intense, ominous silence broken only, whether in fact or fancy Dick could not tell, by the heavy breathing of thousands. The sun came out more brightly and poured its light over the town and the river, but it did not reveal the army of the Sioux swallowed up in the undergrowth on the far bank. So well were they hidden that their arms gave back no gleam.

Dick forgot where he was, forgot that he was bound, so tense were the moments and so eagerly did he watch the base of the hill. When a long time—at least, Dick thought it so—had passed, a murmur came from the village below. The men were but scouts and had gone away, and no white army was near. That was Dick's own thought, too.

As the murmur sank, Dick suddenly straightened up. The black speck appeared again before his eyes. New horsemen stood where the three had been, and behind them was a moving mass, black in the sun. The white army had come!

Bright Sun suddenly turned upon Dick a glance so full of malignant triumph that the boy shuddered. Then, clear and full over the valley rose the battle cry of the trumpets, a joyous inspiring sound calling men on to glory or death. Out from the hill came the moving mass of white horsemen, rank after rank, and Dick saw one in front, a man with long yellow hair, snatch off his hat, wave it around his head, and come on at a gallop. Behind him thundered the whole army, stirrup to stirrup.

Bright Sun, Rain-in-the-Face, and Young-Man-Afraid-of-His-Horses darted away, and then Dick thought of the freedom that he wanted so much. They were his people coming so gallantly down the valley, and he should be there. He pulled at the rawhide, but it would not break; he tried to slip his wrists loose, but they would not come; and, although unnoticed now, he was compelled to stand there, still a prisoner, and merely see.

The horsemen came on swiftly, a splendid force riding well—trained soldiers, compact of body and ready of hand. The slope thundered with their hoofbeats as they came straight toward the river. Dick drew one long, deep breath of admiration, and then a terrible fear assailed him. Did these men who rode so well know unto what they were riding?

The stillness prevailed yet a little longer in the Indian village. The women and children were again running up the river, but they were too far away for Dick to hear them, and he was watching his own army. Straight on toward the river rode the horsemen, with the yellow-haired general at their head, still waving his hat. Strong and mellow, the song of the trumpet again sang over the valley, but the terrible fear at Dick's heard grew.

It was obvious to the boy that the army of Custer intended to cross the river, here not more than two feet deep, but on their flank was the deadly quicksand and on the opposite shore facing them the hidden warriors lay in the hundreds. Dick pulled again at his bonds and began to shout: "Not there! Not there! Turn away! " But his voice was lost in the pealing of the trumpets and the hoof beats of many horses.

They were nearing the river and the warriors were swarming on their flank, still held in leash by Bright Sun, while the great medicine man, Sitting Bull, the sweat pouring from his face, was making the most powerful medicine of his life. Nearer and nearer they rode, the undergrowth still waving gently and harmlessly in the light wind.

Dick stopped shouting. All at once he was conscious of its futility. Nobody heard him. Nobody heeded him. He was only an unnoticed spectator of a great event. He stood still now, back to the tree, gazing toward the river and the advancing force. Something wet dropped into his eye and he winked it away. It was the sweat from his own brow.

The mellow notes of the trumpet sang once more, echoing far over the valley, and the hoofs beat with rhythmic tread. The splendid array of blue-clad men was still unbroken. They still rode heel to heel and toe to toe, and across the river the dense undergrowth moved a little in the gentle wind, but disclosed nothing.

A few yards more and they would be at the water. Then Dick saw a long line of flame burst from the bushes, so vivid, so intense that it was like a blazing bar of lightening, and a thousand rifles seemed to crash as one. Hard on the echo of the great volley came the fierce war cry of the ambushed Sioux, taken up in turn by the larger force on the flank and swelled by the multitude of women and children farther back. It was to Dick like the howl of wolves about to leap on their prey, but many times stronger and fiercer.

The white army shivered under the impact of the blow, when a thousand unexpected bullets were sent into its ranks. All the front line was blown away, the men were shot from their saddles, and many of the horses went down with them. Others, riderless, galloped about screaming with pain and fright.

Although the little army shivered and reeled for a moment, it closed up again and went on toward the water. Once more the deadly rifle fire burst from the undergrowth, not a single volley now, but continuous, rising and falling a little perhaps, but always heavy, filling the air with singing metal and littering the ground with the wounded and the dead. The far side of the river was a sheet of fire, and in the red blaze the Sioux could be seen plainly springing about in the undergrowth.

The cavalrymen began to fire also, sending their bullets across the river as fast as they could pull the trigger, but they were attacked on the flank, too, by the vast horde of warriors, directed by the bravest of the Sioux chiefs, the famous Pizi (Gall), one of the most skillful and daring fighters the red race ever produced, a man of uncommon appearance, of great height, and with the legendary head of a Caesar. He now led on the horde with voice and gesture, and hurled it against Custer's force, which was reeling again under the deadly fire from the other shore of the Little Big Horn.

The shouting of the warriors and of the thousands of women and children who watched the battle was soon lost to Dick in the steady crash of the rifle fire which filled the whole valley—sharp, incessant, like the drum of thunder in the ear. A great cloud of smoke arose and drifted over the combatants, white and red, but this smoke was pierced by innumerable flashes of fire as the red swarms pressed closer and the white replied.

Some flaw in the wind lifted the smoke and sent it high over the heads of all. Dick saw Custer, the general with the yellow hair, still on horseback and apparently unwounded, but the little army had stopped. It had been riddled already by the rifle fire from the undergrowth and could not cross the river. The dead and wounded on the ground had increased greatly in numbers, and the riderless horses galloped everywhere. Some of them rushed blindly into the Indian ranks, where they were seized.

Three or four troopers had fallen or plunged into the terrible quicksand on the other flank, and as Dick looked they were slowly swallowed up. He shut his eyes, unable to bear the sight, and when he opened them he did not see the men any more.

The smoke flowed in again and then was driven away once more. Dick saw that all of Custer's front ranks were now dismounted, and were replying to the fire from the other side of the river. Undaunted by the terrible trap into which they had ridden they came so near to the bank that many of them were slain there, and their bodies fell into the water, where they floated.

Dick saw the yellow-haired leader wave his hat again, and the front troopers turned back from the bank. The whole force turned with them. All who yet lived or could ride now sprang from their horses, firing at the same time into the horde about them. Their ranks were terribly thinned, but they still formed a compact body, despite the rearing and kicking of the horses, many of which were wounded also.

Dick was soldier enough to know what they wished to do. They were trying to reach the higher ground, the hills, where they could make a better defense, and he prayed mutely that they might do it.

The Sioux saw, too, what was intended, and they gave forth a yell so full of ferocity and exultation that Dick shuddered from head to foot. The yell was taken up by the fierce squaws and boys who hovered in the rear, until it echoed far up and down the banks of the Little Big Horn.

The white force, still presenting a steady front and firing fast, made way. The warriors between them and the hill which they seemed to be seeking were driven back, but the attack on their rear, and now on both flanks, grew heavier and almost unbearable. The outer rim of Custer's army was continually being cut off, and when new men took the places of the others they, too, were shot down. His numbers and the space on which they stood were reduced steadily, yet they did not cease to go on, although the pace became slower. It was like a wounded beast creeping along and fighting with tooth and claw, while the hunters swarmed about him in numbers always increasing.

Custer bore diagonally to the left, going, in the main, downstream, but a fresh force was now thrown against him. The great body of warriors who had been hidden in the undergrowth on the other side of the Little Big Horn crossed the stream when he fell back and flung themselves upon his flank and front. He was compelled now to stop, although he had not gone more than four hundred yards, and Dick, from his hill, saw the actions of the troops.

They stood there for perhaps five minutes firing into the Sioux, who were now on every side. They formed a kind of hollow square with some of the men in the center holding the horses, which were kicking and struggling and adding to the terrible confusion. The leader with the yellow hair was yet alive. Dick saw him plainly, and knew by his gestures that he was still cheering on his men.

A movement now took place. Dick saw the white force divided. A portion of it deployed in a circular manner to the left, and the remainder turned in a similar fashion to the right, although they did not lose touch. The square was now turned into a rude circle with the horses still in the center. They stood on a low hill, and so far as Dick could see they would not try to go any farther. The fire of the defenders had sunk somewhat, but he saw the men rushing to the horses for the extra ammunition—that was why they hung to the horses—and then the fire rose again in intensity and volume.

Confident in their numbers and the success that they had already won, the Sioux pressed forward from every side in overwhelming masses. All the great chiefs led them—Gall, Crazy Horse, Young-Man-Afraid-of-His-Horses, Grass, and the others. Bright Sun continually passed like a flame, inciting the hordes to renewed attacks, while the redoubtable Sitting Bull never ceased to make triumphant medicine. But it was Gall, of the magnificent head and figure, the very model of a great savage warrior, who led at the battle front. Reckless of death, but always unwounded, he led the Sioux up to the very muzzles of the white rifles, and when they were driven back he would lead them up again. Dick had heard all his life that Indians would not charge white troops in the open field, but here they did it, not one time, but many.

Dick believed that if he were to die that moment the picture of that terrible scene would be found photographed upon his eyeballs. It had now but little form or feature for him. All he could see was the ring of his own blue-clad people in the center and everywhere around them the howling thousands, men mostly naked to the breechclout, their bodies wet with the sweat of their toiling, and their eyes filled with the fury of the savage in victorious battle—details that he could not see, although they were there. Alike over the small circle and the vast one inclosing it the smoke drifted in great clouds, but beneath it the field was lit up by the continuous red flash of the rifles. Dick wondered that anybody could live where so many bullets were flying in the air; yet there was Custer's force, cut down much more, but the core of it still alive and fighting, while the Sioux were so numerous that they did not miss their own warriors who had fallen, although there were many.

The unbroken crash of the rifle fire had gone on so long now that Dick scarcely noticed it, nor did he heed the great howling of the squaws farther up the stream. He was held by what his eyes saw, and he did not take them from the field for an instant. He saw one charge, a second and third hurled back, and although he was not conscious of it he shouted aloud in joy.

"They'll drive them off! They'll drive them off for good! " he exclaimed, although in his heart he never believed it.

The wind after a while took another change, and the dense clouds of smoke hung low over the field, hiding for the time the little white army that yet fought. Although Dick could see nothing now, he still gazed into the heart of the smoke bank. He did not know then that a second battle was in progress on the other side of the town. Custer before advancing had divided his force, giving a little more than half of it to Reno, who, unconscious of Custer's deadly peril, was now being beaten off. Dick had no thought for anything but Custer, not even of his own fate. Would they drive the Sioux away? He ran his tongue over his parched lips and tugged at the bonds that held his wrists.

The wind rose again and blew the smoke to one side. The battlefield came back into the light, and Dick saw that the white force still fought. But many of the men were on their knees now, using their revolvers, and Dick feared the terrible event that really happened — their ammunition was giving out, and the savage horde, rimming them on all sides, was very near.

He did not know how long the battle had lasted, but it seemed many hours to him. The sun was far down in the west, gilding the plains and hills with tawny gold, but the fire and smoke of conflict filled the whole valley of the Little Big Horn. "Perhaps night will save those who yet live, " thought Dick. But the fire of the savages rose. Fresh ammunition was brought to them, and after every repulse they returned to the attack, pressing closer at every renewal.

Dick saw the leader at the edge of the circle almost facing his hill. His hat was gone, and his long yellow hair flew wildly, but he still made gestures to his men and bade them fight on. Then Dick lost him in the turmoil, but he saw some of the horses pull loose from the detaining hands, burst through the circle, and plunge among the Sioux.

Now came a pause in the firing, a sudden sinking, as if by command, and the smoke thinned. The circle which had been sprouting flame on every side also grew silent for a moment, whether because the enemy had ceased or the cartridges were all gone Dick never knew. But it was the silence of only an instant. There was a tremendous shout, a burst of firing greater than any that had gone before, and the whole Sioux horde poured forward.

The warriors, charging in irresistible masses from side to side, met in the center, and when the smoke lifted from the last great struggle Dick saw only Sioux.

Of all the gallant little army that had charged into the valley not a soul was now living, save a Crow Indian scout, who, when all was lost, let down his hair after the fashion of a Sioux, and escaped in the turmoil as one of their own people.

Chapter XIX
A Happy Meeting

When Dick Howard saw that the raging Sioux covered the field and that the little army was destroyed wholly he could bear the sight no longer, and, reeling back against the tree, closed his eyes. For a little while, even with eyes shut, he still beheld the red ruin, and then darkness came over him.

He never knew whether he really fainted or whether it was merely a kind of stupor brought on by so many hours of battle and fierce excitement, but when he opened his eyes again much time had passed. The sun was far down in the west and the dusky shadows were advancing. Over the low hill where Custer had made his last stand the Sioux swarmed, scalping until they could scalp no more. Behind them came thousands of women and boys, shouting from excitement and the drunkenness of victory.

It was all incredible, unreal to Dick, some hideous nightmare that would soon pass away when he awoke. Such a thing as this could not be! Yet it was real, it was credible, he was awake and he had seen it—he had seen it all from the moment that the first trooper appeared in the valley until the last fell under the overwhelming charge of the Sioux. He still heard, in the waning afternoon, their joyous cries over their great victory, and he saw their dusky forms as they rushed here and there over the field in search of some new trophy.

Dick was not conscious of any physical feeling at all—neither weariness, nor fear, nor thought of the future. It seemed to him that the world had come to an end with the ending of the day.

The shadows thickened and advanced. The west was a sea of dusk. The distant lodges of the village passed out of sight. The battlefield itself became dim and it was only phantom figures that roamed over it. All the while Dick was unnoticed, forgotten in the great event, and as the night approached the desire for freedom returned to him. He was again a physical being, feeling pain, and from habit rather than hope he pulled once more at the rawhide cords that held his wrists— he did not know that he had been tugging at them nearly all afternoon.

He wrenched hard and the unbelievable happened. The rawhide, strained upon so long, parted, and his hands fell to his side. Dick slowly raised his right wrist to the level of his eyes and looked at it, as if it belonged to another man. There was a red and bleeding ring around it where the rawhide had cut deep, making a scar that took a year in the fading, but his numbed nerves still felt no pain.

He let the right wrist sink back and raised the left one. It had the same red ring around it, and he looked at it curiously, wonderingly. Then he let the left also drop to his side, while he stood, back against the tree, looking vaguely at the dim figures of the Sioux who roamed about in the late twilight still in that hideous search for trophies.

It was while he was looking at the Sioux that an abrupt thought came to Dick. Those were his own wrists at which he had been looking. His hands were free! Why not escape in all this turmoil and excitement, with the friendly and covering night also at hand. It was like the touch of electricity. He was instantly alive, body and mind. He knew who he was and what had happened, and he wanted to get away. Now was the time!

The rawhide around Dick's waist was strong and it had been secured with many knots. He picked at it slowly and with greatest care, and all the time he was in fear lest the Sioux should remember him. But the sun was now quite down, the last bars of red and gold were gone, and the east as well as the west was in darkness. The field of battle was hidden and only voices came up from it. Two warriors passed on the slope of the hill and Dick, ceasing his work, shrank against the trunk of the tree, but they went on, and when they were out of sight he began again to pick at the knots.

One knot after another was unloosed, and at last the rawhide fell from his waist. He was free, but he staggered as he walked a little way down the slope of the hill and his fingers were numb. Yet his mind was wholly clear. It had recovered from the great paralytic shock caused by the sight of the lost battle, and he intended to take every precaution needed for escape.

He sat down in a little clump of bushes, where he was quite lost to view, and rubbed his limbs long and hard until the circulation was active. His wrists had stopped bleeding, and he bound about them little strips that he tore from his clothing. Then he threw away his cap—the Sioux did not wear caps, and he meant to look as much like a Sioux as he could. That was not such a difficult matter, as he was dressed in tanned skins, and wind and weather had made him almost as brown as an Indian.

Midway of the slope he stopped and looked down. The night had come, but the stars were not yet out. He could see only the near lodges, but many torches flared now over the battle field and in the village. He started again, bearing away from the hill on which Custer had fallen, but pursuing a course that led chiefly downstream. Once he saw dusky figures, but they took no notice of him. Once a hideous old squaw, carrying some terrible trophy in her hand, passed near, and Dick thought that all was lost. He was really more afraid at this time of the sharp eyes of the old squaws than those of the warriors. But she passed on, and Dick dropped down into a little ravine that ran from the field. His feet touched a tiny stream that trickled at the bottom of the ravine, and he leaped away in shuddering horror. The soles of his mocassins were now red.

But he made progress. He was leaving the village farther behind, and the hum of voices was not so loud. One of his greatest wishes now was to find arms. He did not intend to be recaptured, and if the Sioux came upon him he wanted at least to make a fight.

A dark shape among some short bushes attracted his attention. It looked like the form of a man, and when he went closer he saw that it was the body of a Sioux warrior, slain by a distant bullet from Custer's circle. His carbine lay beside him and he wore an ammunition belt full of cartridges. Dick, without hesitation, took both, and felt immensely strengthened. The touch of the rifle gave him new courage. He was a man now ready to meet men.

He reached another low hill and stood there a little while, listening. He heard an occasional whoop, and may lights flared here and there in the village, but no warrior was near. He saw on one side of him the high hill, at the base of which the first cavalrymen had appeared, and around which the army had ridden a little later to its fate. Dick was seized with a sudden unreasoning hatred of the hill itself, standing there black and lowering in the darkness. He shook his fist at it, and then, ashamed of his own folly, hurried his flight.

Everything was aiding him now. If any chance befell, that chance was in his favor. Swiftly he left behind the field of battle, the great Indian village, and all the sights and sounds of that fatal day, which would remain stamped on his brain as long as he lived. He did not stop until he was beyond the hills inclosing the valley, and then he bent back again toward the Little Big Horn. He intended to cross the river and return toward the village on the other side, having some dim idea that he might find and rescue Albert.

Dick was now in total silence. The moon and the stars were not yet out, but he had grown used to the darkness and he could see the low hills, the straggling trees, and the clumps of undergrowth. He was absolutely alone again, but when he closed his eyes he saw once more with all the vividness of reality that terrible battle field, the closing in of the circle of death, the last great rush of the Sioux horde, and the blotting out of the white force. He still heard the unbroken crash of the rifle fire that had continued for hours, and the yelling of the Sioux that rose and fell.

But when he opened his eyes the silence became painful, it was so heavy and oppressive. He felt lonely and afraid, more afraid than he had even been for himself while the battle was in progress. It seemed to him that he was pursued by the ghosts of the fallen, and he longed for the company of his own race.

Dick was not conscious of hunger or fatigue. His nerves were still keyed too high to remember such things, and now he turned down to the Little Big Horn. Remembering the terrible quicksand, he tried the bank very gingerly before he stepped into the water. It was sandy, but it held him, and then he waded in boldly, holding his rifle and belt of cartridges above his head. He knew that the river was not deep, but it came to his waist here, and once he stepped into a hole to his armpits, but he kept the rifle and cartridges dry. The waters were extremely cold, but Dick did not know it, and when he reached the desired shore he shook himself like a dog until the drops flew and then began the perilous task of returning to the village on the side farthest from Custer's battle.

He went carefully along the low, wooded shores, keeping well in the undergrowth, which was dense, and for an hour he heard and saw nothing of the Sioux. He knew why. They were still rejoicing over their great victory, and although he knew little of Indian customs he believed that the scalp dance must be in progress.

The moon and stars came out. A dark-blue sky, troubled by occasional light clouds, bent over him. He began at last to feel the effects of the long strain, mental and physical. His clothes were nearly dry on him, but for the first time he felt cold and weak. He went on, nevertheless; he had no idea of stopping even if he were forced to crawl.

He reached the crest of a low hill and looked down again on the Indian village, but from a point far from the hill on which he had stood during the battle. He saw many lights, torches and camp fires, and now and then dusky figures moving against the background of the flames, and then a great despair overtook him. To rescue Albert would be in itself difficult enough, but how was he ever to find him in that huge village, five miles long?

He did not permit his despair to last long. He would make the trial in some manner, how he did not yet know, but he must make it. He descended the low hill and entered a clump of bushes about fifty yards from the banks of the Little Big Horn. Here he stopped and quickly sank down. He had heard a rustling at the far edge of the clump, and he was sure, too, that he had seen a shadowy figure. The figure had disappeared instantly, but Dick was confident that a Sioux warrior was hidden in the bushes not ten yards away.

It was his first impulse to retreat as silently as he could, but the impulse swiftly gave way to a fierce anger. He remembered that he carried a rifle and plenty of cartridges, and he was seized with a sudden vague belief that he might strike a blow in revenge for the terrible loss of the day. It could be but a little blow, he could strike down only one, but he was resolved to do it—he had been through what few boys are ever compelled to see and endure, and his mind was not in its normal state.

He turned himself now into an Indian, crawling and creeping with deadly caution through the bushes, exercising an infinite patience that he might make no leaf or twig rustle, and now and then looking carefully over the tops of the bushes to see that his enemy had not fled. As he advanced he held his rifle well forward, that he might take instant aim when the time came.

Dick was a full ten minutes in traveling ten yards, and then he saw the dark figure of the warrior crouched low in the bushes. The Sioux had not seen him and was watching for his approach from some other point. The figure was dim, but Dick slowly raised his rifle and took careful aim at the head. His finger reached the trigger, but when it got there it refused to obey his will. He was not a savage; he was white, with the civilized blood of many generations, and he could not shoot down an enemy whose back was turned to him. But he maintained his aim, and using some old expression that he had heard he cried, "Throw up your hands! "

The crouching figure sprang to its feet, and a remembered voice exclaimed in overwhelming surprise and delight:

"Dick! Dick! Is that you, Dick? "

Dick dropped the muzzle of his rifle and stared. He could not take it in for the moment. It was Albert—a ragged, dirty, pale, and tired Albert, but a real live Albert just the same.

The brothers stared at each other by the same impulse, and then by the same impulse rushed forward, grasped each other's hands, wringing them and shouting aloud for joy.

"Is it you, Al? How on earth did you ever get here? "

"Is it you, Dick? Where on earth did you come from? "

They sat down in the bushes, both still trembling with excitement and the relief from suspense, and Dick told of the fatal day, how he had been bound to the tree on the hill, and how he had seen all the battle, from its beginning to the end, when no white soldier was left alive.

"Do you mean that they were all killed, Dick? " asked Albert in awed tones.

"Every one, " replied Dick. "There was a ring of fire and steel around them through which no man could break. But they were brave, Al, they were brave! They beat off the thousands of that awful horde for hours and hours. "

"Who led them? "

"I don't know. I had no way of knowing, but it was a gallant man with long yellow hair. I saw him with his hat off, waving it to encourage his men. Now tell me, Al, how you got here. "

"When they seized us, " replied Albert, "they carried me, kicking and fighting as best I could, up the river. I made up my mind that I'd never see you again, Dick, as I was sure that they'd kill you right away. I expected them to finish me up, too, soon, but they didn't. I suppose it was because they were busy with bigger things.

"They pushed me along for at least two miles. Then they crossed the river, shoved me into a bark lodge, and fastened the door on me. They didn't take the trouble to bind me, feeling sure, I suppose, that I couldn't get out of the lodge and the village, too; and I certainly wouldn't have had any chance to do it if a battle hadn't begun after I had been there a long time in the darkness of the lodge. I thought at first that it was the Sioux firing at targets, but then it became too heavy and there was too much shouting.

"The firing went on a long time, and I pulled and kicked for an hour at the lodge door. Because no one came, no matter how much noise I made, I knew that something big was going on, and I worked all the harder. When I looked out at last, I saw many warriors running up and down and great clouds of smoke. I sneaked out, got into a smoke bank just as a Sioux shot at me, lay down in a little ravine, after a while jumped up and ran again through the smoke, and reached the bushes, where I lay hidden flat on my face until the night came. While I was there I heard the firing die down and saw our men driven off after being cut up badly. "

"It's awful! awful! " groaned Dick. "I didn't know there were so many Sioux in the world, and maybe our generals didn't, either. That must have been the trouble. "

"When the darkness set in good, " resumed Albert. "I started to run. I knew that no Sioux were bothering about me then, but I tell you that I made tracks, Dick. I had no arms, and I didn't know where I was going; but I meant to leave those Sioux some good miles behind. After a while I got back part of my courage, and then I came back here to look around for you, thinking you might have just such a chance as I did. "

"Brave old Al, " said Dick.

"You came, too. "

"I was armed and you were not. "

"It comes to the same thing, and you did have the chance. "

"Yes, and we're together again. We've been saved once more, Al, when the others have fallen. Now the thing for us to do is to get away from here as fast as we can. Which way do you think those troops on your side of the village retreated? "

Albert extended his finger toward a point on the dusky horizon.

"Off there somewhere, " he replied.

"Then we'll follow them. Come on. "

The two left the bushes and entered the hills.

Chapter XX
Bright Sun's Good-by

Dick and Albert had not gone far before they saw lights on the bluffs of the Little Big Horn. Dick had uncommonly keen eyes, and when he saw a figure pass between him and the firelight he was confident that it was not that of a Sioux. The clothing was too much like a trooper's.

"Stop, Al, " he said, putting his hand on his brother's shoulder. "I believe some of our soldiers are here. "

The two crept as near as they dared and watched until they saw another figure pause momentarily against the background of the firelight.

"It's a trooper, sure, " said Dick, "and we've come to our own people at last. Come, Al, we'll join them. "

They started forward on a run. There was a flash of flame, a report, and a bullet whistled between them.

"We're friends, not Sioux! " shouted Dick. "We're escaping from the savages! Don't fire! "

They ran forward again, coming boldly into the light, and no more shots were fired at them. They ran up the slope to the crest of the bluff, leaped over a fresh earthwork, and fell among a crowd of soldiers in blue. Dick quickly raised himself to his feet, and saw soldiers about him, many of them wounded, all of them weary and drawn. Others were hard at work with pick and spade, and from a distant point of the earthwork came the sharp report of rifle shots.

These were the first white men that Dick and Albert had seen in nearly two years, and their hearts rose in their throats.

"Who are you? " asked a lieutenant, holding up a lantern and looking curiously at the two bare-headed, brown, and half-wild youths who stood before him in their rough attire of tanned skins. They might readily have passed in the darkness for young Sioux warriors.

"I am Dick Howard, " replied Dick, standing up as straight as his weakness would let him, "and this is my brother Albert. We were with an emigrant trail, all the rest of which was massacred two years ago by the Sioux. Since then we have been in the mountains, hunting and trapping. "

The lieutenant looked at him suspiciously. Dick still stood erect and returned his gaze, but Albert, overpowered by fatigue, was leaning against the earthwork. A half dozen soldiers stood near, watching them curiously. From the woods toward the river came the sound of more rifle shots.

"Where have you come from to-night? And how? " asked the lieutenant sharply.

"We escaped from the Sioux village, " replied Dick. "I was in one part of it and my brother in another. We met by chance or luck in the night, but in the afternoon I saw all the battle in which the army was destroyed. "

"Army destroyed! What do you mean? " exclaimed the officer. "We were repulsed, but we are here. We are not destroyed. "

The suspicion in his look deepened, but Dick met him with unwavering eye.

"It was on the other side of the town, " he replied. "Another army was there. It was surrounded by thousands of Sioux, but it perished to the last man. I saw them gallop into the valley, led by a general with long yellow hair. "

"Custer! " exclaimed some one, and a deep groan came from the men in the dusk.

"What nonsense is this! " exclaimed the officer. "Do you dare tell me that Custer and his entire command have perished? "

Dick felt his resentment rising.

"I tell you only the truth, " he said. "There was a great battle, and our troops, led by a general with long yellow hair, perished utterly. The last one of them is dead. I saw it all with my own eyes. "

Again that deep groan came from the men in the dusk.

"I can't believe it! " exclaimed the lieutenant. "Custer and whole force dead! Where were you? How did you see all this? "

"The Sioux had tied me to a tree in order that the Indian boys might amuse themselves by grazing me with arrows—my brother and I had been captured when we were on the plains—but they were interrupted by the appearance of troops in the valley. Then the battle began. It lasted a long time, and I was forgotten. About twilight I managed to break loose, and I escaped by hiding in the undergrowth. My brother, who was on the other side of town, escaped in much the same way. "

"Sounds improbable, very improbable! " muttered the lieutenant.

Suddenly an old sergeant, who had been standing near, listening attentively, exclaimed:

"Look at the boy's wrists, lieutenant! They've got just the marks than an Indian rawhide would make! "

Dick impulsively held up his wrists, from which the bandages had fallen without his notice. A deep red ring encircled each, and it was obvious from their faces that others believed, even if the lieutenant did not. But he, too, dropped at least a part of his disbelief.

"I cannot deny your story of being captives among the Sioux, " he said, "because you are white and the look of your eyes is honest. But you must be mistaken about Custer. They cannot all have fallen; it was your excitement that made you think it. "

Dick did not insist. He was the bearer of bad news, but he would not seek to make others believe it if they did not wish to do so. The dreadful confirmation would come soon enough.

"Take them away, Williams, " said the lieutenant to the sergeant, "and give them food and drink. They look as if they needed it. "

The sergeant was kindly, and he asked Dick and Albert many questions as he led them to a point farther back on the bluff beyond the rifle shots of the Sioux, who were now firing heavily in the darkness upon Reno's command, the troops driven off from the far side of the town, and the commands of Benteen and McDougall, which had formed a junction with Reno. It was evident that he believed all Dick told him, and his eyes became heavy with sorrow.

"Poor lads! " he murmured. "And so many of them gone! "

He took them to a fire, and here both of them collapsed completely. But with stimulants, good food, and water they recovered in an hour, and then Dick was asked to tell again what he had seen to the chief officers. They listened attentively, but Dick knew that they, too, went away incredulous.

Throughout the talk Dick and Albert heard the sound of pick and spade as the men continued to throw up the earthworks, and there was an incessant patter of rifle fire as the Sioux crept forward in the darkness, firing from every tree, or rock, or hillock, and keeping up a frightful yelling, half of menace and half of triumph. But their bullets whistled mostly overhead, and once, when they made a great rush, they were quickly driven back with great loss. Troops on a bluff behind earthworks were a hard nut even for an overwhelming force to crack.

Dick and Albert fell asleep on the ground from sheer exhaustion, but Dick did not sleep long. He was awakened by a fresh burst of firing, and saw that it was still dark. He did not sleep again that night, although Albert failed to awake, and, asking for a rifle, bore a part in the defense.

The troops, having made a forced march with scant supplies, suffered greatly from thirst, but volunteers, taking buckets, slipped down to the river, at the imminent risk of torture and death, and brought them back filled for their comrades. It was done more than a dozen times, and Dick himself was one of the heroes, which pleased Sergeant Williams greatly.

"You're the right stuff, my boy, " he said, clapping him on the shoulder, "though you ought to be asleep and resting. "

"I couldn't sleep long, " replied Dick. "I think my nerves have been upset so much that I won't feel just right again for months. "

Nevertheless he bore a valiant part in the defense, besides risking his life to obtain the water, and won high praise from many besides his stanch friend, Sergeant Williams. It was well that the troops had thrown up the earthwork, as the Sioux, flushed with their great victory in the afternoon, hung on the flanks of the bluffs and kept up a continuous rifle fire. There was light enough for sharpshooting, and more than one soldier who incautiously raised his head above the earthwork was slain.

Toward morning the Sioux made another great rush. There had been a lull in the firing just when the night was darker than usual and many little black clouds were floating up from the southwest. Dick was oppressed by the silence. He remembered the phases of the battle in the afternoon, and he felt that it portended some great effort by the Sioux. He peeped carefully over the earthwork and studied the trees, bushes, and hillocks below. He saw nothing there, but it seemed to him that he could actually feel the presence of the Sioux.

"Look out for 'em, " he said to Sergeant Williams. "I think they're going to make a rush. "

"I think it, too, " replied the veteran. "I've learnt something of their cunnin' since I've been out here on the plains. "

Five minutes later the Sioux sprang from their ambush and rushed forward, hoping to surprise enemies who had grown careless. But they were met by a withering fire that drove them headlong to cover again. Nevertheless they kept up the siege throughout all the following day and night, firing incessantly from ambush, and at times giving forth whoops full of taunt and menace. Dick was able to sleep a little during the day, and gradually his nerves became more steady. Albert also took a part in the defense, and, like Dick, he won many friends.

The day was a long and heavy one. The fortified camp was filled with the gloomiest apprehensions. The officers still refused to believe all of Dick's story, that Custer and every man of his command had perished at the hands of the Sioux. They were yet hopeful that his eyes had deceived him, a thing which could happen amid so much fire, and smoke, and excitement, and that only a part of Custer's force had fallen. Yet neither Custer nor any of his men returned; there was no sign of them anywhere, and below the bluffs the Sioux gave forth taunting shouts and flaunted terrible trophies.

Dick and Albert sat together about twilight before one of the camp fires, and Dick's face showed that he shared the gloom of those around him.

"What are you expecting, Dick? " asked Albert, who read his countenance.

"Nothing in particular, " replied Dick; "but I'm hoping that help will come soon. I've heard from the men that General Gibbon is out on the plain with a strong force, and we need him bad. We're short of both water and food, and we'll soon be short of ammunition. Custer fell, I think, because his ammunition gave out, and if ours gives out the same thing will happen to us. It's no use trying to conceal it. "

"Then we'll pray for Gibbon, " said Albert.

The second night passed like the first, to the accompaniment of shouts and shots, the incessant sharpshooting of the Sioux, and an occasional rush that was always driven back. But it was terribly exhausting. The men were growing irritable and nervous under such a siege, and the anxiety in the camp increased.

Dick, after a good sleep, was up early on the morning of the second day, and, like others, he looked out over the plain in the hope that he might see Gibbon coming. He looked all around the circle of the horizon and saw only distant lodges in the valley and Sioux warriors. But Dick had uncommonly good ears, trained further by two years of wild life, and he heard something, a new note in the common life of the morning. He listened with the utmost attention, and heard it again. He had heard the same sound on the terrible day when Custer galloped into the valley—the mellow, pealing note of a trumpet, but now very faint and far.

"They're coming! " he said to Sergeant Williams joyfully. "I hear the sound of a trumpet out on the plain! "

"I don't, " said the sergeant. "It's your hopes that are deceivin' you. No, by Jove, I think I do hear it! Yes, there it is! They're comin'! They're comin'! "

The whole camp burst into a joyous cheer, and although they did not hear the trumpet again for some time, the belief that help was at hand became a certainty when they saw hurried movements among the Sioux in the valley and the sudden upspringing of flames at many points.

"They're goin' to retreat, " said the veteran Sergeant Williams, "an' they're burnin' their village behind 'em. "

A little later the army of Gibbon, with infantry and artillery, showed over the plain, and was welcomed with cheers that came from the heart. Uniting with the commands on the fortified bluff, Gibbon now had a powerful force, and he advanced cautiously into the valley of the Little Big Horn and directly upon the Indian village. But the Sioux were gone northward, taking with them their arms, ammunition, and all movable equipment, and the lodges that they left behind were burning.

Dick led the force to the field of battle, and all his terrible story was confirmed. There were hundreds of brave men, Custer and every one of his officers among them, lay, most of them mutilated, but all with their backs to the earth.

The army spent the day burying the dead, and then began the pursuit of the Sioux. Dick and Albert went with them, fighting as scouts and skirmishers. They were willing, for the present, to let their furs remain hidden in their lost valley until they could gain a more definite idea of its location, and until the dangerous Sioux were driven far to the northward.

As the armies grew larger the Sioux forces, despite the skill and courage of their leaders, were continually beaten. Their great victory on the Little Big Horn availed them nothing. It became evident that the last of the chiefs—and to Dick and Albert this was Bright Sun— had made the last stand for his race, and had failed.

"They were doomed the day the first white man landed in America, " said Dick to Albert, "and nothing could save them. "

"I suppose it's so, " said Albert; "but I feel sorry for Bright Sun, all the same. "

"So do I, " said Dick.

The Sioux were finally crowded against the Canadian line, and Sitting Bull and most of the warriors fled across it for safety. But just before the crossing Dick and Albert bore a gallant part in a severe skirmish that began before daylight. A small Sioux band, fighting in a forest with great courage and tenacity, was gradually driven back by dismounted white troopers. Dick, a skirmisher on the right flank, became separated from his comrades during the fighting. He was aware that the Sioux had been defeated, but, like the others, he followed in eager pursuit, wishing to drive the blow home.

Dick lost sight of both troopers and Sioux, but he became aware of a figure in the undergrowth ahead of him, and he stalked it. The warrior, for such he was sure the man to be, was unable to continue his flight without entering an open space where he would be exposed to Dick's bullet, and he stayed to meet his antagonist.

There was much delicate maneuvering of the kind that must occur when lives are known to be at stake, but at last the two came within reach of each other. The Sioux fired first and missed, and then Dick held his enemy at the muzzle of his rifle. He was about to fire in his turn, when he saw that it was Bright Sun.

The chief, worn and depressed, recognized Dick at the same moment.

"Fire, " he said. "I have lost and I might as well die by your hand as another. "

Dick lowered his weapon.

"I can't do it, Bright Sun, " he said. "My brother and I owe you our lives, and I've got to give you yours. Good-by. "

"But I am an Indian, " said Bright Sun. "I will never surrender to your people. "

"It is for you to say, " replied Dick.

Bright Sun waved his hand in a grave and sad farewell salute and went northward. Dick heard from a trapper some time later of a small band of Sioux Indians far up near the Great Slave Lake, led by a chief of uncommon qualities. He was sure, from the description of this chief given by the trapper, that it was Bright Sun.

Their part in the war ended, Dick and Albert took for their pay a number of captured Indian ponies, and turning southward found the old trail of the train that had been slaughtered. Then, with the ponies, they entered their beloved valley again.

No one had come in their absence. Castle Howard, the Annex, the Suburban Villa, the Cliff House and all their treasures were undisturbed. They carried their furs to Helena, in Montana, where the entire lot was sold for thirty-two thousand dollars—a great sum for two youths.

"Now what shall we do? " said Albert when the money was paid to them.

"I vote we buy United States Government bonds, " replied Dick, "register 'em in our names, and go back to the valley to hunt and trap. Of course people will find it after a while, but we may get another lot of the furs before anyone comes. "

"Just what I'd have proposed myself, " said Albert.

They started the next day on their ponies, with the pack ponies following, and reached their destination in due time. It was just about sunset when they descended the last slope and once more beheld their valley, stretching before them in all its beauty and splendor, still untrodden by any human footsteps save their own.

"What a fine place! " exclaimed Albert.

"The finest in the world! " said Dick.

The End